AWA

The Extraor...... journey
of Vivienne Marshall

2017 Benjamin Franklin Silver Award

2017 Next Generation Indie Gold Award

2017 Literary Classics Gold Award

2017 Literary Classics Silver Award

2017 Book Excellence Award

PRAISE FOR
The Extraordinary Journey of Vivienne Marshall

"Following acclaimed *Method 15/33*, Shannon Kirk sheds her thriller threads and dons a chimeric cloak. . . . Kirk captures a phantasmagoric vision. . . . Ceaseless hope and the importance of letting go of life—and the things that complicate it—are key to this uplifting tale. One word in the title says it all: Extraordinary. . . . sheer poetry, a book to read many times. Or give to friends as an extraordinary gift."

—L. Dean Murphy, Bookreporter.com

"There's so much joy in this book, I'm surprised it doesn't burst. Enough love to light a galaxy. Imagination with a capital I. Shannon Kirk is a ferocious talent."

—Elisabeth Elo, author of *North of Boston*

"Kirk brings a sense of magical realism [where] one could read the tale strictly for the beauty of its language. . . . This is one gifted writer, and [this is] one gorgeous, uplifting, and powerful book."

—Dawn Reno Langley, award-winner author, #LitChat

"Amazingly imaginative, gut wrenching and heartwarming novel . . . a keeper shelf, page-turner."

—The Reading Frenzy, rating it 5 out of 5 stars

The Extraordinary Journey of Vivienne Marshall

The Extraordinary Journey of Vivienne Marshall

SHANNON KIRK

REPUTATION BOOKS

THE EXTRAORDINARY JOURNEY OF VIVIENNE MARSHALL

Published by Reputation Books, LLC
reputationbooksllc.com

Book Design: Lisa Abellera

ISBN 978-1-944387-08-2 (paperback)
ISBN 978-1-944387-10-5 (hardcover)
ISBN 978-1-944387-09-9 (e-book)

First printing: September 2016
This paperback edition published: April 2018

10 9 8 7 6 5 4 3 2 1

Reputation Books

To my mother who told us about the Stuck Duck, and thus it is her story. To my father who told us about selling shoelaces at Christmas, and thus it is his story. I was one of the lucky ones, born to a selfless wild-heart woman and an alien beamed down from Planet Shubondalay. Thankfully, this interspecies connection resulted in a house of tales.

To my brothers, Brandt, Mike, and Adam, faithful towel boys in any devastating game of Monopoly.

To Beth Hoang, the Jessica to my Josie, the Armadillo to my Sunshine, my Uncle Chester. My sister cousin. My tough-love first-draft reader.

To Heather Wright, the only person with whom to take a mud slide. My very best friend who gets me through.

To Kristin Francoeur, her mother's magnolia tree is quite lovely, indeed.

To Lachlan Cameron, a real-life priest, a real-life inspiration.

For Michael, my husband, who listens to all of this and provides his guidance like a true guardian angel. Without him I would be untethered and lost.

For Max, the one and only Max, for whom all these stories are told, because he is the center of the universe.

Lastly, to the unnamed taxi-man. I hope you catch up on your skiing in Heaven some day, but not soon. If I were Vivienne, I'd surely choose your Heaven to inspect. When I rode in your car, I had started this book months before, not knowing whether to keep trying or whether to give up. And when you said, "There must, must be a Heaven. I need to catch up on my skiing," even though I wasn't even talking to you, well, that's when I wondered if signs were seeking me, or me seeking them.

Chapter I

I should have stopped. I should have looked both ways. I should have taken my head out of virtual clouds and my eyes off the text. I suppose it was foolish, so cliché, so very postmodern of me to die by one word, but that's what I did. I just had to read the most recent Facebook updates. What are you doing, Susan Talgar of High School? What are you doing this very second? I must, must know. Aha, good one, you've played ASCEND in Words With Friends!

Imagine me a whole person, clicking along in my red birthday shoes, absorbed in a moving crowd. Imagine the merciful weather and how Mother Nature allowed a jacket-free stroll, so too, the cleansing fragrance of new flowers and new leaves and new air, as if the sky itself were spring-fed. Do you see us oblivious to the hope of this May day? We're all, I and these busy strangers, collectively hypnotized; we trance-walk while brain swallowing the billions of informational bits and bytes our personal devices provide, leaving us displaced and unaware; except, everyone stops for the Do Not Walk. Everyone, that is, but me. Apparently, I'm the only one lucky enough to have a friend as genius as Susan Talgar, the only one slapped stymied by her superhuman word play.

The shoulder-high grill slams my side, and I fly forward and up, cartwheeling like a boneless doll, my forehead a fulcrum to my flipping body. Tiny pebbles sink into my nose and cheeks—all of this is undoubtedly fast, yet for me, so slow.

After scraping my arms, legs, and face skin in a burning slide and landing crumpled, I focus, perhaps for three seconds tops, on two things. One is the juxtaposition of my red heels embedded in an iron grill of some beastly truck—armored, fire, delivery, I don't know, a big truck. How the laws of physics conspired to create this truck/stiletto collage is beyond my paltry scientific knowledge as a freelance editor.

The other thing is my opened leather bag, the strap of which has been ripped off. The bag's top flap with the silver buckle slaps a manhole cover like a finger keeping beat on a table. The inside is disgorged, and the contents spilled. Papers and pictures cycle in a ground wind and curl around the shins of stalled pedestrians, some with hands to mouths, some sheltering children's eyes, some screaming, one woman throwing up. The contents of the bag, which were so important only minutes ago, fly to the subway entrance and paste against the windows of stores and restaurants along the way: the manuscript I'd finished editing for my client author, my lovely son Ivan's little league picture sets, and Jack's (Ivan's father) proposed summer custody plan—the same it's always been since Ivan was born.

Also thrown from the bag is *The One and Only Ivan*, the book I was reading to Ivan at night—he loves the main character, a gorilla, and I don't think it's just because he has his name. *Ivan* slants open-faced on the curb, the pages flying in gusts. All of these items scattering, slapping, curling, flapping, flipping, irrelevant to onlookers who recoil upon view of broken me—everyone too shocked to gather the details of my precious life.

Three seconds pass, and whatever sirens I might hear fade, as does the sunlight, as does the clunking of the truck's sputtering engine. People point with no sound, and their motions blur to white and then black.

What was that word? *Ascend?* Oh you cruel, clever world. You dirty little devil. You nasty, nasty trickster. You got me again.

Chapter II
Noah

I find myself in a lovely park with a lush, colorful canopy and a wood plank path. I follow this aisle past subtle streams and feel the sun reaching and winning to bathe my face. I walk along. Day slips away, and a twilight falls.

In a twinkling air, I come upon a narrow bridge. Only pedestrians and golf carts can pass over, or the native deer and occasional buck who dominate the fields beyond. This bridge with hand-carved rungs and gaslights, it is beautiful, don't you think?

All around the bridge and deep down into the valley below, twisting, zigzagging tree limbs fight for space from ground to sky, as if one thousand people are in a sweater party, all trying on sweaters, pulling them over heads, stuck on arms and elbows, pulling them off, stuck again on arms and elbows. Crooked, bent, long, short, stilted, stretched, high and low, everywhere knobby limbs. And they're old, like an elephant's trunk with matching elephant knees and their bands and wrinkles earned by years of wisdom. Same color too: nature's gray and brown.

The leaves rustle in a quick jostle, as if chuckling themselves at the joy of it all. Looking above treetops as dense as broccoli, I can't remember a sky more perfect, except in a painting I saw by Van Gogh. You know the one, *The Starry Night*, with its planet-earth blue—just like that, that color, that quiet. Stuck in this thick cerulean are dancing white, yes, true white stars; reflective strings from their tips stretch across the ocean sky to touch point with a star of like kind.

I feel no chilling breeze. I feel no aching heat. I think the gold glow of the gaslights is a vaporous metallurgy equalizing my body temperature with that of the air—as if my skin is blending with the night and there can be no difference between me and this scene.

Somehow I reach the foot of the bridge and I wonder why I haven't been here before or if I have been here before. How did I miss such a wonderful place? Have I been cheated? Was everything else and everywhere else in my past meaningless? Why did I have to go through all the trouble if this was here for me, why?

Something, someone, is standing across the way, across the bridge. His hands are in his pockets. He is watching me. Silent. In the glow of the gaslight, he appears around thirty-five, my age, as if he had continued to age as I had aged. As if he had not been crippled and later died, all before we turned twenty-four. His blond hair is more tightly cut than the free waves he had when we were young, but his blue eyes still scatter light. And he is walking. Noah. Walking. With strong and definite steps to me. He sweeps his hair with his hand, and the sailor rope bracelet I sent him in rehab drops to the cuff of his jacket. I steady my balance on the rail of the bridge, shaken to know he ever wore it.

I am looking at Noah, yes Noah, waiting for me at the other end of the bridge. My love, my Noah, the one I would have married had his spine not snapped, had he given me a chance to overcome the odds with him. I recall practicing vows, wearing my mother's wedding dress. Sure, my after-school charade may have just been a dreamy teenager wish for my next-door boyfriend, but everyone back then, before the snap, sensed the depth.

I try to run across the bridge to jump into his arms, but he holds a hand in a palm-wide fan.

"Stay. Stay. I'll come to you," he says.

Noah is the one who comes to greet me here. Scratching my ring finger with my thumbnail, I feel the absence of something that was never there. I picture Jack, my son's father, but see Noah before me. Two aches. Two tempests. Two loves who collectively spanned most of my life.

Noah places his warm hand upon my forehead, pinning a stray hair with his thumb, and pauses to study my eyes. So close he is, after all these years, and the endless seconds without him vanish in the devilish wink he gives. His sweet breath of subtle honey, I taste his breathing once again. A stone pressing my chest lifts, but air is also sucked out of my lungs. And when he leans in and whispers, "Calm now, Vivienne," his lips hover near my cheek and brush my skin in a slide. Although he provides only a skim of a passing blow, I remember something. I remember a kiss so very long ago.

"Vivienne, I cannot wait to show you the possibilities," he says, as if this is a proper greeting after so long.

"Noah?"

"There will be plenty of time for reminiscence and explanations as we explore the options."

"Options?"

"Yes, the options you have in creating your Heaven."

Options? Heavens? Before I can formulate the nine hundred questions I obviously have, a blinding white washes everything out. Blink. Gone. And some man is adjusting tubes in my nose.

I am saturated in morphine, every possible narcotic, so I do not have a Hollywood reaction of yelling or demanding answers. A metallic halo braces my head and neck, forcing my direct view on the can light in the white ceiling and the bleached sheet draped high to my chin. Straining my eyes to roll around, I find more white. The man with the tubes speaks medical words to someone out of my immediate circle of sight. His puffed, pasty cheeks and round nose make me think of someone named O'Brien or McAfee or Callahan. You know: the Irish look.

Every nerve in my body pulses, and a monitor by the headboard blasts a fire siren, which calls the man to depress its flashing buttons. And these white walls, this white blanket, these white sheets, this line of liquid they've plugged into my veins, their medicines and their whispers, the casts encasing me in a plaster exoskeleton—all of this, everything, every word, chokes me in a hard reality. I long to return to the vivid bridge. I try to bite my lip in anguish; I learn I have no such capacity.

The presumably Irish man places two fingers on my exposed wrist and studies my opened eyes. "I'm your nurse, darlin'. The sedatives and painkillers will kick in again in a few seconds. Calm, darlin'. Count down with me.

"Eight. Breathe.

"Seven. Breathe.

"Six. Now breathe.

"Five.

"Four.

"And three, darlin'.

"Two.

"One.

"One, breathe, calm darlin'."

A warm wave soothes me indeed, *calm darlin'*. By my encasement and my immobilization, I know the deep nausea I sense is a cover to indescribable pain, all of which is held at bay by a thin panacea of narcotics. One slight drop in whatever chemical level my nurse maintains will send me to the depths of hell. The devil of torture awaits his chance to repeatedly pulverize my bones with a bulldozer and impale my organs with a dull pitchfork.

The man-nurse, apparently satisfied with the pulse he secured with his countdown, dabs lightly the crow's-feet around my blinking eyes with cool water on a cotton ball.

"Hi there. We didn't think you'd wake up today," he says.

"What's up?" I manage to gurgle from lips that seem wired shut.

The man-nurse laughs. Oh, a good hearty laugh with his wide, fat shoulders bouncing like a shaken Jell-O mold. "Whhhoooo, whhooooo, whhooooo, haaaaa, so yes, we got a comedian here, this one," he says, checking a clamp on my finger and writing dashes and checks in a chart, which is wedged between his soft belly and left wrist.

"Mmmm," is all I muster in response.

"Girl, you did some work on yourself, honey. Had to pick a fight with some big ol' truck, eh? Didn't ya momma tell ya they all made a' steel? You precious, darlin', precious."

Wait a second. *Am I in some southern hospital?* Shouldn't he have said, *You're wicked banged up, doll, but I got ya back.* Last I knew I was in downtown Boston, crossing Boylston, and then—oh dammit to hell—I zombie-walked in front of a truck.

"Where am I?" I think ten minutes pass in my effort to conjure this question.

"You're in Massachusetts General Hospital, Mass General, darlin'. The grand ol' ICU. You been out one whole day. It's Wednesday. Mmmhmmm. Docs had you in surgery for ten hours. Did a fine job, ya ask me."

"Where (cough) (pause) (breath). You (pause) (pause). From?"

"Is that what ya gonna worry 'bout? Where little ol' me from? Aren't you precious. Aren't you downright plain pretty, Precious."

I blink is all. A. Slow. Measured. Blink. Talking, I find, requires nuclear energy on this side of the white lights.

"Well, darn. Not many people ask me much. Most my patients not real chatty up here in the ICU. Had a lady in a coma one whole year. She had no one to read to her but me. Now my lady surely didn't ask where I was from. They took her two nights ago. Those angels. Took her 'round two in the a.m. I mean, I didn't see the angels myself, but maybe I heard a whisper, or somethin'. I was in the middle of an article 'bout Carmel Valley Ranch in Carmel, California. Sounds jus' perfect, and my lady, well now, I thought she might be smiling too . . . maybe it was the drugs though. But then, a howl, a whoosh, and I look up. No more smile. No. Jus' a flat, straight line of closed lips, which, unfortunately, matched the one on her heart monitor.

"Well now, my lady, two of us, just two lonely birds on this old round rock. I'm from deep, deep, Mississippi, Precious. Deep down there where an alligator is a pet. I'm a gay, white man with a round, proud belly, and I miss me some fishin' at my good ol' auntie's house! You like that, Precious? I see you smilin'. I got dozens o' stories for you, darlin'. You just keep fighting for me, okay?"

I want to hug this big, gay gem. I want to kiss his moony face, smooth his fly-swept hair, and tell him I love his accent. I want to be his friend, read travel magazines with him, linger through long lunches of wine and beer and fried southern food, and gossip and chat, hear his "dozens o' stories," and figure out why he thinks he's alone on this "old round rock." In life, I fall easy like this. Sometimes a mere wink in my direction or a simple shimmer of light in a stranger's eyes topples my swiss-cheese walls. I have a weakness for kindness and an addiction to storytellers.

Even though I'm semi-conscious, I catch the dimmed glint in my nurse's eyes, the slight droop of his lids, and the ever-so-subtle curve of his spine in an almost defeat. He has that humor, a funny little jiggle, but my man-nurse is masking some sorrow, I can tell.

I want to ask him his name and what's bothering him, but I'm thirsty, and my eyelids weigh twenty pounds each. And the only strength I can gather is the strength to have one last, coherent thought: *I need to get back to that bridge.*

The bed beneath me sways. The ceiling lights swirl. My nurse hangs his red-blotched face over mine. Squinting a concerned disappointment, he says, "No, Precious, come on girl, fight. I have to tell someone—hell, any living, listening soul—stay with me and I'll tell you a secret. You're the only one I got in this ward who might listen, and I know you won't tell no one. Fight, Precious, come on girl."

Secret? Why is he looking so nervously over his shoulder? I don't even know this man. What is his name?

Black. Nothing. Nothing.

Click, click, and I find myself in a visible spectrum. Just like that in a snap, back at the end of the glorious bridge, with the arms of trees everywhere, the Van Gogh sky, the stringy, white stars, the chuckling leaves, and Noah right before me. Waiting. Above and around, as though framing him, are those age-old, wise elephant tree limbs.

I think of an article I read once about a famous tree named *L'Arbre Du Tenere.* Early in my career, I worked for a publishing house. One of our novelists included an excerpt in his manuscript on a colony of aspen connected below ground by a complex root system. Biologists say the trees, although they appear as individuals, constitute one organism. The largest, weighing six million kilos, is named Pando (or Trembling Giant) and occupies a plateau in Utah.

As fate would require, in addition to being the largest organism on earth, Pando is also the oldest, at eighty thousand years old. I thought Pando might be a good metaphor for life, which is exactly what the author thought and why he used it in his book. At the time, I was training to be a legitimate editor, and my grunt job was "fact-checker," so I set out to verify the Pando piece. In this way, I stumbled upon and was thus distracted by a wholly different tree, *L'Arbre Du Tenere*, the exact opposite of Pando: alone and in the dessert.

> L'Arbre Du Tenere has become a living lighthouse; it is the first or the last landmark for the azalai leaving Agadez for Bilma, or returning. The birds rest at the foot of the tree. Attracted from afar by its presence, they come to shelter, thinking they will find water and green foliage. Unfortunately, it is death that is waiting. It is not a mirage, but just the same it is not a spring where turtledoves and crows and the pressing sparrows can drink. *Abstract of Commandant des A.M.M., Michel Lesourd, of the Service central des Affaires Sahariennes, 12 May 1939*

. . . Not a spring where turtledoves and crows and the pressing sparrows can drink . . . and thus, poetry from a military observation, a spear for deeper meaning in an empty, deadened scene. I always

thought of Noah in the sadness of the tree, alone out there in the desert. I printed the page of the lifeless vegetation and tacked it to my wall, above my book-cluttered desk. I'd contemplate this image every day and worry about that long-gone tree, how no other trees grew around it, and how nothing but vultures clawed its carcass. Perhaps I pictured Noah, sitting vigil on a cracked limb.

I face him on the bridge. "Are you his soul? Noah's soul? Am I imagining this?"

"Don't worry, it is me, Vivienne. Even if you were imagining this, delusions can be therapeutic. But you are not imagining this."

"Then what is this? A dream?"

"Not really. No."

"Have I died, Noah?"

"Not quite yet."

"I'm going to die, aren't I?"

"Oh, you will definitely die."

"I mean, like, I'm going to die now, very soon."

"Most likely."

"How soon?"

"Hard to say. Not up to me."

"Who then, who decides?"

"Well, no one specific. Some of it is up to you."

"Soon though. You said soon."

"In all likelihood, very soon."

Very soon. I am going to die. This is how he tells me. A matter-of-simple-objective-fact. As though we were making dinner and I asked if we had any more garlic, and he had to break the bare truth: "Not much, about one clove, sorry." As though I hadn't been missing him since the day of his accident: twenty whole years.

Truthfully, at first, I think, *Okay fine.* So I die soon. This is rather nice actually. I like this bridge, I like these trees, this sky, those stars. I like being here with him. I like to see him stand again, use his legs again. It's been so long. So many years. My last memory of Noah is with atrophied legs, born of a vicious unuse, and we were so young.

And then I have a horrible realization: I am going to die soon. What will happen to my eight-year-old son? Who will hold him through nightmares? Curate his growing mind? Who will rack their brain for new plot lines, every morning, every night, to satisfy his insatiable requests for "more stories, Mama?" Who will feel as complete as I do just to see him happy to listen? Jack will try his damnedest, but he's only one side of the parental equation.

Only this last weekend, Ivan and I cuddled in Ivan's single bed, snug under his robot blanket. I read him *The One and Only Ivan,* and he laughed at the dog in the story and grew teary when the character named Ivan, a gorilla, was sad. As he fell asleep to me reading, butterflies tickled my heart to see his floppy, blond curls bounce to the beat of his deep snoring. I too nodded off, only to awake with one arm prickly from blood loss, cradling my Ivan, and the other holding *Ivan*.

"What about Ivan? I can't leave Ivan," I say, straightening from leaning against the bridge rails.

 "Let me show you something, Vivi."

"You called me Vivi."

"I always call you Vivi, Vivi."

"You haven't . . ." But the point is futile, and Noah interrupts my thoughts anyway.

"Vivi, step down, come down here below the bridge."

We hop down a hill that props one end of the bridge, and we skate along a skinny dirt path between those knobby trees. The leaves are chuckling, roaring, ruffling on high and full.

At a grass-covered door embedded in the hill, Noah pulls on a birch branch handle, and we enter. Much like a hobbit hut, inside is a small earthen room. Unlike a hobbit hut, a window serves as one wall, with a view of, I assume, the floor of the valley and the stream that snakes beneath the bridge. Roots poke through the low dirt ceiling and scrape my hair as I make my way to the window wall. Thinking again I'd see the world outside, I am stunned to view Ivan, my son, in his room, holding a picture of me. Not a stream. Not a valley floor. Not the trunks of those trees.

"Does this mean I can see him anytime I want? Come here, look out for him?"

"He already has guardians. Look closer."

I lend my face to the glass, wiping away nonexistent clouds. Straining, at first I see nothing but Ivan holding my picture. The curtains in his two windows blow into his room, tickling the top of his hair.

"Look closer, at his windowsills," Noah says.

Tilting my head as though an angle would cure my blindness, I note what appears as two faint, gray, barely visible funnels, sitting behind those billowing curtains.

"They watch him. He has more than most," Noah informs in a low voice.

"Why are you whispering?"

"I don't want to interrupt them."

Them?

One of the funnels twists to me, and I can only guess it heard our talking or coiled in my tension, for the smoky mist haunts my eyes to the point I rub them.

"Vivienne, this was a one time deal. We cannot come back. Not while Ivan is alive. You have to let this Ivan go. This is very difficult, trust me I know, but you will have an image of him until he arrives."

I fly out of the hill hut as if my body is on fire. Noah follows. Outside, we're on the floor of the forested valley. The trees are the walls of a deep well, and we are two stones thrown to the depths. The leaves have stopped laughing, and the trunks seem to sag. After sprinting to the shallow, bubbling stream, I wheeze in an effort to expand what feels like collapsed lungs. Noah comes up behind and flattens his hand on my back.

"Vivi, I'm sorry. Sometimes I get confused here, and I still make mistakes. I shouldn't have taken you to view the living. All of this is too soon. Too unbelievable. Listen, please. Breathe, Vivi. Ivan is fine. In fact, he is more fine than most. Some people have no one to preside over them. You didn't until I came. If you're lucky, you have one, only one to track your way—as herald or sentry or something in-between, I do not know. If you're very lucky, two or three. Viv? Two for Ivan? Do you know what this means? There must be great things in store. But listen, you can't think of him now, okay? I know it's hard, but you need to focus on something else. Vivi? Vivienne?"

Noah searches the depths of my eyes and the corners of my face for evidence I'm listening; his hands grip my shoulders. I look up and into his blue eyes, stall, stare, and resurrect the hypnosis of my youth, the comfort of melting into him and forgetting the world. My back loosens a notch of tension.

"I can give you a gift. Ivan is with you. There is no such thing as time here, as you measure the hours in the living world. And also, you can have everything you ever wanted or dreamed of or might dream of—I've told you, there are options."

Noah explains that I will die soon and he wishes to make the transition easier. He says I can create my own Heaven by testing other peoples' Heavens, whether they are already dead or still alive. "Time," he says, "doesn't exist. Those who are living now, you can see their Heavens, either because time has folded and they are here, or simply because you hold their image with you. Just accept these new physical rules. Don't get too bogged down in applying science to it all. It won't make sense to your alive mind anyway." According to him, by checking out other afterlives (again, even people who are still alive), I might get some ideas. One restriction, however, is set to protect me: I am not permitted to select the Heaven of anyone in my immediate family. Not my son, my mother, or my father. "You'll confuse life with death, or death with life, if you do that. They'll be in your Heaven anyway, so don't get caught up in theirs. Please try to have fun, explore the options." He swallows and inhales as though consuming air and says the next line slower, a gentle ache in his voice on the verb: "Walk with me through them."

"What's the catch? You're acting guarded, especially with the restrictions on my choice."

He settles his attention on a twig wedged between two rocks in the valley stream; he bends to pry it out. After taking what seems like minutes to contemplate my question, all the while hand-rolling the twig as though a talisman to collect the words he clearly struggles to find, he stretches his gaze above the wrinkled limbs and returns a serious self to me.

"Vivienne, in life and in death there are always catches. Consequences. Aftershocks. I am only permitted to guide you through your options. I may not comment upon them, or, as I hope I am suggesting, I may not warn of possible dangers—consequences, catches, whatever you want to call them. Even the eternal ones." Not one crease or any hint of joy appears along the borders of his sweet face. I encase his warning and bury the disquiet within my fear.

To halt me from interrupting the solemn mood with pressing questions, he places a finger on my opening lips.

"Vivienne, please, please. Let us have this time to see the possibilities."

I don't want to test his resolve; he seems so stern and sad, but hopeful too. And I want to be hopeful. So I say nothing.

He goes on to explain how I should give my selections some thought, but whatever Heavens I choose, they should belong to people who touched my life in some meaningful way. "Course correctors," he calls them.

The adventure sounds like my life. In my job with the publishing company and now as a freelance editor, I sift through varied settings: fiction, non-fiction, memoirs, fantasies, whatever is the story *du jour* paying the utilities for my and Ivan's New Hampshire home. But I have no idea whose Heavens might inspire me to build a blissful afterlife. The offer is as preposterous as a waitress who brings a tray of desserts, only to ask whether you'd prefer the melting lava of chocolate or creamy caramel tart or divine almond soufflé or perfect *tres leches* cake. *Uh, all of them please.* But course correctors' Heavens? This seems impossible. I close my eyes to think on a choice to begin this strange odyssey.

Chapter III
Lachlan

A candied-blossom aroma fills my hospital room. The delicate vapor is how purple would smell if colors had odor: floral with a taste of sugar. I blink awake and ever so carefully toggle my eyes to find the source of the scent. Sure enough, on a bedside table, pastel cones of a lilac bouquet burst from a round, glass vase. It is May; they are in full bloom. My man-nurse has his back to me. He heel-spins to meet my eyes and places his clipboard, which presumably holds my chart, on a tiny steel sink.

"Oh hey, darlin'. We were hoping you'd come around to join us earlier. Your son left some hours ago. He'll be back in the mornin', don't worry. Tomorrow's Friday already. You were snorin' like a salmon-stuffed grizzly today, Thursday. Just wanted you to know. And your boy, he is doin' just fine. Fine, young, strong boy. Father's a cute one, whhooooo, you got a story on that one, don't ya, darlin'!" In a lower voice, as he leans closer, he adds, "Saw his wife too. And damn, they been married as long as your boy been on this rock." He pulls back, dare-winking me with screwed eyebrows, as though I have a secret to tell and he knows exactly the pattern of my camouflage.

Sure, Jack's "a cute one" all right. Just try and avoid his beguiling green eyes, the pupils themselves the size of quarters. Go ahead, try not to daydream about his sinuous legs suffocating your hips. For advanced players, I dare you, take a hit of the drug-like arousal caused by the splotches of birthmarks on his muscled forearms and creamy chest. "A cute one" is a vast understatement: Jack's physical presence is like a male selkie, enchanting you to crash upon the rocks.

"What, you already smilin'? You just woke up. You're a devil, Precious, a devil and some trouble." He wags a finger while jamming his other hand on his hip like a fine southern lady in a flop-rim, frilly hat.

I am indeed smiling at him. I love people who get straight to the point, who ask the pregnant question. Here my nurse is really asking, "How do you have a son with a married man and he comes and brings your son and his wife to visit you?" Well, now, I do have a story there, and I want to tell my nurse, but first things first.

"What is your name?"

"Marty, darlin'. Name's Marty."

I want to hear about my son, want to find out if my mother was able to rise and attend, assume my father has been throttling doctors' necks for answers, and already heard Jack, my boy's father, has come to witness the downfall—the definite end to things. I know I have profound choices to make also—Heavens—yes, I'm fully cognizant of the two dimensions I inhabit. Frankly, I'm not inclined to quarantine death from life: Marty's liberal injections of morphine likely allow me easy acceptance of varied realities. Nevertheless, I wince at thinking more on my loved ones or landing on Heavens to survey. Instead, with the few vocal resources I have, I narrow my attention on who is present before me.

"Are you lonely today, Marty?"

"Well holy rollin' hell, Precious, ain't you just like me. Getting right down to it. Is that how it's gonna be between us? I knew I'd love you when they carted you in."

I loll lazy eyes in my best attempt to urge him to keep talking.

"Darlin', you know what? I ain't sad today, no. Met a splendid little boy who misses his mama and his fine, fine father. Mmmmm, yes, very fine. Then I get to talk to you. So everythang feather fine, ya see." He swallows deep to pause and to make it true. Then, with a lighter tone, back to conspiracy, he continues.

"You know my lady, the coma lady who died a couple nights ago? I told ya 'bout her yesterday, yeah? I got her things here with me. Ain't no one came to claim 'em. Don't go tellin' no one. I probably should'a turned 'em in. Anyway, anyway. This ain't my secret, though. No, no. Maybe we save that part for later, okay." Marty lowers his lids and drops his shoulders, seems to lose a bit of his nerve. I try with straining eyes to get him to keep going. Sure enough, after his pause of silent introspection, he jolts to once more.

"So, Precious. I got my coma lady's journal here. Want I should read you a page?"

Even though I ache to shake a violent YES, I chin stretch an ever so slight and slow yes, all I can gin up. Marty provides a duplicitous grin, the kind you share with a best friend when a devious and delicious plan comes together. He makes quick inspection of the windless hallway to ensure we are alone, which it seems we are and will be, for our world is well into a deep, dark midnight. The nonchalant hum of the fluorescent hall lights barely have enough energy to invade my low-lit room.

Marty sidles a chair next to my bed and from a bag at his feet, produces a tattered leather book. He opens to the first page and reads: "*Diary of Celia Jones. March 16, 1973. This day I delivered my baby son. I watched the nuns at the convent from behind the trees; how they shrieked to discover my infant in the basket by the bushes. One dropped the note. Another hurried to retrieve it, fluttering across the lawn. I'll see her forever in her black robe, habit askew in her frenzied effort to capture my words—those words, destructive, world-rocking evidence caught in an updraft and plastered to a cobblestone. One might consider cruel extortion with those words, but I ran. How shocked the nuns acted, not at the baby, but at the announcement in my note of the father's name—his illustrious, famous name, at least in 'these here parts.' As soon as my child was safe, I escaped, passing a priest in my exit, who watched with folded arms.*"

At this point, flickers of light blot my focused vision, and my heart begins to pound too loudly. Maybe Marty's story worked to raise my blood pressure dangerously high, maybe it was his mention of a priest, which led to the spike, and also my first selection. Monitors shriek while Marty yells, "Hang on, Precious. Now hang on!" Lord only knows what miracles of medicine they'll perform. I black out.

The next thing, Marty's gone, and a muted white light shines down upon a green pleather chair in the corner of my hospital room. A second vase filled with purple lilacs is set on a footstool. In the chair sits Noah.

"Vivienne," he says.

My voice is easier to find with Noah in the room. "Noah," I say, as though the entire scene is perfectly normal and expected. I do not understand why his being here is immediately acceptable, understandable. Perhaps the mystery was already solved, buried within my living soul, and only the edge of death reveals this peaceful, knowable truth.

"Have you thought about a Heaven you'd like to visit, or sample, I should say?"

"Yes."

I surprise myself with this answer. I guess I chose when Marty said "priest" and I ruminated on the choice in-between Marty and Noah, a time when I believe my body and soul rested.

"Needs to be someone who taught me a lesson, but can't be my parents or son, right?"

"Yes, that's right." His liquid eyes trap me in a familiar wish to blend with him, hold him, talk endlessly—catalogue observations and thoughts, no matter how mundane.

"Well, okay then." I pause. I'm pretty sure whose Heaven I should visit.

"Noah, when I was a freshman in college, I lived with a friend and her family in Queens. I was lonely, sad a lot. You know, by then there was my mother and her . . . well, and, of course, what had happened to you. Anyway, suffice it to say, I was not happy, so I threw everything into school. My friend and I shared the basement. Her parents and brothers had the upstairs bedrooms."

"I remember."

"You remember?"

"I wrote to you there after my accident. All our letters. And Vivienne, before you begin, we should talk. . . . I can't say how sorry . . ." He moves to stand, intending, I believe, to approach my bed and encapsulate me in physical and verbal apologies.

Even as I lay dying, I claw the sheets, choking the fabric to avoid an outburst. But no cotton can quiet my dormant emotional pain. When even a pebble invades the space between people strongly connected, tempers can jump in the instant of one wrong word.

"Why, Noah, why did you leave?"

I jerk my head and torso toward the hall door, pausing in his and my silence. Having cranked so swiftly, I realize I am neither braced nor casted. Inspecting my unbroken arms, I no longer understand my own limbs.

"Never mind, no. Don't say anything. Never mind. I can't think about that right now."

"Oh Vivienne, I . . ."

"No, no, not now. Please."

"Okay, okay. We don't have to. . . . Please . . . continue your story." He backs into sitting once again, tapping the air with a flat hand as reassurance that he'll acquiesce to the heightened emotion in the room.

"Yeah. Okay. So, okay. So, anyway, my friend's name was Delia, but everyone called her Diamond. She was a clone of Rapunzel—long, curly, blonde hair, and a rabbit's nose. Her hobby was to fabricate wedding veils out of the scrap laces she scrounged from merchants in the bowels of Manhattan. She sprinkled her creations with crystal dust and sold them wholesale to mom-and-pop bridal shops throughout Long Island. Her youngest brother, Lachlan, swore she crushed real jewels for her dust, and hence her name, Diamond. I was nineteen at the time; so were you. Lachlan was ten."

Noah settles into the chair, arching his back while winking at me to continue. And although only thirty seconds ago I wanted to fling him across the room, I now wish to consume his body in a long, soul-taking kiss. I wink back, continuing my tale.

One day Diamond's mother asked me to babysit Lachlan. It was summer, but I was taking a summer course and I was stressed about a paper I had to write on the psychology of aesthetics. Diamond was off with her veils, so they left me with Lachlan. I figured I'd let him watch TV. He was a good kid.

About half an hour goes by and here comes this little thing, practically skipping into the dining room where I was studying, papers scattered everywhere on the table. Like a cherub he appeared—puff of blond hair, thick, like a Brillo pad, with tight curls if he didn't wash and dry and brush the mop.

"I'm taking you somewhere," he announced.

"Lachlan, come on buddy, I have to finish this. Go pop in a movie or something," I said.

I hadn't showered in days. Hair in a somewhat ponytail, misaligned sections having missed the band.

"You need to take me somewhere. You need to see this place. You need to leave this house," he said.

I thought, *You're just a kid, kid. Why do I need to do anything you say?* But here's the thing. He, at the wizened age of ten, spoke like a white-beard professor, directing the youngest of pupils through the simplest of fundamentals: calm, all-knowing, the holder of indisputable truth. Dumbledore in jeans and kid Air Jordans. He challenged me with unblinking eyes; his were older than mine in that moment. I agreed to go.

Lachlan hops in my rusted, brown, hand-me-down Ford and buckles himself without me telling him to do so.

"Get on the highway, south, get off Exit 33. I'll tell you more when we get there," he said. And then he did a child's, closed-mouth smile, looked at his dangling sneakered feet, and stared out the passenger window. Through the reflection, his eyes danced about at the sights, bouncing around the world outside, yet his head stayed still. Except to give one more set of directions at the end of the ramp at Exit 33, he remained silent.

We arrived at a fifteen-foot gate, arched at the top. *Fieldcrest Botanical Garden* was forged in iron cursive on a brick wall.

"Why are we at a garden, Lachlan?" I asked.

"You need to be here today," he said.

"I need to be here?"

"Yes."

"When have you been here? Has your family taken you?"

"No. I've never been here."

Then I got chills.

"What do you mean? How do you know about this place?"

"We passed it once. Couple of years ago, I think. I thought you needed to see it."

"Why?"

"I'm not sure. I just think you do. Are you mad?"

"Mad? Why would I be mad? I might be confused, not mad."

"Maybe you should walk around."

This kid was ten. He was ten. Let's not forget that.

So we entered the gate, paid for our tickets, and drifted to a tended path. I was used to being muddled in the trap of Queens. Queens is gray. Gray stone, gray brick, gray concrete, with little relief by way of the burnt orange of dumpsters and billboards and transit signs. Otherwise, gray on gray on gray. If man constructed Hell, he would draw inspiration from pockets of Queens. And here I found myself in this oasis near the end of the LIE. Bursts of manicured reds, blues, and yellows in the wildflower beds. Honeysuckles with hummingbirds. Golf-course, rolling lawns. Trimmed trees and shear-shaped bushes. Butterflies, bees, and probably some faint, invisible fairy somewhere in the lime-green leaves. Quiet too. In the entrapment of Queens, bus horns and sirens blare twenty-four seven in a constant undulation of dying and replenished noise—a pinched, pulsing nerve on the spine of Manhattan. But here, in this botanical nirvana, I could hear the buzz of a bee, so too, a cloud slide by overhead, like a pillow moving across the sheets.

I sat between a forsythias bush and three boxwoods and reclined to bended elbows to lay in the grass atop my cardigan.

Ensconced in green, I melted into the blue sky. Lachlan skipped around, sketching in a flip-pad with an eraser-less pencil he'd packed in his back pocket. Some time passed before he plunked down, crossed-legged beside me.

"What do you think?" he said.

"I'm calmer here," I said.

"Is that good?"

"Yes, Lachlan, that is good."

A yellow butterfly landed on my toe. We watched his wings fold up, fold down, and flutter off to skim a bed of rolling petunias. Without him, we daydreamed our separate ways for a good forty-five minutes. You know that tingling you get sometimes when you're thinking about nothing at all, those small clips of time when you're not planning or remembering or worrying and your brain is light, has no weight, and it feels, well, good? Free.

Anyway. We had to leave at some point.

Actually, I felt compelled, perhaps torn, to leave because I remembered the day's albatross, that damned paper on the psychology of aesthetics—or was it the topic philosophy? Can there even be a science behind beauty, some mental measurement attached?

Having finished the story about Lachlan, I focus again on Noah.

"Noah, when do people take you from a damaging routine and force a silence upon you in a place of beauty? Who does this? Not everyone. It stuck with me.

"I think a lot about that day and about Lachlan's leadership. I was lucky to have listened to him. He planted an invaluable seed in my mind, probably the most valuable seed. The yellow butterfly landing on my toe was the most important thing to have happened to me the entire day—the only worthwhile achievement. Sure, I got an A on the psychology, philosophy, whatever-it-was paper on aesthetics. Sure, I didn't slow down, much. But I gained an insight that I should strive to live in real time, which was a new concept to me at that age. I'm not saying I ever mastered—or even came close to—living in the now, but at least I aimed to do so. I had some Mt. Everest hurdles after this whole Lachlan day: my reaction to your death, the rollercoaster with Jack, my unwed pregnancy. So it's not like I floated through life like some all-peaceful swami or anything. Anyway, as I got older, I went to botanical gardens when I needed to, by myself. Nature is my church.

"Lachlan became a priest. I want to see his Heaven."

CHAPTER IV
The Reserve of a Priest

Things quickly get bizarre. The lights flicker fast, and I suddenly understand that I am indeed on my way to see Lachlan's Heaven—Lachlan, who has not yet died. I recall how Noah told me to simply accept these new physical laws, accept too how time is not as I understand time, and so I do, but again, again, everything is bizarre. Noah rises to hold my hand within the flashing lights.

As my extremely brief stint at ballet (two classes) taught me, hold on to your tutus.

Almost as soon as I select Lachlan's Heaven, a flash of bright white shocks my hospital room, I'm pulled by my feet, I'm vertical to the ground, and my unclasped hair falls free and up, horizontal with the floor. I spin in a sort-of liquid, which rolls smoothly on my skin, but I am not wet. Flash again. I'm on a boat, and my father is fishing off the side.

All of this is natural. Normal. Acceptable. My father is peaceful and casting off the bow, and I know he won't let even a black fly bite me. So I am safe, and this must be a pleasant place. Odd though, because my father has not died yet. But neither has my mother, so where is she?

My father half-twists as he reels in a bass, "Oh hey, Viv."

"Hey Dad," I nod to him.

Noah is beside me with his hand on my shoulder. My father kindly acknowledges him with a bounce of his elbows, while maintaining the tension on his reel and line. A narration begins, booming over us on the boat and to others, who are undefined, on the shore:

"There is a place where all the windswept boats go, a beautiful forest with sky-high trees, a Narnia for freshwater vessels and toys." I look up to find where the announcement is coming from, but my body jerks back because the boat speeds up, and we're going fast and straight down a channel. My father reels in his bait and holds onto the edge. Clouds streak under the speed of the boat, and then a green, from trees, starts to mix with the blurred white.

The air, the sky, the world itself, becomes greener and greener.

We slow, and the green and brown of the trees become distinct, but are confused with the emerald air. We slow more and come upon a clearing and idle. We arrive in a magical place. All around a round, blue reservoir are trees at least three hundred feet tall, all of which are backlit by shades of green. The trees are the light, airy, fun kind—oaks, sycamore, banyans, and birch, not dark and dense, like evergreens. I don't think your common redwood or gnarly pine would dare root in this kingdom, for he would be the gloomy court jester.

Incalculable gold treehouses perch at varying heights, and a solarium—created by a hole in treetops—allows gentle morning rays to spill upon a hut at the shoreline. I've never seen anything like this before, not even in an imagined fantasy. With the dancing blue of the water and the jade-to-lime pulsing in the sky, it's as if a summer meadow has been inverted to hug me in my favorite colors. The temperature is similar to my first night on the bridge, an equalization of degree between my skin and the air—a blending comfort—like floating in a warm lake on a warm day. A scent of delicious sugar wafts about.

The narrator continues his explanation: "Please take stock, look all around. A lot of work going on in The Reserve. Over here, by this dock, the river empties into the reservoir, see the steady stream of lost freshwater items. Everything must be sorted so when their owners come to find them—in their afterlife—they may regain their eternal memory of fun. No lost items with bad memories come to this place. No tipped canoe that led to a drowning. No motorboat that blew up and burned a chest. No fishing pole that poked an eye out. We have good river fun, fine summer times, great lake trips, dreams on streams. So many love romps in swamps, we've lost count. That's all. That's the fun.

"Oh, now wait, hush everyone, quick, a rare one coming down the pike. You're right on time, here comes a shark-bitten knee-board. Oh, how hilarious. Look there, at the sky screen, see those kids laughing, peeing their shorts, slapping each other's backs, all over some dumb river shark who bites their board, drags it underwater, and appears to surf it himself. Oh, a rare one. A good one. Alright, enough, enough, moving on, heading over to Command Central, the lifeguard hut by the sycamore. We'll meet our CSO, Chief Sorting Officer."

As our boat nears a straw hut adorned with surfboards and seemingly hundreds of red whistles hanging from orange ribbons, several people become more visible and audible. Many are dressed in either parrot-print shorts or flowered sundresses. They huddle before a man in a Kelly-green bathing suit with purple turtles dancing at the hemline and a matching purple t-shirt. Flip-flops are his shoes. He is doling out instructions, and I can hear him as clear as if no other voice exists, but his back is to me. The boat's engine must startle him because he turns and reveals himself. Before me is Lachlan as a grown man. Same Brillo-pad mop of blond hair.

He laughs when he sees me. "Vivienne! I'm so glad you're here. So you're checking out my Heaven, huh? Isn't it great?!"

"Lachlan, this is unreal." I step off the boat, and he leads my movement by holding my hand and guiding my steps. Noah joins us too. My father shows no intention of abandoning his fishing, for in this place the bass are the size of ponies.

"Hang on one minute, please," Lachlan says, in the most courteous, caring way, as if I am the only guest he has ever had, or ever will have, and he has been waiting an eternity for my arrival. This, even though I am most certainly not his only visitor in this forever bliss. I squint, my eyes trembling with coming tears—which I fight back—to feel so special.

Lachlan addresses the crowd around him and finishes his assignments. "Okay, folks, we have a surplus of new inventory to get through today. It's mid-May. Serious thunderstorms raced throughout the southeast and deep into Florida this past week. Lots of lost stuff. Greg [his brother], you're on fishing lures. Diamond [my old friend], you're on canoes with Mom. Sam [I don't know who this is], you're on rafts," and so on go the instructions. His subjects file off.

Diamond hugs me, kisses my cheek, and hooks my pinky finger with her pinky finger—we're like two little girls, skipping off to play. Lachlan and Noah follow, both walking with their hands behind them, heads bent in a mutual quiet, as if they are complicit in a scheme about me. No one says a word.

I wander away from Diamond as she begins her sorting work so I can scan the minutia of the stations circling the reservoir. Each station holds a different sign: "Canoe Division," "Kayak Division," "Weathered Docks Division," "Fishing Pole Division," "Miscellaneous Division," etcetera, etcetera, around the reserve the Divisions continue. One person at each Division casts a pool hook, grabs at their individual assignments, drags the items to shore, and places them in refined piles, by like kind, as though stacking wood blocks tight to begin a game of Jenga. Another person holds a clipboard to inventory the details about each article: size, color, date of collection, and any other identifiable features. Upon a whistle indicating completion of a pile, a forklift wheels onto the scene, scoops a completed stack, back-wheels into a three-point turn, and disappears down one of the winding stone dust paths. The operation is rather organized, corporate almost, but without the mindless drone of fluorescent lights or the soul-sucking politics of six-sigma affairs.

The seemingly constant stream of lost things continues to flow to the reservoir, but one item catches my eye: a black box bobbing in the water. I inch closer to the shoreline for better view. A gold clasp bounces in a wind-wave. The shape of the object: rectangular. Division sorters crowd the beach, and a suntanned man shuffles the sand in his bare feet. "A floating briefcase. Well I'll be chucked corn," he yells. One side of the case is water-warped, revealing piles of cash inside. Some bills have escaped, and so a trail of US one hundreds float in a snakelike dance across the top of the water—Benjamin Franklins, flat and weightless. A crewmember in the Miscellaneous Division hooks the briefcase and drags her to shore.

What? How? What?

Not a soul answers my internal questions, yet I understand by the onlookers' slit-side-eye inspection of my reaction that this discovery might connect to me somehow. *How?*

But before I might quench my curiosity, music interrupts, filling the air from above, and all around, on high. A swamp-mystical violin solo resonates from the limbs of a patch of white birch, which vibrate like tuning forks. The haunting, yet hypnotic, rhythm reaches in and tugs my heart, weaves through my hair, tingles my scalp, and kisses my eardrums. My mind is electrified into a lovely light. Light, light, feathers in my head. I may have lifted off my feet.

There may be no notes to compose this melody, but maybe an artist on earth prays for his masterpiece, and hence will come to him upon a lightning strike, this song.

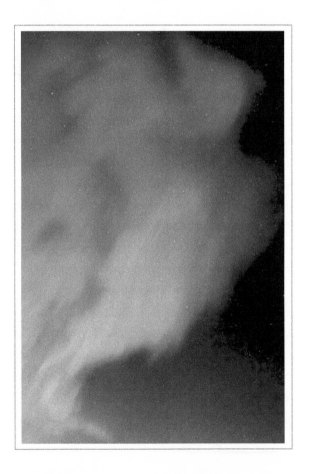

"Do you like my Heaven?" Lachlan asks.

"I am in love. I can't love anything more," I say.

"Come here, sit with me." He gestures to a deep-green bench with a sign affixed to the back: "Masconomo Park."

"Do you like this bench?" he asks.

"Yes, of course. Is it from a real Masconomo Park?"

"Indeed," Lachlan laughs. "You're starting to get this, aren't you?"

"I don't know about that."

Lachlan was a boy when I knew him, so to see him whimsical over a park bench makes sense: He's still somewhat childish, although trapped in the body of a man-aged priest.

A waft of fresh-baked bread comes over the reservoir, along with the nut-chocolate scent of an Italian roast coffee. Soon enough, a young woman in red pants, white t-shirt, and red apron peddles up on an antique-green bike, a basket tied to the front. She hops off, opens her basket, and hands me a cardboard tray; she delivers another to Lachlan. Inside each tray is a hot, crusty bun, a chunk of milk chocolate, and a white mug filled with coffee, mine already calibrated perfectly (I taste from my quick sip) with heaping spoons of sugar and steam-frothy milk.

"Breakfast," she says.

I like how her pigtails bounce, and I love the blue ribbons holding her hair in place. I double-love her large-framed, half-moon, coral glasses with diamond dust accenting the corners of each eye.

"Thank you," I say. She peddles away to others in The Reserve.

"So now you've met Sissy," Lachlan informs upon the nudge of his shoulder to mine. "I often spend 'months' [he air-quotes months] in a treehouse, leaning against her back and reading books. Sometimes she opens a shop full of hand-sewn clothes, beyond these trees here, basically whenever she feels like opening the rainbow-painted doors." Lachlan points to a place obscured by the high trees.

So there's more.

Seemingly done with her morning routine around The Reserve, Sissy speeds off, winding away on the stone dust paths and disappearing into the trees. Watching her, I feel I could be her, and I long to read all of Gabriel García Márquez's books while leaning against her back and drinking her coffee and eating her chocolate.

A summer wind silences the music. I wash the crumbs of the crusty bread down with two swigs of that marvelous coffee and let a square of chocolate melt in my warmed mouth.

"Shall I continue?" Lachlan asks.

"Please," I manage, but with tightened lips, for I don't want him to see my chocolate-stained teeth. Noah is watching me from beside a tall oak near the water's edge. The blue reflections rise like sonic circles around him, and the green glow from the trees appears as though all of Ireland has dissipated to mist. Framing him, moss drips from a banyan's low-lying limbs like moonshiners' beards. I believe he exposes a slight craving, subtly bouncing his pupils from down to up and resting upon my eyes, not flinching when I catch him.

"Vivienne, you wonder why this place. When I was a priest, I worked hard every day, thinking, listening. Thinking, thinking,

thinking, and reading. I loved to study, I did. Don't get me wrong. And I hope I helped some people. If I had to choose again, I would do nothing different. But, so much quiet analysis of things real and unreal, tangible and celestial. Thinking about what scripture might mean because of just one word. Ah, the miles of research into one word, its evolution and varied meanings. So on. So much research. So much writing."

When Lachlan pauses his story to breathe deep, I think on his words and about my editorial job and the obsessive days I'd spend altering an author's scene by replacing one word. Re-jiggering a pivotal sentence might require hours of contemplation, research, reference to my dog-eared and stained thesaurus, and a package of red pens. Throw the word "beep" onto a page and you might inadvertently imply technology, when in fact, the author intends none.

"One summer, I vacationed at another priest's lake house in New Hampshire. A week of fly-fishing on Upper Suncook Lake. The very first morning, I woke up before my friend. Him, by the luau pit, the priest filing fishing poles." Lachlan directs with a nose nod, and the priest, indeed filing fishing poles, waves in return. I sip my coffee and add a bite of chocolate to mix on my tongue.

"The sun was coming up over the trees, and I saw two things floating by the dock: a child's float—a blowup dolphin—and a woman's rope and rubber sandal. Now this was a clean lake. Pristine. Not very populated. Odd, to me, for these two mismatched items to be swept away. I wondered whether their owners recognized their loss and if they had had fun times with them. Maybe I was being weird to think and wonder so—about what? About objects? Nevertheless, I knew whatever the owners thought of this plastic dolphin and rope sandal were happy thoughts.

"This was the lightest moment of my life, Vivienne. The sun was rising, the sky was navy coming in to cornflower blue, and a suggestion of red-to-pink hinted behind some corpulent clouds. I believe God came to stand with me that morning. I even put my hand on my shoulder expecting to meet His there.

"As for the dolphin and the sandal, there was no religion behind my wishes. These were easy thoughts, and I was not performing mental gymnastics around some arcane text or theory. I asked myself, might I like an occupation in which I find lost things, an easier routine with less exhausting analysis and study and more happiness?"

As Lachlan reminisces on his own question, I ask myself the same thing.

He pauses, looks to the ground, and chuckles to himself. "But I never allowed myself to answer that question until I lay on my deathbed, for in that moment, my vow was complete. I was free to finally answer my then decades-long, pending question and said to myself, 'Yes, I do.' And so, Vivienne, I created this place, my Heaven. Of course, I added my favorite music and people and other things that you haven't even seen yet. Can I show you the blowup dolphin and the sandal?"

"Please, Lachlan, show me."

We lift off the bench and hand our trays to a man in farmer overalls collecting trash from around The Reserve. Sauntering past the Miscellaneous Division, Noah stays an obliging distance behind, watching, it seems, just me, smiling at my smiling. The glistening treehouses overhead line the winding path we follow.

Lighter and lighter the air brightens, sparser and sparser the trees clear, when at once the world breaks free of the forest, and we arrive upon an untamed scene. It appears as though ten thousand rainbows and all of Hawaii have been blended in some fantastic hurricane, and out came a confetti of paradise. Stretching for miles, a patchwork of interconnected pools and an adjoining ocean shimmer in a diamond glaze.

To our right rises a forty-foot tall, rough-hewn log barn with startling red doors. Adjacent is Sissy's shop, which I know instantly from the wild stripes of colors on the cabana-style building, but also from her sign: "Sissy's Vintage Clothing, More Colors Than You Care To Count. Open When I'm In The Mood."

Acknowledging Sissy's shop with a nod as we pass, Lachlan escorts me up the ramp to the barn. "The Miscellaneous Barn," he announces. "This is where we keep the most prized and rare finds. Somewhat of a Freshwater Memory Museum. The FMM we call her. Come in." As punctuation on his direction, he heaves open the wide doors, which creak only a fraction when first nudged, but then glide as though the hinges are caked in butter.

A mellow, cooling air greets us, along with filtered lights that beam through the spaces between the slits in the roof's logs. The floor sparkles in a recent polish, as though the concrete had, only a minute before, set and dried. A picnic table centers the space, on which is an ice-cold pitcher of water and a pyramid of cider doughnuts, whose medicinal vapor of cinnamon and apple dissolves whatever apprehension you might impossibly still hold.

Lachlan explains, in a proud manner of grinning and pointing and hurriedly moving wall to wall, how all the shelves on all four walls of the sky-scraping barn house the best finds from the Miscellaneous Division. And as his grand finale, he directs me to a lacquered black wood case on the back wall. Noah bites his lip as he inches closer, and I feel his crave intensify as my own core heats. It's as though in his closeness to my body, our combined aura explodes in red.

Behind glass doors, lights up-shine the objects within. Each has a brass plaque, which detail their significance:

Item #1: A Blowup Dolphin
Lost on a lake one hot July morning. Swept away in a slight, slight wind. No more to it. Upon view of the floating dolphin and its mate, a woman's sandal (see below), Our Lachlan conjured up this Heaven. He felt the hand of God on his shoulder during the morning's red-pink-to-blue sunrise.

Item #2: A Rope Scandal
See Dolphin (above).

Lachlan peels off to address some questions from a surfer dude in pink swim trunks, who is somewhat frantic about a crate of popping arm floaties. Noah and I float off to survey the many items on the shelves of the barn. Along the way, we read all sorts of engraved plaques, most of which are far more detailed than the ones for the dolphin and the sandal. "Anyone who works the

Miscellaneous Division may write the plaque for special miscellaneous finds," Lachlan yells from the opposite corner. I note his information and store that nugget deep, intrigued by this prospect like a magnet to metal.

Many plaques reveal stories about love, which shouldn't surprise me, for fresh water corners the market on that most ancient emotion. From first love to engagements to lost loves reuniting, the reservoirs, rivers, lakes, bayous, and valley streams, all hold tight to the kisses and near misses and close-skin, blessed aching that come with love. While other themes populate the shelves—stories about salvation or just plain fun—Noah and I hover on the plaques about love. One calls to me, but I'm not sure why. It seems so connected to a tug I feel in my heart.

> Item #330015: A Band of Gold
>
> He was so nervous as he knelt before her, so dry-heaving sick that this beauty that graced his life would awake upon his proposal and run to a better suitor. His fingers shook, he babbled on, he fumbled, and he fell. In his distress, he dropped the 1/2 carat stone set in thin gold, and All That He Could Afford was swept away in the lake's current. He gasped. She gasped. He said, "Ele, darling, I'm so sorry, I wanted to ask—" but she cut him off, "You were going to ask—" but he cut her off, "I lost your ring, if you would have blessed me, I was going to ask . . ." and tears actually came to his eyes. "I would have said yes." "Would have?" "Would have and do." And he smiled wide, as wide as the sun, which dried

his watering eyes. "But the ring," he said. "I don't want a ring. A ring is silly, you fool. Just tie some lake grass around my finger and we'll be done with it. I'll go plan a party, or two." For Eleanor Sanderstorm (maiden name) loved to plan parties.

A week later, Eleanor walked into a tattoo parlor and asked the resident artist to ink her a band of green. She had him also include, in the tiniest of black cursive, "Permanent Lake Grass." Her proud fiancé stood at her shoulder in awe at how she winced not once under the prick of that needle.

As I run my fingertips across the engraved words, I wish to comfort the man in this plaque for losing his ring and to congratulate him for his bride. Lingering far too long, I reluctantly push myself to move on and side-step to a series of water-warped books. Suddenly, the bright red doors of the summer barn open. In walks Lachlan's father with the Miscellaneous Division inventory keeper (which I know from his clipboard). They carry with them the bloated briefcase with the money I had seen floating in the reservoir. *Now, what*, I think again, *would ever be happy about a lost briefcase full of money? And why does it seem connected to me?* But as I run to discover the reason, white lights shock me to the concrete floor, and I once again tumble to my hospital bed.

CHAPTER V
The One and Only Ivan

I 'm trying to read the rest of the book my mom was reading to me before she died. *The One and Only Ivan*. I will write in the margins what I'm doing each time I read it. Like now. Like this note. A girl named Eleanor (but calls herself Ele) moved in today, May 24, 2012, two days after Mom died. Also my ninth birthday, but I don't care about my birthday. Ele is nine too. I first saw her chasing birds in her backyard. She stopped to watch me read *Ivan* in my backyard. She wore a red, ruffled skirt with red pants underneath and a white shirt with a black dot on her belly. I rubbed my eyes because I thought she was a giant ladybug. Ele says me and Mom's house looks like a fancy wedding cake. Ele's house is white with black shutters—she's the new girl next door. She jumped the skinny river and asked if she could read *Ivan* with me. She said she likes how my name and the book's name is Ivan. She also said she's my best friend now, if I agree. I'm pretty sure I agree.

May 18–June 1, 2013, One year since Mom died. Me and Ele read *Ivan* in the kitchenette Mr. Sanderstorm built her. I explain how I write notes in *Ivan*. Ele holds my hand. Ele understands. We talk about our "problem" and think we've found a solution. We're not going to tell anyone. And I'm not even going to write about it in *Ivan*.

June 12, 2013, Me and Ele read *Ivan* because we solved our "problem" today. I can't write what we did in case anyone finds out. We hope this means they can't separate us. We can never tell anyone our secret.

I miss Mom so much. Read *Ivan* over and over. ~~JHT~~ ~~JHT~~ ~~JHT~~. June 13–November 30, 2013.

May 22, 2014, Another anniversary of losing Mom. Read *Ivan* all day and plan to every year.

July 12, 2017, Ele broke her arm today when a car swiped her and knocked her off her bike. But Super Ele jumped up out of the road gravel, popped her forearm back into place, and gripped the bone in a hand-cast. All the while, like some fantastic action hero, she scanned the license plate of the car that sped away, focusing as though distance meant nothing to her laser eyes. She got back on her bike, whizzed past me without speaking or blinking, marched into Mr. Jurnot's house, called the cops, ratted out the hit and runner, and then, when she was sure her report was in, asked to be taken to the hospital. Not once did she shed one tear. I, on the other hand, vomited. Jack, my dad (I call him Jack sometimes just to tease him), had to hold me through the night while I sobbed out of fear of losing my Ele. I am fourteen, I shouldn't cry, I guess. But I've loved Ele since I was nine, and now understand I am in love with her, which scares me, but makes me live, all at the same time. I don't care what the other boys my age think. They don't understand. I again checked, and as I expected and knew full well, my and Ele's "secret" is safe. Read *Ivan* from 3-7 a.m., until everyone woke up for work or summer camp. I wish Dad wouldn't leave me alone today. I miss Mom.

August 1, 2021, I am hiding *Ivan* in Ele's suitcase right now, before she leaves for her college and I leave for mine. She is so scared to go—I know she is, but she won't admit it—sending *Ivan* is the only thing I could think of to show her how much I'd miss her. Breaks my heart, the book and her leaving. No doubt she will be the smartest and prettiest and toughest girl at Wesleyan. Ele, I love you so much. Good luck in college, my love.

August 2, 2021, This is Ele. Ivan said I had to write this note. I was so upset when I found *Ivan* in my bag, I actually cried. Me! I cried! Anyway, I called the old tenderheart and read Ivan to him over the phone all night long. I will return *Ivan* to Ivan at Christmas Break.

December 21, 2021, Christmas break. When Ele handed back my precious copy of *Ivan*, I asked her to go to the lake with me. The weather was strangely warm, no snow in sight. After our picnic, I took her to the dock, got down on one knee, but dropped the ring I had saved for over a year to buy. Since we were by the spot where the river enters, the current caught Ele's intended ring and gurgled it away. Despite all of this, she said she'd marry me, and she was happy to tie a piece of lake grass around her finger as her band. Then we read my old notes in *Ivan*, as we cuddled up in the back of my cranky, old VW. Ele says that next week she's going to have an engagement ring tattooed on her finger, and if I didn't know her better, I'd think she was kidding. Eleanor Sanderstorm will be my wife, Ele Marshall.

CHAPTER VI
Marty

"Friday morning, Precious. Time for your cocktails," Marty announces as I awake. "How 'bout I add an extra splash of vodka in this here Bloody Mary, hmm." He needles some narcotics into a hanging silicon bag, which sends liquid to stream along a tube through a hole cut in my left arm cast, and into my veins. Heat prickles under my skin. "And since you're my favorite patient, how 'bout I add some extra vodka by throwin' in some al-kee-hol soaked celery. You like that, Precious? I see you smilin'. Old Marty's got your cure." Marty wrinkles his round nose and bounces those fat-padded shoulders of his. "Your boy Ivan is here. Just ran to get a doughnut in the cafeteria with his papa and your papa. Left you a picture." Marty displays a drawing of a stick-figure woman in a hospital bed, bandaged top to toe, but with a red-crayon smile over the wrappings on her face. A warped Red Sox #1 hat hovers over her Ernie-style circle head. In a corner of the drawing, Ivan has written, "Please Get Better Mama, Red Sox Tix Came! I Love

You! Ivan." Although baseball bores me to the point I wish for golf instead, my boy loves Big Papi, and so I get him tickets each summer and we share gallons of Coke and dozens of pretzels in the bleachers.

I read Ivan's card, and a cavity in me widens, as though my ribs have parted to allow a burning fire to till my chest. My heart sinks to an abysmal place. Whatever remains of me throbs. A gravitational weight and a universal heat, which I had never realized before, pin me to the sheets, reminding me I am painfully alive. Suddenly an excruciating feeling of swelling tissue in each limb threatens to beat through the plaster casts, which causes me to flush and wish to vomit. Marty sees the signs of torture and opens a valve in my drug line.

"They'll be back any minute, darlin', just you hang on."

Marty said Ivan, Jack, and my father are here. But I'm sure he once again did not mention my mother. I worry she's hurting, and I lament in a thick guilt that perhaps she's truly unwell. Yet, still trying to grab hold of the promise of relief-giving narcotics now saturating my blood, I don't have the strength to ask where she is or whether she's been to see me. Since my heartbeat rises in volume on the monitor, I set my intentions on a less emotional course. At least for me, that is.

"Your lady?" I mumble, meaning, *Marty, please tell me more about your coma patient who died and left her journal.*

Marty closes his eyes and lowers the syringe in his hands. Two clicks of the wall clock pound in the silence. But Marty soon revives, a marathoner at mile fifteen urging himself to keep going.

"Precious, got her journal right here. Been readin' to ya all night. You probably didn't hear a word, though. We thought we lost ya yesterday. You been dippin' deep elsewhere, yeah. Listen though, I can give ya a recap. What with my lady's journal and your mysterious little romance," and he added on a wink, "your ahem, romance, with your Baby Daddy and my coma lady's journal, we got *Days Of Our Lives* all up in here. So, here ya go, my lady, she left her baby boy with the nuns. Turned a cold shoulder to his pink puffed butt. Moved herself north to Boston. Seems she had an affair with a married Federal Judge, a rather well-known Federal Judge, one President Nixon may have tapped to be next in line for the U of Old S Supreme Court. She was his court reporter. Uh huh. Yeah.

"The Judge, he did try, she wrote, to give her money to raise that boy, but she flat-down refused. Not sure why." Marty allowed a deeper droop in his shoulders, upturned a reverse steeple to quiet his fidgeting fingers, and cast his eyes so low they matched his dropped voice. But like a balloon that soars quickly in an updraft, he jumped his spirits so fast, I couldn't read well enough into the lowered demeanor. "So this Federal Judge, he's a good man. And when the nuns call him up and tell him they got a baby with his name on it, he—"

A knock at the door cuts Marty off. Four people enter: Ivan, Jack, Marcus Marshall, my father, and a man who must be my doctor—I haven't consciously met him yet. Not my mother, which unfortunately does not surprise me. Ivan lights upon sight of my opened eyes and jolts to grab my right hand, which is the only part of my torso not in cast. I wiggle my fingers to touch his chin, and he nuzzles into the movement. His tears wet my fingertips.

"Mama, Mama, Mama. You're awake."

The heart monitor erupts with noise, and the fire in my chest likewise explodes in flames. Like a referee calling a dust-clearing strike, the doctor pushes everyone away from my bed.

Marty holds dominion over my face. In a hush-soft, deliberate voice, he addresses me while locking into my visual vertigo. "Precious, if you want to visit with your boy, you're going to have to calm now. Calm now, Precious. Ready, count backwards with me. Ten, now breathe, nine, eight, breathe darlin', seven, whhooo, six, five now, four, there girl, there girl, breathe, breathe, three, two, and one, Precious, one. You fine, you fine. Calm."

The monitor settles some, yet the empty fire pit of my heart flames again, this time with the added pleasure of swords stabbing my lungs, the muscles of my sides, my back, and my stomach, and I'm sure some sadist jams sticks wrapped in barbed wire down my throat. My thoughts too, I can't even begin to describe how dreadful. Worse yet, a startling thought tempts me to acknowledge an unacceptable admission: *I don't want to stay.* I swallow this diabolical pill to the nether regions of my bruised amygdale: *No, no. Not acceptable. I must want to stay. I must want to stay. But Ivan. Is this harmful for him? Does he suffer to see me like this? Noah, where are you?*

Jack and my father gently approach, each red-eyed with sorrow. I think the sight of me awake in this state must be worse than the image of me out cold: a suffering human vs. an unfeeling corpse.

"Baby, I'm so glad you're up. Your doctor has only a second, so we need to talk with him before he runs. Give us a sec," my father says.

Jack tells Ivan to sit on the green guest chair while he and my father consult the doctor. The trio of men, my father, Jack, and the doctor, soft-shoe to my feet. But Ivan cringes when he looks at the chair, inching backward away from it, so Marty crouches next to him to distract him with his multi-faceted watch.

At the foot of my bed, the doctor produces a silver wand and scrapes the bottom of my left foot, which is the only part of both my legs not already in cast. I don't feel a thing. I don't even involuntarily twinge like you're supposed to. Nothing.

In a murmur, the doctor informs Jack and my father, "Based on her x-rays, she has a 1 percent chance to ever walk again. If she doesn't fade, like she did yesterday, and she can fight her way out of this, you'll have to prepare the house for wheelchair living."

House? Strange. I haven't thought of my house even once, my big house with Ivan. Our home. Just the two of us.

My father sucks in his bottom lip, squares his shoulders, and covers my calf with his big dad hand, as though joining me in my corner in this bout with dread; he lifts his chin to the doctor, as if saying, *My daughter and I will prove you wrong.*

For his part, Jack, handsome Jack—espresso-brown-silky-hair Jack—follows my father's hand and squints his eyes in a way hidden to all else but me, for I've always caught his vulnerabilities, and not-well-hidden jealousies. He walks to my side and crumples to his knees, in confession, or realization, I don't know. His arms hang above his head, his hands clasped together in one strained fist. To witness this breakdown from the man I love causes me to sob internally, my heart flatten to paper.

The deep groan he summons muffles the click of his wife's shoes; she enters the room the very next second. And so, she finally sees what I've always known.

Truth be told, she's always known. She doesn't flinch. Instead, Ivan escapes Marty to run to her and repeats what the doctor said. Kneeling to his level, she listens face-to-face and doesn't blink her brown eyes as he talks. She smooths his hair with gentle strokes and kisses his scalp. And I am relieved Ivan has someone solid in this mess to hold him tight. Jack is a great father, yes, but she will have to fill the maternal void.

As for Jack, I am sad for him, to have never said the words when it mattered. This too, my confession, which I afford myself, dying here: I have no regrets, I said everything long ago. However sorrowful I am for Jack, however much I'd still take and console him, my body tenses to see Ivan so unraveled. If only I could shout to Jack, *GO TO IVAN, LEAVE ME, GO,* but I struggle with the energy, my lids lower and close, and the monitor squeals once again. My ribs stab whatever organs remain within.

Whenever I catch Jack in these moments of truth, I remember the time I met him. There we were, fresh off our first jobs as post-grad nobodies and entering real jobs as gainful adults. We were twenty-four. One year and some months since Noah died.

In our first meeting, a surge of energy shook my shoulders, sound fell up—leaving me in a vacuum—and I'm sure white spar-kles and blurring orbs took the place of dust caught in the midday sun. You know how it is when you're sideswiped in a human collision. Out of nowhere, someone stands firm in your path, demanding undivided attention. You might as well have a concussion; you might as well fall into a coma. At least, this is the feeling I remember. In reality, Jack sat across from me in an armless chair in the glass-walled lobby of our new employer, Harry Von Franklin Publishing, Boston. Jack didn't speak, and neither did I, for we did no more than suspend time in a mutual stare. I never understood that moment, but it happened alright. "You're Vivienne?" he said. And I said, "You're Jack." And we said nothing again, his green eyes watching my blue eyes, and vice versa, slowly, not urgently nor worried about how the other might interpret the act. Back then, Jack had the same full hair and lean soccer body he had when he fell at my hospital bed. A full-on temptation.

Our new employer, H.V. he said to call him, set us off to meet with a group of author agents at Grub Street, a writers' haven in downtown Boston. For the next three months, Jack and I followed up on their queries, reading the piles of draft novels and novellas and short stories and poems they sent us. We shared space and hours and coffee and nearly every meal in our brick-townhome-turned-office in Boston's Beacon Hill. "Find me the next *Anna Karenina* or *War and Peace, One Hundred Years in Solitude,* or John Irving. Whatever, I don't care, just find it, and don't come out of this office until you both agree you've struck gold," H.V. instructed. I was pretty sure I was never going to agree with Jack: I wasn't going to be the one to end our joint project. Damn the future of literature.

While Jack never asked me out on a proper date, he gave me no reason to think we weren't on a constant date anyway, for he kept up those suspended stare sessions, each time forcing a sound-less vacuum upon me. I couldn't imagine he wasn't weightless too, floating in the same bubble. He was all I thought about, and he was the only one to have ever made me forget about Noah.

One day Jack brought a cider doughnut into our shared closet office. The cinnamon apple aroma mixed with the coffee I had just poured. "Some new bakery on Charles Street was giving these out. I've been dying to share it with you for three blocks," he said, tearing the doughnut in half, taking his and handing me mine. What transpired thereafter is a story in itself, and I do hope to explain. But here I am in a hospital dying, a doctor having announced to the men in my life I would likely never walk again, *if*, stressing *if,* I survived.

My beautiful Ivan lunges for my bedside, tears staining his little face, that face, that perfect face, a size I can fit in one hand. He grabs my casted arm, feathering the plaster with his twig fingers, "Mama, Mama, no. He says you won't walk. Just like your friend Noa . . ."

I don't hear how Ivan finishes his sentence, because I black out. Maybe Marty's "vodka cocktail," or maybe the shock, but my brain cannot take the information, my desecrated heart cannot withstand the emotion, and my body trembles, riddled in pain. So I leave for a respite with Noah.

As I blink, I look to the green guest chair with the lilacs at its side. There sits Noah, waiting.

"This Marty. You already care about him, don't you?"

"I do, Noah."

What about the others. Will you mention the others?

"He's funny. I like him too. And Ivan. Ivan is a strong boy, Vivienne. And your father, he's been through so much. He'll get through this too."

And Jack? Will you mention Jack? Acknowledge him?

Three purple petals cascade to the floor, which Noah watches, his shoulders tensed to his neck. A quick blackout fogs him to wavy, as though he sits behind rainy glass. Crisp sight returns, however, with Noah grasping tight to the arms of the chair, holding firm. He burrows his eyes into mine, stealing away any lingering thoughts on Jack, trumping him even in short-term memory. How he looks at me, how he does this, owns me with his eyes, is not unique to his heavenly self. He's done this before. And I suppose I do it to him.

CHAPTER VII
Firsts

There are those inevitable firsts. First Bite, First Word, First Step, First Birthday—a lot of important firsts when you're young, a dense and packed assembly line of firsts, at first. And then the firsts start to disappear: First Glance, First Hand Hold, First Kiss, First Love. Full stop. A flatline actually, right after First Love, like you came to the end of the Earth and out before you is the end of everything; here there doesn't seem to be any promise of more firsts on your horizon, only a white and windswept glacier, and not even a polar bear roams in its forever. I shared a lot of firsts with Noah.

We grew up in the same New Hampshire town, Milberg, about forty minutes (twenty minutes once they built the highway) from Manchester. When we were in grade school, McDonald's, Milberg House of Pizza, and the Tree Branch Bar & Grill were basically the only restaurants for miles, unless you were a veteran, in which case, you could enjoy the Fish Fry at the windowless VFW.

"Downtown" consisted of a yard-sized park with a white gazebo, which forever suffered peeling paint. The grass of the park yellowed and browned, but was usually mowed, or at least when the town scrounged enough funds to attend to such things. Also in downtown were an operating 1870 country store with penny candy, a video store the size of a large bathroom, a barber, and a library, which was really a rust-red house.

Way back when I was a child, Noah and I lived in a development of about fifty cape-style homes. Mine was yellow, his white, side by side with adjoined back lawns.

Our moms were best friends. Our dads were best friends. Our nineteen-year-old moms got pregnant around the same time, and as fate would require, delivered around the same time. I was born on May 14, 1977, four weeks after Noah, who was a mid-April baby. They sometimes called us "spring birds." We lived next door to each other for the first fifteen years of our lives. From literally Day One, we were introduced as best friends. Differences defined us as separates, of course: He had blond hair; I had black; he was male; I was female. But the differences ended there for the most part.

Our dads, best college buddies who'd scored a couple of honeys (our moms) on spring break in Daytona, worked office jobs while our moms raised us and made the homes. My dad owned his own small company at the time, a shoe store he'd grown since he was a boy—having started with one product, shoelaces, which he first sold from a box under a department store window in Manchester. He had taken night college courses as a partial hiatus from the constant energy he gave his business. So when I say "office job," I mean he worked inside. Noah's dad was a regular-old accountant. He'd do the hour-forty-five commute on Highway 93 to and from Boston, consistently voicing his displeasure to anyone who would listen.

The guys chose to buy homes in the same housing development in Milberg because they wanted to appease their best-friend wives, who suffered nostalgia for their native Florida homes. The best thing to do, everyone agreed, was to "keep the girls together."

Early on, as in, we could have been three, when Noah left me at the end of our day, I felt so deeply saddened and incomplete, like one of my legs or lungs had dislodged and crossed the yard to skip in another house or breathe in another bed, without me. At five, we held hands, for the first time.

By age eight, pressure brewed on Noah's side to join the neighborhood boys more. So we soon began to play together only on weekends. And since I wasn't a tomboy and, to this day in my death, loved my mother's spike heels and makeup, I wasn't about to start head-butting soccer balls just to be around Noah. But after what happened, I would give anything to go back and stitch myself to his side for every second of his healthy life. I would have feigned interest in football. I would have cleaned his soccer cleats.

But alas, at age eight, a first break-up, of sorts. Still. We had our secret weekends, without the boys. And we had a tree fort with more espionage and make-believe ginned-up within those wide-pine walls than all the works of Clancy and Tolkien combined. We also acquired a semi-tractor trailer truck, and more firsts to come.

When we turned ten, Noah's father, Mr. Vinet to me, decided he couldn't take "the fucking bullshit traffic" and "asshole drivers" anymore, so he quit KPMG, much to the very audible distress of Noah's mother. He bought himself a retired semi from a local potato chip distributor and placed the rusty beast in Noah's side yard, adjacent my side yard. His plan was to restore the truck and open his own moving company. Inside this steel shell were at least three hundred boxes of unopened bags of chips: the mini-bags, like they give you with pre-made sandwiches at company lunches. We're talking a child's dream here: thousands of bags of Doritos, Frito-Lays, Cheese Puffs, Fried Onions, Lay's Potato Chips, Ruffles, and the holy grail of all snacks, the glorious, incomparable Cheetos. I have no idea why the distributor sold the truck with all this gold product still within, and I never asked.

Noah didn't allow anyone else but me into the hull of the truck, which restored my toddler's affection for my old friend. So in return, I didn't open the subject up to even my mother for discussion. Although, Noah and I did enjoy the crustless baloney sandwiches and Tupperware pitchers of Kool-Aid she'd surreptitiously leave by the back hatch. I think I caught her watching us a couple of times, hiding behind a willow tree, vacillating between a serious contemplation of our antics and a red-faced giggle she'd stifle by doubling over. When beckoned home for meatloaf or tuna casserole or Steak Hoagie Sunday dinner, whatever was the recurring weekly meal, I'd enter the back of our two-over-two yellow Cape, kick my Keds in the "mudroom" (as my parents referred to the two-foot-square notch by the door), and skid to her hip in my socks. She'd cloak me closer with one arm while rinsing something in the sink with her other. Her long, skinny fingers would rake my skull, and we'd embark upon our nightly charade:

"Where you been, babydoll?"

"Oh, just playing with Noah."

"Yeah. Where?"

"Around."

"Mmmm. You want to know what I've been doing?"

"Sure, Mama."

"Been wiping this crusty floor and making you a meatloaf."

I'd wrinkle my nose and laugh in tandem to her laugh. She'd kiss my nose. She smelled of rose.

Noah and I would tiptoe into the back of the semi when Noah's father was off setting up his new office, and we'd lay among the boxes of chips, eating like rooting pigs. We'd hide in the upturned boxes, and we'd rest on the corrugated floor when we were full. We didn't have much light, and it didn't occur to us to bring flashlights, until the last day. So most of our time was spent eating chips in the dark and playing in boxes. We hauled markers and glue and duct tape and transformed empty boxes into spaceships, then we'd battle in space with our spray-paint ray guns.

A year churned by, and there remained bags of chips.

On May 14, 1988, after a day of enjoying my eleventh birthday cake, Noah and I met up at 11:11 p.m., synching our twin cereal box watches to the very specific, agreed-upon time. We feather-stepped past snoring parents in our separate homes to converge in our combined backyards. Noah would have traipsed by décor in twin to the décor I slid by, for our mothers frequented New England yard sales and flea markets—stuffed with antiques given the region—as their constant "Girl Outings." Our homes mirrored the other in a budgeted eclectic: original oil paintings with scratched frames, workbenches from old barns shortened into coffee tables, blue bubble glass lamps, and painted seaman chests. Our colonial decorated Capes were staged better than the other boxy Capes in the development, which were invariably walled with pastel carpets and sparsely furnished with particle board "furniture sets." And since our interior set us apart, I formed a sense of pride, a fire that I might achieve more in life, if I tried. Like my mom.

The Psychology? The Philosophy?—of Aesthetics. What was that paper on?

It doesn't matter. I suppose. Or maybe environment means everything.

My mother, Jessica, with the large breasts. Noah's mother, Josie, with the plump butt. Together they called themselves, buoy and anchor. But to me, Josie was Noah's Mother, Mrs. Josephine M. Vinet, carekeeper of my heart. Strangely, I kept her at bay, never choosing to burrow into her arms when she'd scoop in for a hug. In retrospect, I think I wanted her to consider me an equal, not a child, rather, another of her kind: a precious guard charged with keeping Noah near and safe and happy.

Did we both fail? Did anyone?

Alas, Noah and I met at 11:11, new eleven-year-olds, shivering in the cool night air. A shooting star whizzed past billions of white pinpricks in the cloudless, moon-bright sky. I'd forgotten my pink bunny slippers, so I folded my feet together and balanced on one flamingo leg. My Smurf pj's afforded little warmth. Noah's blue flannel bottoms flirted with being out of season, but sure seemed smart on that cold May night. His Teenage Mutant Ninja Turtle T-shirt was just plain ridiculous.

We entered the old semi hunched, as though our posture would conceal our absence from our separate beds. Inside, the stale air warmed us, as did the comfort of our First Home together, which we lit with red, boxy flashlights. I'm talking about the ones with the rubber nipple button and giant rectangular battery.

For the first time, we noticed our adolescent trail: smears of red and orange and black spray-paint covered the walls of the trailer; our spaceships, on which we'd taped paper cups as buttons, were now warped, the cup-buttons loose; crumpled chip bags littered every square inch; and an armload of stuffed animals held watch in the corners. Noah took my hand, as I lifted mine to his. We must have both thought the same thing, which was, *I play with stuffed animals and boxes, is that okay?* I think we were both scared of what would come next in our growth. Then the moment passed when I saw the last bag of Cheetos and fell to my knees.

"No way, I'm getting those Cheetos," Noah yelled.

"Nuh-uh, I saw first."

"No way, Viv, they're mine. It's my dad's truck."

"Your dad gave this truck up eight months ago when your mom made him go back to work."

"VIVI! Come on! It's my birthday."

"It's my birthday, dumbass."

Noah pounced at me, grabbed the bag out of my hands, and I tackled him to the ground. Hollow echoes of taut steel ricocheted in accompaniment to our tussle. We dropped our flashlights. One rolled flat so the beam shot a moving diagonal-horizontal; the other teetered on end, beaming a dancing vertical. The lighting mimicked the shifting spotlights of a circus calling patrons to the

Greatest Show on Earth. A puff of empty bags floated up around us. As I wrestled for the coveted snack in his clenched claw, Noah opened the bag and extracted a fistful of Cheetos. Somehow, I was able to do the same from the same bag, at the same time.

We both chewed, me on top of Noah, while a horrible fact of biology dawned upon us in the now settled illumination of our boxy flashlights. Within a trail of light, the undeniable squirming of worms became visible. Cutting lines through the orange dust staining our hands, teeny, tiny meal worms, a whole colony's worth, on one palm. Old chips that aren't fully sealed get worms, you see. We had been eating these worms, or worm larvae, for months, I believe, but we'd never brought flashlights before, and we hadn't paid much heed to the staleness. So we didn't taste nor see nor feel—until that First Light—the infestation of our bagged delicacy.

Noah placed his hand over my mouth to muffle my coming scream, which was odd, because I did the same to him. And then the First Wildest Thing in all my life happened. Noah, who was pinned beneath me, by my full eighty-five pounds, stopped screaming, sat up, and took my face in his cheese-and-worm-covered hands so he could direct my lips to his. He kissed me for the first time. First Kiss. Then the Second Wildest Thing in my life happened: I felt bad that Noah had eaten worms. This is when I realized I *loved* him. First Love.

CHAPTER VIII
Armadillo to the Rescue, Part 1

nother deep, dark midnight beyond the half-pulled shades welcomes me back to the hospital. Someone must have brought in a lamp and shut off the overhead canister bulbs, for a gold glow has softened the room. One purple petal from the somewhat-still-fluffy lilacs falls to a puddle of this gentler light on the linoleum floor. Also, a close friend or family member, only someone who knows me well, must have added my favorite music: Jakob Dylan sings his poetry in a gravely voice from an iPad by the sink. Noah stretches his legs into an angle from the green pleather chair and steeples his fingers to his chin. I can tell he's waiting for me to announce a Heaven I'd like to survey.

"Noah, remember when they took Armadillo away?"

"Of course. How could anyone forget that whole scene?"

I have a friend named Armadillo. A dark-skinned Greek who shot bows and arrows. Armadillo's parents both worked and left their only child under the care of her eighty-year-old grandmother after school and in the summer. Nana Armadillo let us be in the back-yard or the basement while she watched soaps or did crosswords. It was the late eighties, the heydays of non-orchestrated playdates, no plague of Big Brother monitoring of children, no equalization of talents or engineered fairness for all. Life was kill or be killed. We were savages, unscheduled and free. We were fine. Sort of. Well, some of us.

None of the other girls our age wanted to play with Armadillo because she'd made the taboo admission that she preferred Garbage Pail Kids to Cabbage Patch dolls. As she explained, the former were "more realistic." Also, she flatly remarked at lunch one day—not really intending, I think, to be mean, just stating what were to her objective facts—that Strawberry Shortcake seemed rather "insipid and too pink." None of the other girls understood what "insipid" meant, and I had to look the word up. Nevertheless, everyone else shut down when Armadillo dissed the hottest dolls on the market. Armadillo didn't really notice since she was always spending recess with her nose buried in the art books or Judy Blumes or archery magazines she toted around. In reflection, if I had to characterize Armadillo, I'd say she was a nerd crossed with Pocahontas crossed with Bob Dylan in his painting years. So to me: a perfect mix.

Armadillo lived in a single-level, brown ranch, up the hill and down the hill from Noah and my housing development. Given her family's penchant for archery, a fifty-foot gallery was clear-cut into their pine and oak four acres to make a shooting range. A negligible stream flowed on the surface of forest moss between her rustic-but-manicured and her neighbor's inapposite junkyard land. From this body of fresh water, dime-sized frogs flourished, thus infesting Armadillo's lawn by the hundreds.

By age thirteen, Armadillo graduated from target construction to designing her own feathers for the ends of her arrows. Her father stocked her with all the supplies: bleached white feathers, a rainbow of dyes, a kit of tiny paintbrushes, a vice, and a magnifying glass. The set-up was similar to fly-tying. Armadillo would ask me to sit with her after school in her hobby-stocked basement, while she painted her feathers on a ten-foot-long tavern table. A couple of swinging garage lamps buzzed above, zapping us into an incandescent hypnosis.

I drew Armadillo targets of the words we hated, like "Algebra" and "Training Bra." She shot the letters dead center every time. Besides Noah, she was my best friend. She was whom I stuck with during the weekdays while Noah was with the boys.

In the summer of our thirteenth year, Armadillo and I often wore matching moccasins and fringed suede skirts—leftover Indian Halloween costumes—and layered each other's hair in squaw braids. We'd sneak off with Armadillo's real arrows to spy across the frog stream to the backyard of twin boys next door. Oh how we hated those boys. They, by the way, were not part of Noah's crowd—they were outcasts, and for good reason.

One otherwise hot summer day, their father came home with a dog, whom the imbeciles named Maggie. Maggie was a black lab fleabag, who would howl at the moon and cry dog cries when it rained. A month into the neighbors' ownership, the cards were dealt for old Maggie: the dog was a beating toy, alone and abused, as evidenced in the patches of fur soon missing from her emaciated torso and rickety hind legs. We began to deliver heated announcements of the regression to our parents, usually while eating dinner at the other's house. But not enough time lapsed for any adult to take preventative measures.

On July 4, 1989, the demon boys hit Maggie's hindquarters, precisely on a black patch of exposed skin, and as the poor mutt yelped and cried and huddled on a dirt patch in their junked yard, those mongrels wrestled and punched each other, arguing over who had flung the lucky shot. As simultaneous periscopes, Armadillo and I sprouted up from behind our hiding rock to see Maggie in her stooped state and an open gash on her back left leg. Lifting synchronized binoculars, we examined her death wound, a green oozing hole of pus and gangrene. Our combined, forming brains had soaked in enough biology to diagnose this battered dog as good as dead, actually worse, suffering to death. We lowered our lenses and lifted our eyelids to peer each other in mirror to the other. I'm pretty sure there was a split second when we were one being, plotting the murder of twin boys. I was the first to break the unstated pact. Armadillo glared on.

I coughed to bring her to her senses, but she uncoiled her crouched legs, while raising her bow in the boys' direction. Her trigger fingers danced a two-step twitch, as she squinted her eyes to aim. I pulled the hem of her fringe skirt to summon her back down, hissing in her ear, "Army, no. You can't shoot them. Come on, let's get back."

"Fucking inbreds. They deserve to die," she said.

I'd never heard Armadillo swear before that moment. Armadillo was always scooping up those dime frogs and gently placing them back in the stream, taking care to warn me to walk softly on her lawn so I wouldn't harm them. She'd whistle at mama birds too, as if congratulating them on their nest of eggs. So to hear her suggest a living being should die, that startled me to realize we had entered the war zone. Affirmative action was afoot.

That night, while everyone else ooh and awed at the town-sponsored fireworks, we worked in her basement long into the night, wearing, the whole while, our Indian gear. We ate cheese-steaks and buttered popcorn for dinner, and a six-pack of Coke came and went. Armadillo was ominously dark and quiet in her work, painting one feather with the fixation of mad genius, especially fond of a red she mixed from the dyes her father gave her and a beet she pulled from her mother's garden. The blood of that squished vegetable dripped off her working fingers and trailed up her forearms. Each time I tried to talk to her, I'd have to say her name twice, three times, before she heard me. "Army, Army . . ." She'd shoot up startled, snapped back into the world of the conscious. "What?" she'd ask. "Nothing, never mind," I'd say.

Armadillo kept going, mixing dye, measuring, painting, the magnifying glass her only lens, her pupils the size of sand dollars. When at last she stepped aside, I peeked upon her microscopic masterpiece. God, she was talented. There on her feather was a world of smiling dogs, dancing upright on hind legs, holding paws in a circle, and kicking Rockette style around a blood-red fire. Dead center rose Maggie like a flame, balancing on the backs of the miserable twins. A spit over a roaring fire seemed to wait for the boys, who were hog-tied and silenced with apples shoved in their mouths. When I craned up from viewing her feather, Armadillo was writing something in black ink on a sheet of target paper. She turned to me, grabbed the feather, Superglued it to a naked arrow, and said, "Let's go to bed now." As we marched upstairs, I did think it curious how she carried the arrow with the new dancing dog feather, her bow, and the target paper. Usually these things stayed in the basement. But I wasn't about to question Armadillo.

We crawled into bed, still wearing suede skirts. I kicked off my moccasins, allowing them to land in a jumble. Armadillo, on the other hand, bent to the floor and lined her Indian shoes to face the door. The full moon lit her room in a shade of haze-blue; her shades and curtains were undrawn. I tried to snuggle in to my side, bear-hugging her stuffed pelican from our fieldtrip to the Stoneham Zoo.

I didn't hear a night cricket.

I didn't hear a faucet drip.

I didn't hear the house creak or a furnace groan.

I didn't even hear that full moon pulse.

A void of nothing for a good long minute.

And then we heard it: Maggie moaning, begging in her calls for the sweet hand of mercy, *Please come to me Night Death, take me from this misery.* Armadillo flipped quickly to face me; one Pocahontas braid fell along her upturned shoulder. She seemed calm, happy she had her reason. Pushing my bangs to the side, she said, "Sunshine, here we go." Without so much as a squint to check my answer, she jumped out of bed and landed in her moccasins, as though Wonder Woman cuffing into her power bracelet. "Come on," she said. I shuffled into my own shoes, but with none of her superhero grace.

I followed Armadillo's possessed path, out into the back-yard, crossing her shooting range, stepping over the frog stream, tiptoeing between bull pines, and landing behind the heart-shaped boulder we'd crouched behind. She climbed atop and, with the full moon as her backdrop, stood with the straight back of a master ballerina. I swear someone in my housing development set off a round of contraband fireworks and scattered the clear sky with a confetti of red, white, and blue—but perhaps that's my rose-colored nostalgia illuminating the stage of my dramatic memory.

Maggie stopped yelping in the shadow of the warrior on the rock, opened her body, and unclenched her trembling muscles. Armadillo nodded to Maggie's plea, stuck the target paper with her writing to the blade of the dancing-dog arrow, pulled the bow back, her trigger fingers steady this time, and let go her missive in a motion so deliberate, it seemed all she'd done was flick her ten-thousandth cigarette.

The note was impaled by the arrow and stuck to the tree Maggie was tied to. We tiptoed toward Maggie, passing rusted barrels and doorless cars. Once there, Armadillo crouched to hug the shivering dog and whispered to me to untie her rope. When I did, I saw her sign in the tree: "I'm coming for you next, Bitches."

The next day, everyone knew who shot the arrow and sent the message.

But that night, probably the most suspenseful night of my life, we carried Maggie to Armadillo's basement and stayed up all night spooning her water and hugging her and crying into her wounds. Naively we thought classical music might give her rest, and stupidly, we were afraid to wake Armadillo's parents, afraid they'd make us return her, or afraid we'd crossed some unstated boundary. But I don't think waking them would have made a difference: We'd already waited too long. Armadillo's parents awoke at dawn to find us gently stroking Maggie behind her ears, soothing her into an inevitable death. Later that morning, the vet put her down.

There was the troublesome issue of Armadillo's threatening message, which created a somewhat tricky legal and mental health issue.

Armadillo took full credit or blame, depending on how viewed, and said she sent her threat without my knowledge, for she waited until I fell asleep. After she spent an hour in juvie, they hauled in Dr. Claire Coello, Child Psychiatrist, who I soon dubbed, "Satan." In short, Satan led Armadillo's parents to the conclusion that Armadillo would fare much better at a special school for the "artistically inclined" in LA, "where passions can be free and thus tempered in expression." This may have been the turning point in Armadillo's aging, the point where she and others began to recognize the powers of her frightening intellect.

On the day of Army's incarceration, my mother skipped into my antique-lace-curtained bedroom. Sweat glistened her neck, and her thick, blonde hair swayed in two ponytails. She smelled of dryer sheets mixed with the scent of rose lotion, and thus, she cleared the burdensome air with her crispness and flowers. Her constant athletics costume lit my beige room in fantastic colors:

fluorescent blue running shorts and a fuchsia running tank. She lunged her long, lean legs to leap up on my four-poster canopy bed and curl around me like a mother cat.

"Vivienne, come on, babydoll, I know you weren't asleep when Armadillo shot that arrow," she said, while brushing my hair with her red-painted nails. She nearly purred in her coaxing for truth.

"But Armadillo would never hurt anyone."

"Vivi, do you really believe so?" And here she twirled around my back to face me like a haunting, taunting devil ghost, the kind who tempts you to eat the whole cake.

"I really believe it, yes, Mama. Don't you?"

"Here now. I respect you for defending a friend. And, of course, I know Army wouldn't hurt anyone. Nothing is more evil than a senseless act on the helpless, a child, an animal. And those boys are the evil ones. Besides, you would never have let her hurt those boys anyway. But I'd like to pluck their fingernails out."

And then I shook from the extreme of it all. When I was done quaking off the emotion, she kissed my cheek and said her signature line, "I love you too much. Too much." She soldier-jogged to the pull-up bar in the hall my dad had installed for her. One hundred pull-ups a night was her regimen, for she was in training for her annual waterski solo competition, and to me she was the most beautiful woman in the world.

Unfortunately, I don't look a thing like my mother. I inherited my dad's wiry, Italian, black hair, blue eyes, and hem-every-pair-of-pants-I-buy genes. Strangers used to stop my mother to ask if she was my Swedish *au pair*.

Nevertheless, the worst news I received in my life to that point was that Armadillo would be moving to Los Angeles to enroll in a school for the artistically inclined. I lost my Armadillo.

But because tragedy likes to stack upon tragedy, making you wish with each new one for the known evil of the former one, the day after her moving truck inched out of town, I stumbled upon a new black. When you're down, they keep kicking, a steel-toed boot straight to the kidneys.

In my journey home from the bus stop, one day post-Armadillo, I scraped my feet in a pathetic shuffle, not caring about how overnight the green canopy now sprouted red leaves too. My gray zip sweatshirt provided enough warmth, but soon, I could tell, it would not. I did not break my blank concentration for the group of girls catcalling me to join them in drawing rainbows and purple pools on the sidewalk with chalk; no, my mind's eye saw Armadillo nose-clouding the glass of her family's car, as if breathing out a farewell as she passed on by. I limp-wristed a flick of my lunchbox in the girls' direction, intending to get home, throw my bags in the mudroom, and flop on the couch to eat chocolate chip cookies without the chocolate chips, which is what I hoped my mother made during the day, because this is how she cheered me up.

The girls chalked on, not used to my presence anyway and thus unruffled when I dismissed them. *I want Armadillo*, I whined to myself. How self-indulgent I was, wallowing in my own pity. If I could go back in time and shake myself, I would, for I had zero perspective. Zero, that is, until the next minute passed.

I scraped along. Subconsciously, I'm sure I perceived the chaos at the end of the block, the spiraling noises and emergency colors that grew more definite upon my approach. The blue reflections, so far off, became flashing lights. The red glow, so far off, so too became flashing lights. A low drone rumbled from the earth, masking itself as fall's soundtrack, only to increase bass, ratchet the volume, and blossom into sirens. Alerts blared insistent, as I lifted my chin from my chest and pinched my shoulders from a slouched posture. I picked up my pace, no longer shuffling. Reality invaded me with each pop of my Keds: pop, pop, pop, pop, my rubber soles pressed and popped along the sidewalk, as though ripping suction cups off a window. Awareness screamed, became a truth undeniable.

An ambulance roared up our street to join the fire truck in front of our yellow house. Two men in jumpsuits burst open my front door from within and stood to the side to . . .

Stood to the side to allow two other firemen carry my mother on a stretcher to the paramedics with black bags on the lawn. She was gasping, clutching her chest, her body jumping as though electrocuted. Her beautiful face was solid gray.

I will never forget the shade of her skin. When she stopped writhing, when her body lay unmoving, when the man jammed paddles on her chest to shock her, and when I watched from five feet away, her skin remained, solid gray.

They diagnosed her with a variety of critical and chronic ailments, all of which had her heart at the core. She spent two days in the ICU fighting with all of her ventricles, only to lose in the end when the cardiologist added her name to the "need" column on the donor list.

Sometime during the third day, they stabilized her, awoke her from her narcotics nap, and upgraded her condition to "stable but guarded." Surgeons had worked like clockmakers, banding and sautering and patching and welding, all to make her tick until such time that replacement cogs and pins and wheels arrived from some yet unknown donor factory. At least, this is how my dad explained the medical words to me.

The first night I was permitted to visit her, I wailed into my mother's chest, "It's my fault, Mama, it's my fault. It's because you always say you love me too much. You love me too much and now your heart is bursting."

My mother spoke in a solemn tone and cupped and lifted my chin with her hands as though she were angry. To make the heaviest of impressions, she said in the sternest of voice, "Now you listen to me, young lady, you know hearts can't swell from love; they swell from clogged arteries and genetic anomalies. And guess what, you got my genes. So you're going to be smarter about the functions of the heart. And by functions of the heart, I do not mean the mystery of love, which is a matter solely for the soul. If you do not feed the soul with love, your soul cannot produce the blood your heart needs to pump through your veins. And that is real science there, girl. So the fact I love you too much is the science that's kept me alive for years, probably much, much longer than this great God intended," and here she pointed at the ceiling towards God in her sermon, almost shaking her fist at Him in defiance. She whispered to the ceiling, "I am not done. You're not taking me yet."

I didn't ask whom she was talking to.

CHAPTER IX
Armadillo to the Rescue, Part II

My father told the principal I needed a couple of weeks out of school to process our new life. When we were home, he left me with my paternal grandmother and aunt (my mothers' parents kept her constant vigil), who cleaned our house with the obsession of people unable to cope with illness. They also made elaborate meals no one ate.

A week into this routine, with no one really watching me, I slipped off to Armadillo's empty house. Of course I knew where the spare key was hidden: Armadillo and I put it under her target hay bale, precisely so I could hide in her bedroom closet and scare off potential buyers. Neither of us could fathom the thought of feet other than our own in her house.

I creaked in through the backdoor and encountered for the first time, the feeling of a shell of four walls that remains once a family leaves. The silence was like sound stripping off me, being sucked away to bleed to the outside, as if the walls were not insulated. Thinning further, the siding became rows of cracks to me then, a facade that gave no barrier to wind whipping in and out. An unnatural darkness crept of spiders up my spine, and not because the lights were off. This was the tangible feeling of loneliness, and I learned I didn't like it.

Armadillo's parents had staged the ranch with the bare minimum of functional furniture. A couch. A coffee table. No blankets on beds. No frills or tchotchkes. Without Armadillo's arrows everywhere, without crossword books slung over armchairs, without a pile of her mom's beets shoved in the sink, and without her dad's jacket resting on the counter, it was as if Reagan's Gorbachev had said, *Nah, on second thought, we fight. Here, I press 'dis button. Boom.*

But this vacancy I'd stepped into did not deter me. I went to Armadillo's closet, like she and I planned, and found the spot—literally marked with a duct-taped X—where we thought I'd hide to make ghost noises when buyers came to inspect the house. I never imagined I'd come to cry myself blind in the corner where her hamper once sat.

Apparently I must have fallen asleep on this first outing to post-Armadillo's. Or, perhaps I'd fallen into an abyss of grief with my endless mind prayers: *Please, God. Please, please, God, please don't take my mother. Please, God, please please, God, please don't take my mother. Let her live, let her live, letherlive, letherlivelether-liveletherliveletherlive.*

My grandmother and aunt thought I had run away. Cops were called. Only Noah figured to check Armadillo's house. He waited until everyone stopped asking him questions on where I might be and climbed out his bedroom window and ran up the hill and down the hill to Armadillo's ranch. He knuckled her window, which startled me, and I crawled to open the closet. When I saw his bright eyes and wavy hair, I ran to let him in at the back door, and sobbed a body sob into his chest. He shimmied our combined, sloped bodies out of view. Our motion was like a slow dance, in which the man leads a drunken woman slumped upon his chest.

The next day we returned to Armadillo's after renting VHS tapes under my father's name from Milberg Video Magic: *Mannequin, Roxanne, Splash, Big, the NeverEnding Story, Back to the Future*, and a couple of Chuck Norris movies. Our chair was Noah's old beanbag, which we dragged up the hill and down the hill.

With a bowl of hot popcorn and M&M's mixed together, we hit play on *Splash*. I rested in the crook of his arm as we folded into each other on our beanbag. He never once loosened his grip around my shoulder; twice he blew my bangs from my eyes, looked away from the movie, and kissed my forehead to make sure I wasn't crying. Each frame of that movie allowed me to escape my mother's downfall and Armadillo's absence, all within the clutch of Noah's warmth, his kisses, the taste of salt and butter and chocolate, and the image of a woman with fins.

The next day, I determined I couldn't bear to sleep in my yellow house where I expected my mother to walk in and curl around me like a mother cat. During the day's visit, her color drained to gray again, and her heart monitor, to me, sounded as though it was warning of a nuclear meltdown. When the nurses came, they pushed me to the hall, yelling how they needed to clear the room immediately. My mother screamed, "Don't you push my baby. Don't you take my baby away!" Stretching both arms in my direction, she said, "Vivi, come back in here, you mark my words, I will not leave this earth before you. I love you too much, too . . ." But the nurse kicked the door so hard, I fell backwards into the hall and didn't hear the "much" I expected. I practically hurdled over some slack-jawed stranger and hid in the hospital bathroom for an hour. When I got home, Noah was waiting on my front steps.

"I can't sleep here tonight," I said.

"Let's sleep in the fort," he said with air quotes around "the fort."

We told my grandmother and aunt we were camping out. And because it was 1990, they gave in without much of a battle. With sleeping bags and pillows, we trod up the hill and down the hill to our brown ranch, unwatched. The air was an even temperature, not too hot, not too cold, and the tug of fall's cocoon was beginning to tether us into a cabin comfort. The hint of a distant wood fire made me think of carving a pumpkin.

Noah and I lay in Armadillo's bed that night, each in our own sleeping bags. We were only thirteen. Still, the subject did come up.

He rolled to his side, him, on what was once Armadillo's side of the bed.

"We could run away," he said.

"What do you mean?"

"Like, we leave right now. Walk out of town. Get on a bus. Go to Florida. I've got seventy-six bucks buried in the backyard. I bet we could get jobs at Disney. They need all those elves and all, and we can totally do that. Also, probably wouldn't cost much to live because they have like a campground on site. So we'd just need a tent. We already have sleeping bags."

"My dad has a tent in the garage he uses for fishing trips."

"Okay, so we could take your dad's tent and the money and go."

"Also, I got a hundred fifty bucks from my birthday and Christmas. In First Century bank though, downtown. We'd have to wait until tomorrow so I can do a withdrawal."

Silence. We thought about this. I gave the whole idea serious consideration.

"But, Noah, what would we be? Boyfriend and girlfriend, like a couple?"

"Uh, I guess so."

"Does that mean we'd have to, you know . . ."

"What?"

"You know."

"You know, what?"

"Come on. You know what I mean. Like, the stuff they do in beds. Grown ups."

"Oh, like hump or something?"

"Noah!"

"Well, that's what it is. Randy told me he watches his sister and her boyfriend doing it up in their attic."

"Seriously?"

"Yeah, seriously."

"He's such a perv!"

"Yeah."

"Anyway. Would we have to do that stuff?"

"So, maybe? Why? You think we shouldn't?"

"I just, I don't know."

Silence again. We thought about this. I gave the whole idea serious consideration.

"Viv, can I kiss you for real?"

"You always kiss me."

"I mean, like in the movies. On the lips for a while."

"Uh, okay."

We wormed our sleeping bags closer and our noses clanged awkwardly. After tilting and readjusting our heads just so, Noah met my lips, and we did our best to copy the moves of Tom Hanks and Daryl Hannah. At first, his lip skin on my lip skin slipped in a weird wetness. But after crashing buck teeth, we got into a groove, my heart grew warm, and lightning shot scattershot within my body; electricity surged out of my arms and through the top of my skull. I think we did pretty darn well for ourselves, in our first make out session. We kept practicing the long-kiss, even with some jutting tongue action, and once our jaws were sore, we closed our eyes and fell asleep, holding hands under conjoined pillows. I didn't think once about my mother or Armadillo during those blessed five minutes.

Our resolve to run away increased the next day when we arrived back home to discover my mother would be in an induced coma for at least a week. Noah and I stood shoulder to shoulder like those creepy twins in *The Shining*, as my grandmother delivered the news. Nana knelt on the kitchen's white and blue linoleum with my mom's apron around her waist. How it angered me to see her in Mama's apron. Her hands smelled like wet, raw turkey, for indeed we'd interrupted her stuffing a Cornish hen. While she hurried to wash blood from her fingers, Noah spun me to face him. "You get the tent and your bank stuff. Meet me at Armadillo's in half an hour. Don't forget your bike," he said. His voice was lower than the rumble of blood and water in the sink.

Two hours later, after a surprisingly easy stop to withdraw my life savings, we were halfway to Manchester, New Hampshire. We paused on a country road in Candia by a golf course for a break. The divot between the road and the rolling farmland provided a good slant upon which to set our bikes. White clouds of cotton candy dominated the sky, but a defiant blue fought for space among the white, refusing to be denied. Behind a knotted oak—whose leaves had begun to turn red and orange—Noah and I leaned against each other's backs and ate some kind of cold fish casserole we had taken from the stash of neighbors' well-wishing food deliveries.

A red cardinal sat on a limb overhead and once or twice swooped to dance for us.

"Viv," Noah said, his back to my back.

"Yeah," I said, knowing he was seeing me and I him even without having to face each other. His back felt hot on my back.

"Viv?"

"Yeah?"

"When we get down to Florida, should we call home?"

"I think we should lay low for a little bit. I miss my mom so much already, and I so want to call her if I could call her and she wasn't . . . she wasn't. Ugh! I can't stay around this anymore and I seriously want to go." My eyes grew wet.

"Me too. I was just making sure you were still with me."

"Noah, I'm with you." I swallowed tears, determined to be angry and forgetful. The tears fell anyway, but I betrayed the emotion by continually wiping my mouth and cooling my voice, so Noah would keep talking.

"Do you love me, Viv?"

My heart fluttered, my cheeks flushed in heat, and my throat closed as though I were choked.

"Viv?"

"Yes?"

"Do you love me?"

The tears stopped; I said nothing.

"Vivi, it doesn't matter anyway. I wanted to know, because I love you."

The cardinal swooped between Noah and me.

"Well I can't imagine life without you, so I guess that means I love you," I said.

"Good."

He leaned his head against my head, and I against his, and we rolled together as though our minds were kissing. Two cats curled on a pillow in a window, purring in our sleep in the sun.

We finished our fish casserole, which we had jammed into pods of Reynolds Wrap, and cast the spent foil into our empty lunch bags. Leaning together once more, we looked to the sky.

"Viv?"

"Yeah."

"I hope we packed some brownies."

Two hours more, we boarded a bus in Manchester. Miraculously, we had enough for two one-ways to Florida, and not surprisingly, we had only $20 left as our nest egg.

Our route had planned stops in Hartford, Connecticut, Trenton, New Jersey, Greensboro, North Carolina, somewhere in Georgia, Pensacola, Florida, and at last, the holy land: Orlando. We sat in the middle of the half-filled bus; the blue and red and gray cloth seats afforded no warmth in the inexplicably (given the fall season) over-air-conditioned tube. The windows yearned for a heavy dose of Windex. We rolled along, and my eyes dropped lower in sadness with every click of the odometer.

Somewhere between Hartford and Trenton, Noah's complexion took on a shade of pale green. He broke into a sweat and just as quick as if he'd been sucker punched, bent and vomited on the bus floor. Trying to say something, he vomited again, this time all over me. Since I had the window and he had the aisle, I flattened against the side of the bus.

"Noah, what is wrong with you?!"

People dotting the seats around us began to complain about the stench. Whole families moved forward toward the driver.

"What the hell is wrong with him?" Some kerchiefed woman yelled, scrunching her nose and flapping a newspaper to short wind her gnarly mug.

"Noah, Noah?" I asked.

"Viv, I feel so hot. My stomach hurts so b . . ." and then he lost himself again. I removed my sweatshirt and tried to mop his face as tenderly as my mother had done to me, but my efforts were thwarted, and I ruined the only article of clothing I had to spare. I shivered, exposed in my spaghetti strap tank top, no training bra for my mosquito-bite breasts.

I tried to rub his scalp. His back. His arms. His neck. I said, "Noah, it's okay. A lady is telling the bus driver. Can you make it to the bathroom?"

"I can't, Viv, I'll try . . ."

In my indelible memory, his skin went from Wicked-Witch-of-the-West green to pottery clay gray, the color of my mother's skin. I arched in a fear, slamming my back against the smudged bus window.

I tried everything I could think of to soothe him: speaking softly, rubbing his spine, flaring my nostrils at anyone giving us a snarl, wiping his face with my bare hands, edging around him so as to dome over him from the aisle side, as if my scrawny body could shield him. I asked a lady for her bottle of water, and when she hesitated, I ripped it from her hands. "Drink this," I said, resting the bottle on his lips like watering a broken-winged bird. But when he wet the inside of his mouth, he only got sicker. I kissed his scalding forehead because I had no other comfort to offer.

The bus began to slow as the brakes ground to life. With the load the beast had to carry, it lurched upon a full stop, as though saying, *Fine, you need off, go on with you, and hurry up.*

Our bus driver cantilevered a torso turn with his hairy right arm and searched his passengers for the source of the commotion. Once found, he drooped his shoulders in a practiced drudgery—his personal Groundhog Day—and rose in an obligatory reluctance to shuffle to where we sat.

"You kids have to get off. I shouldn't have let you on in the first place. There's a phone booth—come on." He pointed outside the bus to a bank of phones at a roadside rest stop. "I've seen plenty of runaways on these busses in my life, but I've never seen a couple as pathetic as you two." He shook his head, sad, I think, that he couldn't let us be, as though we had failed him in some slice of freedom he might have vicariously had through us.

"Girl, you need to call your mother or his mother or whoever gave you those nice clothes and nice shoes and dentist-perfect teeth. Now get on, I'll help your boyfriend."

I lowered to the driver's authority, thinking, *Boyfriend, he said boyfriend*, and walked up the aisle. Behind me, people slid in their seats to make way for the sick boy to pass. When I heard their physical cringing, I wanted to stop and scissor-kick the fools, Chuck Norris all up in their faces.

By the time I said, "Collect call for," we'd been gone a grand total of eight hours. The driver took the receiver after I said hello to Noah's mother, Mrs. Josephine M. Vinet, the woman I had failed. Turned out, Noah had food poisoning from that fish casserole we'd stashed in aluminum, and so did I, for I started my bout of retching as soon as that awful call ended and Mrs. Vinet was on her way to retrieve us.

A month or so later, Armadillo called.

"Did you get my letters?" I asked. I'd written several to tell her about my mother's decline, the Noah kissing night, and our runaway attempt.

"Yes. I know everything. They said you could come stay with me for a month in California. Until Christmas. You'll come to school with me. Actually, I think our parents already arranged something with our schools because your mom needs the rest. But I said I wanted to ask you."

After packing, I spent the rest of the day with Noah at Armadillo's still-empty house. He said I should go to California so I could get strong again. He also said he'd mail me daily observations and Garbage Pail Kid cards to cheer me up, which he did. One of his seemingly meaningless, but profound in hindsight, notes went like this:

> *V,*
>
> *I spied on my mom today. She did the weirdest thing. No way she knew I was in the kitchen closet recording her phone conversation—but she hung up and said, "Noah, if you think I don't sense you in there, you don't understand what you mean to me." I think she's like an alien or something.*
>
> *Miss you,*
>
> *N*

I learned a few things from Armadillo in the course of my life—especially during our one month together in California, when she healed me a bit. For one, we should stick up for the downtrodden, protect them, avenge them, heal them. I also learned that some people have an art innate and it's best to let them grow in it, encourage it, lest their passions swallow them whole. This lesson I would later apply to myself and also to Ivan. At Armadillo's new school, she flourished as a painter. Later in life, some of her clients said her choice of color seemed to cure those suffering depression, which is something I learned first-hand.

But what I learned most of all from Armadillo was that a best friend is probably the most valuable thing on this earth. Armadillo got me through. One day in California, the sun turned a glowing orange, hanging above a horizon of blue and yellow and a sea of light navy. She walked me to the edge of the water, snagging an abandoned plastic pail along the way. After filling the pail with rocks, she said, "Throw these as hard as you can into the ocean and aim for the doctors who diagnosed your mother." So I did. Ten more times she filled that bucket. There have been times in my life since that I have thrown so many rocks in the ocean, I feared I'd stop the waves.

After I returned to New Hampshire and throughout into our adult lives, Armadillo would send me postcards from around the world. Just last week, she sent one from New Orleans:

> *Arguments with laughter, cigarettes with coffee, an open-door bar with candles for light, a large Renoir wannabee in a white shirt and black beret, the regulars in their chairs on the sidewalk, hunched, and a clinking horse carriage trotting past fill the scene below my balcony. This world is a hazy, perpetual slow motion. If you were here with me, we'd follow that Renoir and make a mystery of his life. Please tell me you see these things in our separation. I miss you, Sunshine.*

The dim lights of the hospital hallway distill through the slats of the shade, casting lines across Noah's somewhat transparent body. He's waiting for me to say my next selection out loud. And although she is still very much alive, I know time doesn't matter, so I announce, "I want to see Armadillo's Heaven."

White,

    pulled by feet through a blue tunnel,

      hair over head,

        bridge,

          sweater party of tree limbs,

          Noah holding my hand.

           Ahhhhhhhhhhhhhh.

CHAPTER X
The Reserve of an Artist

Army,

I stood on your front walk, loving your magnolia tree and its magnolia blossoms. Bees flocked to one meaty bud. They'll plant the tree the year your mother dies, as a comfort, because you like magnolia. This is your Heaven, I've been there. I was just passing through.

Until,

~Viv

(This is the note I'll later ask Marty to write to Armadillo)

Noah and I hike a mountain. Upon arrival at the pinnacle, the same narrator from Lachlan's Reserve explains our where-abouts: "There is a valley with a river made of paint. When you dip your brush in, whatever color you're thinking of comes out. This allows the artist to avoid the frustration of mixing and wasting precious acrylic bases in getting the hue wrong.

"Also in this valley, there is a village and an amphitheater and several art galleries. Ah, but this is just a fraction of this Reserve, for it extends to every location Ms. Armadillo Hanson has traveled and those she has not. Alas, alas, so much to the Reserve of one Armadillo, which, by the way, she has named, Sunshine. Sunshine has been awarded Heaven of the Year for three, ahem, years straight, based upon Armadillo's use of color. Color, of course, is the most prized quality of Heavens. Come, let us inspect."

Noah and I wind our way down the mountain by following a hiking path cut through white birch with yellow leaves. Low-cut, lime-green grass carpets the mountain's floor. Fluorescent blue birdhouses with a bright pink undertone adorn hundreds of the branches along our trek; they sway in the tickles of wind that race through the canopy. Purple finches fly house-to-house, limb-to-limb, and a whistle of a tune bubbles up from the ground.

When we break free of the yellow-green trail and out of the grove of birch, we find Armadillo standing in the mouth of the valley, leaning against a heart-shaped boulder. We are in the bottom of a majestic and green valley, one you might expect in Costa Rica. Mountains on three sides boast roaring, tumbling waterfalls as high as the sky. The front wall of the valley is no mountain, but a glimmering ocean, whose beach glistens in one hundred colors of reflective glass. Along the floor of the valley weaves a multi-color river of paint with tributaries weaving to every nook and cranny of the valley and beyond, to places I simply cannot see. Just beyond Armadillo at her heart-shaped rock is a column of stone pillars.

Armadillo runs to me, grabs me in a love-hug, and twirls me as though she's Julie Andrews singing in the hills of Switzerland. I, her armload of air.

"I have a huge party planned for you tonight! I can't believe you're finally here. I've missed you so much."

"How did you know I was coming?"

"I have my sources," she says and winks at Noah.

I remember they grew up a hill apart. I had forgotten, for I had begun to view Noah as someone different in his adult—his angelic—form, something closer to me than he had been when we were young, if this is even possible. At being reminded, I also remember my life and Jack and the sadness of my son, *oh Ivan*, my parents too, my father's now constant trouble, my mother's constant decline. With these earthly thoughts, so begins a series of physical senses, making me aware of my body, of pain. Indeed, I wonder if a cobra is crushing my arms and chest, about to swallow me. It is as though when I bring to mind my life, my physical body invades, demanding to be felt once again. The ground trembles by the feel of my weakened legs, and colors kaleidoscope, fading to white. Noah dissipates to a transparency. And suddenly I recognize all of this as signs I will fall back into the living. I am surprised at how incredibly distraught I am to leave Armadillo and Noah. While I do want to be with my family, I am not prepared in this moment to leave serenity, so I fight the pull by staring at the ghostly Noah and plead him to help me stay.

"Noah, please," I call out.

He scoops me close. With my body enshrined in his arms, I remember Marty's cure for spikes in my health; I count slowly backwards, *eight, Precious, seven, six now slow, five, Precious, four and breathe, three now good, two, and one, Precious, one.*

Finally I am able to focus on my surroundings and release from Noah. Armadillo stands before me with a wicked grin.

"Sunshine. Here in the, well, spirit. Come on. If you're sampling Heavens, I have a lot to show you before the party starts tonight. I hope you like stargazy pie."

As with any time I caught up with Armadillo in life, I have no clue what she's talking about or what insane itinerary she's got planned, but whatever it is, I'll likely wonder why I've never experienced it before—I'll feel as I felt upon the first night on the bridge: cheated that I've only just discovered something wonderful.

We follow Armadillo through a row of Romanesque, limestone columns set in the center of the valley like vertebrae.

"Cleopatra had these installed in one of her palaces after she met Mark Antony—her palace no living historian has yet unearthed, but which she recreated in her Heaven. She toured me through her intricate hidden rooms and rolling gardens when I visited her Heaven a month ago. Freakin' blew my mind, Sunshine."

I suspect Armadillo is telling a tale, as she is wont to do, and so I listen on, raising my eyes of amused skepticism.

"There I was having ginger tea with Cleopatra in her secret palace and she's stroking the fur on her ten cats, and then snap, literally on the snap of her henna-tattooed fingers, she transports me to the courtyard, and I found myself standing in these wonderful pillars in a mile-wide garden stuffed with pink roses. Cleo laid her gold tiara on a wooden bench and leaned on a pillar, appearing to contemplate some long ago time. She said, 'Mark asked me to marrvy heem out zere, beyond zose roses by zee swans. No one knows zis.' Sunshine, for real. I didn't know how to respond. Right? So I said, 'Cleopatra'—can you believe I was talking to Cleopatra?—'Cleopatra, I sort of like these columns, like a lot.' And she goes, 'Ah jes, vell, they arrre nice. I vas thinking on redecorating actually.' Snap, and she snaps, 'Ju have them. A gift from me to ju. And mayve as a favor to me, ju might paint me somvvthing, Madam Armazillo. I suppose a Queen should have a painting from the woman who keeps vinning Heaven ov ze Year."

"Shut up, Army, you can't be serious."

"Dead serious, girl. Literally. I am literally dead serious. Okay, I was joking. But I had you going for a minute. I have no clue where Cleopatra is in the afterlife, but wouldn't it be cool to find her?"

At this, I burst, crunched in a fit of snort laughing. Armadillo does too. Noah leans against a column and laughs as well. I spit out half sentences throughout my roaring spell, trying to remark on Armadillo's ridiculous vampire accent that might be accurate if Cleopatra were from Transylvania and not Egypt.

As we trail into a sputter of giggles, Noah and I lower ourselves to sitting against the stone columns. Armadillo begins to walk in and out of the columns away and then toward us, in a somewhat looping figure eight.

"When you come upon a row of columns," she says, "do you choose one side to walk along or do you weave in and out combining both sides into a braid of footsteps? This is what I hope I do with my art, blend one side with the other, the life, the death, the colors and layers of both."

"Oh Army, I can't wait to see everything. Can we go now?"

"Yes, I'm dying, woops, not dying, already did that, I'm existing in an eternity to show you."

I start to laugh again.

"Don't laugh. Come on. Get up, there's so much, so much."

"Vat, can't zu jus snap jour fingers, Madam Armazillo?"

Armadillo giggles, "Sunshine, let's go." And she holds my hand to follow her, like we're double Pocahontas, tracking prey once again.

We braid our way through the columns, taking Armadillo's winding lead, and come upon a house on a small mound that presides over a round field, which other houses, on different mounds, also border, making it a quaint community. Our destination house has clapboard siding painted a fern green, which is offset by fuchsia-pink shutters and cedar window boxes overflowing with a bounty of red wave petunias.

"This is one of my galleries," she says. "I call it M, which stands for my muse."

Off the short path leading to the pink front door is an eight-foot magnolia tree with gloss-waxy leaves and heaven-white buds. Not one brown petal or limp leaf corrupts the perfection.

"My magnolia. Someone planted it—while I was still alive—in the front yard of my life house the year my mother died. I couldn't part with this tree even here in death."

Armadillo rubs a wax leaf—like fingers to a kitten's ears—and bows in respect.

"My mother," she says, choking back a tear or a laugh, or both. "Anyway, that was tough, Sunshine, and the worst part was, you were already gone. I didn't have anyone to comfort me through all those years without her, or you."

"Oh Army, I'm so sorry."

"Oh hell, not your fault! Listen to me, carrying on. And I have no right anyway. Whatever the reason was I was meant to have that journey in life, I can tell you I didn't waste the emotion or the lesson. I poured further into my painting, and now I carry what I learned to my M, my beloved M." In a wistful longing, she stares at her Muse house and plucks two gold horse charms, hanging from twine tied around her neck. She seemingly sees something, or someone, in her wordless gaze and wrinkles her nose to chase away the taunting memory. Armadillo has had many life-enveloping love affairs—I, being her best friend in the world, know all the lovely and gory details. I can only imagine the collection of loves she accumulated after my death and through her life. Only she knows the one that continues to tug at her heart, even here in death, and forces her to bounce charms on her chest.

She looks across at the memorial for her mother again, the magnolia tree.

"And besides, my mother, the old bird, lives right there anyway and here you are now." Armadillo points across the field to a glowing blue house with green shutters and sprays of delphinium sprouting out of red window boxes. Mr. and Mrs. Hanson wave to me from their porch. I wave back.

Inside M, a ray of sunlight creeps like a vein along the polished wood floor. Half walls of white plaster define the room into a maze of sorts, and on those half walls hang huge paintings in gold frames.

Noah and I meander through the art maze, soaking in the painted scenes, which are each of an opened windowsill looking upon some distant land. Before each windowsill are realistic, as if photographed and not painted, collections of still-life objects one might find in the far-off place. One painting in particular catches my eye, so I study the details.

Here in this painting is a window opened to a large park, low office buildings, and shops and cobblestone alleys. Within the collection of items on a table before a sill, the following are painted: a bowtie (so real I think I can reach in and grab it for Noah to wear), opera binoculars, a pair of Prada reading glasses, a receipt for a restaurant in Malpensa, a bottle of Montefiore Chianti, two ticket stubs to *La Bohème* at La Scala, and a tear-stained linen handkerchief.

Noah's pensive smile and low lids hide a deep secret. I figure I'll ask later what the suppressed twinkle in his eyes mean.

"Love in Milan," Armadillo says. "You like? Remember when we went there, Sunshine?"

"Sure do. On our way to Genoa. We didn't want to leave Milan, though. We stayed two extra days, right?" I say.

"Remember the guy I met, Giuseppe?"

"Giuseppe! Ohhhhhh, woo, I had forgotten about him."

"Yeah, well, I didn't," Armadillo says, dropping an octave on "didn't." "Giuseppe. Anyway, he was a yummy little treat. He comes from time to time to, well, check in on me. Mmmmmm. Good thing I never got married, because I surely would have been divorced. So many beautiful specimens." She leans in to whisper in my ear, "In my world, God, this collective energy rather, just wants you to be truthful, and I believe I was and am. I was honest with whoever might have crossed my path, and I loved all of them, truthfully. Truth is personal, I find, and it's different for everyone. So I make no comment on others' truths. Does your God want you to deny love for a different truth that man defines? I don't know the answer. I just know I did wind up here, so, who knows."

Oh Armadillo, you guzzled life and here you guzzle death.

But M's floorboards rattle when I continue my thought: *Yet, why is it okay for Armadillo to espouse this philosophy, when I had denied the same to Jack and even myself. Should I have calmed in the hospital? Said something to ease him, the situation?* Like before, as I allow my mind to wander to life, I waver, and Noah once again becomes a rainy vision. I think of a song I recently heard Eva Cassidy sing, "Tall Trees in Georgia." When I'd heard the lyrics, I thought of Armadillo and here I think of them with her before me: *Control your mind girl; And give your heart to one; For if you love all men; You'll be surely left with none.*

A nausea tightens my throat. Armadillo claps her hands in my face.

"Vivi. Vivi. Listen. Ask yourself, are you being truthful?" In a stern jerk of my shoulders, she whips me to view the Milan painting, then whips me to view Noah, who is coming to a better clarity.

"Are you being truthful?" she repeats, in the tough-love tone of a best friend.

"Armadillo, it's fine. Fine. Let's move on," Noah says.

Armadillo gives him a squint, as if to say, *You sure?* And I have no idea what this secret language means.

Am I being truthful? About what? Do I have a different truth from Armadillo? Perhaps.

"Anyway, I painted this picture for you, and I can't believe this is the very one you fall into. Remember how you were upset because *La Bohème* was playing at La Scala and we couldn't afford the tickets? We had only just graduated grad school. We bought a bottle of that there Montefiore Chianti and drank it from a brown bag on a marble step across the street from La Scala. For two hours we watched the parade of women in red gowns and men in tuxedos. You kept telling me how one day you'd find your true love, who would take you to see *La Bohème*."

"You remember that?"

"Remember that? It's seared in my brain."

"Army, I absolutely love this painting. And you even put the receipt from the restaurant in the field in Malpensa. Remember how there was that little abandoned castle by it—we couldn't believe such a thing could exist."

"Yup. Now listen, if you want to go, we can go right now. I designed the scenes so you open into them like opening a door. All of the frames are on hinges." Armadillo opens Milan; behind is not a wall, but the painted-now-real park, the low office buildings, and the shops on cobblestone alleys. A swallow flies up from a tree in the park and flutters for us. So, too, a yellow butterfly. A moped hums and bumps on the stone.

As we step into Milan, a bell rings.

"Oh darn, we can't go right now. Time's up. We need to get ready for the party. Come on now."

Armadillo whisks Noah and me out of M, across the round field, past her parents' electric-blue house, and along a beach littered with smooth beach glass of aqua and orange and blue and red. "Only the rarest of sea glass tumbles here, but *all* of the rare pieces, which explains why there's so much. I use the glass for my sculptures." She nods to a sculpture garden within the grassy dunes to our left. A ten-foot mermaid arches her back; red sea glass studs her hair as though they are rubies. A whale tail rises from a dune as if out of the sea; his blue glass shimmers in the setting sun and against the now fire-orange sky. Countless other sea-themed sea glass sculptures dot the endless dunes. Behind us, the high mountains of the deep valley begin to shade in the coming evening, the rumbling waterfalls creating a mist at their bases.

Armadillo leads us to a narrow path with a driftwood fence on each side, similar to a public easement between mansions bordering a beach. Pastel towels and bathing suits hang in lumps over the pointy tops. Overhead, a thick canopy of oaks sway, housing cardinals and cooing turtledoves.

Before long, twilight grades the light, first to a blue haze and then, upon arrival at an amphitheater carved in a cliff sea wall, a navy blue punched with tiny orange candles. Strings of twinkle lights are strung among the multiple levels of the cliff wall and along the stone seating. It is night in Heaven.

"On the very top of the cliff. That's my home, the glass house. We'll change in there. I have a view of this sea, the valley we just came from, M, Rare Beach-Glass Beach, the sculpture park, and all of the lands of my Heaven."

I drape my arm around my old friend, and we make our way to her glass home on top of the cliff. The ocean roars not tragically, but as orchestra drums calling an audience to attention. Noah clasps his hands behind his back and follows, calmly grinning to the ground.

I think, *Everything you do is so grand, my friend. I can't decide which piece is best.*

Once inside her glass home, Armadillo shoos Noah to a side hall and scampers back to choose our dresses. After we pretty ourselves, Noah appears like a contemplative spectre in the arch of the hall, hands placed patiently in his tan linen pants. The sight of desert sands, their dunes and shadows, under his crisp white shirt stalls me from placing another flower in my hair. With a subtle bounce of my pupils, down to up, I land my craving upon his gold hair, which is combed back but free, easy.

Armadillo vanishes to another room.

I don't move.

And neither does Noah.

A thousand candles seem to light the room and reflect off the glass.

Armadillo tiptoes behind my back, and she too stalls. I can only presume she doesn't know if she should burst the moment she witnesses between Noah and me.

Nevertheless, another bell rings, and the decision is made for us.

"Well then," she says, clapping her hands. "Let's go."

We follow Armadillo to a painting hanging in the foyer, which features a tiny fishing village at night. Christmas lights define a path for a parade of people.

"Mousehole, Cornwall, pronounced 'Mowzal.' You never went there, Viv. But I did. And I never got the chance to tell you about this magnificent feast. So here's my chance."

She opens the painting by pulling on the frame and we enter her painted fishing village. Bulbs of blue, red, and yellow hang on rickety sticks and rope. The swath of partygoers passes, each member carrying paper lanterns and chanting a song I know quite well. They sing without any uniformity and traipse along, dangling their lanterns, some stumbling, some skipping, some cheering at random, and some blowing kazoos. Streamers shoot out without any real timing or sequence.

"Jakob Dylan's 'Nothing But The Whole Wide World.'" I know you love his voice," Armadillo says, acknowledging the music in the air. "So, in life, this village has an annual festival right before Christmas called 'Tom Bawcock's Eve.' Legend has it, many years ago, Mousehole residents were near starvation because their fishermen were stuck at sea in a storm. Tom Bawcock set out in his boat, taking with him his cat. Well the cat apparently sung the storm to sleep, allowing Tom to catch barrels of fish. The villagers guided Tom and his cat back to shore with homemade lanterns. At least, this is how I remember the tale. In celebration, the villagers hold an annual Christmas feast and serve stargazy pie, a pie of fish and potatoes with fish heads sticking out. It's grand fun. It's nuts. Anyway, even though it's not Christmas, I thought we'd throw a

'Tom Bawcock's Eve' celebration for you tonight, because I thought you might like to experience something you never had before."

So, she does it again, gives me something that leaves me feeling cheated for having missed out on it before.

Damn do we enter a raucous party.

We sit at a crowded tavern table in a low-ceilinged bar. English waitresses in handmaid costumes serve us mugs of cold ale, which are so full, the froth slops off the sides. The stargazy pie is served to rousing whistles and whooping applause, and a jug band in the corner goes bananas with a furious folk song. Despite the fish heads sticking out of the gigantic pie, it sure tastes like the best thing I've ever tasted. And here I thought Noah and I had sworn off fish casseroles for an eternity.

When the pie is cleared from the table, one of the waitresses announces that a chocolate cake will be served in my honor. As she toddles off to fetch it, I tell Noah I feel flush and need to cool down. He hooks my arm and helps me outside to a quiet pocket by a post-and-beam fence.

A lull in the air signals me to expect a shock to the ground and a return to the hospital room. Grabbing Noah's arm for stability, I beg, "If we have to go back, please can we please first stop at the Freshwater Memory Museum in Lachlan's Reserve? I'd like to see some more things in the barn, and I want to see if there's a plaque yet for that briefcase of money."

Chapter XI
Freshwater Memory Museum

Noah squeezes my hand; he seems almost excited I would again ask to stay longer.

"Okay. Let's get over to Lachlan's. This way, I think." Out through Armadillo's painting, back by the cliff amphitheater, and through the driftwood fences with bathing suits we run. When we reach Rare Beach-Glass Beach, we sprint down the shoreline. Along the way, I grab a sand-worn bottle top, which matches one I found in life at a boat landing in Gloucester, Massachusetts. That one had a miniscule scrap of a torn love letter inside, or one I imagined. But that is another story altogether.

At a notch in one dune, Noah weaves us down a path, and we find ourselves on the shore of Lachlan's round reservoir. Ripples of waves gently lap at the edge, reaching to touch our toes. Candle-lights strung among the sky-high canopy twinkle above. Everyone who might have been sorting canoes or filing fishing poles is asleep, except one other being in the middle of the water.

A baby grand piano floats atop a raft set free upon the sleeping reservoir, and there plays a man in tails and topcoat, top hat too. A tickle of a sweet song meets my ears. Noah presents me with a gallant extension of his arm to a dance floor, which is made of a patchwork of antique surfboards.

We kick off our sandals, which, frankly, I didn't even know I was wearing. Noah rolls up his pant legs and palms my waist with one hand and my shoulder with the other. The piano player takes Noah's circling finger point to mean he should start a slow love song, one I had never heard before. I feel as though an electrical fire erupts within my chest.

Noah leads me through ballroom twirls and at each stanza creeps his long body an inch closer. Closer. Inching in. His breath heats my neck and jellies my muscles. Gliding to the far edges of the dance floor, one corner to the next, he transforms our ballroom decorum into a tantalizing tango by standing more erect to bend his body over mine. Long strides he takes; I, I follow, I follow. When he folds me backwards over his knee, I ache for his body to never leave mine. Beads of water form on my lips having rolled there off my tongue, and how I wish to use this water to wet his neck. So I move there. Slowly. The song plays on indefinitely, but at long last, trails to a regretful finish. We keep on a beat or two until we realize the music has ended.

And yet, we remain entwined on the dance floor.

Noah lends his head to the space between my chest and collarbone, hanging there, breathing hard, and contemplating another move. He plucks the straps of my dress, loosening them to fall along my arms. Lifting his head high enough to match his mouth with mine and hover there, he breathes in my own breath. I inch closer, even though not a fraction comes between us. He winds his hands into the back of my scalp to cradle my skull and pull me to him. A mixed taste of honey seems raw to me, as if his instinct is my own. And under the Heaven moon, beneath lit candles in trees, we bite lightly each other's lips and press hard in a mutual devouring. I could have stolen his very soul in this moment, and he, mine.

A light on a long limb extinguishes, and the spell we are in breaks. Noah releases me and bows as though I am a queen. And yet, I do not feel an ounce worthy of his heady affection.

Did Jack ever capture me like this? I think so. But did he? When?

"Shall we," Noah says, pointing to the Miscellaneous Division Freshwater Memory Museum. An inviting gold light beckons us to enter.

"Uh, okay." I reluctantly slide my straps to their rightful places and wrestle internally to dampen what had arisen within. The only way to do this is to force my thoughts on something entirely nonsexual, so I picture polishing the banister in my house. That doesn't work, obviously, so I skip to, well, nothing—nothing right now has an innocent connotation. If you have a beating heart, I'm sure you understand.

Not wanting to leave the last moment, I relent and go on, snailing my way along the stone dust path to the museum's entrance. Crickets and an occasional bullfrog form the night music, which holds the reserve in a sleepy mellow. Allowing myself to think only of solving the mystery of the briefcase full of money, I focus on locating its plaque. And yet, before entering the barn I hesitate, recalling my situation, my life, my son, the others at the hospital. *Why am I thinking of a briefcase of money, now? Why? Who am I supposed to be?*

The ground seems to give, as if pulling my feet, and the sight of Noah morphs from clear to rainy to clear. I tense my muscles to fight the dire impermanence.

Tenuous of my slipping state, I walk softly past Sissy's closed and darkened vintage shop and enter the barn on light steps, rapping the open door to announce our presence. Lachlan sits at the center picnic table sharing port with the inventory keeper.

"Vivienne! How great. Noah, welcome, welcome. Come on in you two."

"We can't stay long, I'm so sorry," Noah says, deepening the line between his eyebrows.

I tilt my head, taking in his words. *We can't stay long,* I think with a pang of disappointment—and confusion at the disappointment. *Do I want to live? What is my definition of life now? What is real? What is truth?*

I definitely feel the concrete floor tremble, which I ignore, stiffening against my failing state.

Turning to Lachlan, I ask, "So, I was wondering about the briefcase of money. Is the plaque completed yet?"

The inventory keeper wipes his mouth with a napkin and grins at Lachlan before addressing me. *A little secret between them about me? About what?*

"Vivienne, we're still," he pauses to choose his words, "working on crafting the right prose." He looks to Lachlan for an approving agreement in how he has answered. Once acknowledged, he speeds a polite completion, "Should be done soon though. Please come back."

"Yes, Vivienne, please do come back," Lachlan adds, as he rises and nears Noah. I catch it, I know I do: Lachlan's hopeful wink, not a conspiratorial wink, but a gesture saying, *Hang on, we're pulling for you*, not to me, to Noah, who screws his face in a subtle worry. Lachlan perks up his voice, keeping a tight clasp on Noah's shoulder, "But listen, there's plenty of other things. Here, some port to cap off the night," he says, pouring each of us the blood-red liquid. "Take this and walk around. Stay as long as you like. Read everything."

I try to ask Noah what's wrong.

He waves off my inquiries, saying, "Nothing is wrong," and lamely hides an obvious disconcertion by burying his nose too far in his glass of port. Separated not physically, but because he refuses to answer a single one of my questions, we plod around with our goblets.

Noah rubs his temples, drifting away with almost every step. Still, he denies my concern, saying my medicine must be mixing with my final march, confusing the "doubt of life with the certainty of death." Picking up a plaque, he adds, "Please, Vivienne, let's enjoy the few minutes we have left in this night, these wonderful stories, and do not worry. We are here together now." Since he gives a genuine plead and jumps to a brass plaque, I follow his lead once again.

One particular item stops me. It belongs to my father, Marcus Marshall. Reading the accompanying plaque makes me hopeful that my lovely son Ivan will also find a vocation he loves and will make a success. A prayer, I suppose, is born when I read this plaque.

Item #1533910

After school, Marcus Marshall, fourteen, sat on a corner in downtown Manchester, New Hampshire, under a department store's windows with ever-changing mannequin displays inside. He held a sign scrawled in crayon: "Please, a dollar for my mother and my sister." He didn't care about the boys and girls from St. Joe's, who passed and flicked pennies at his face. The humiliation did not outweigh the hunger.

One day, near Christmas, a man with a red sweater and matching red scarf handed Marcus a box full of new shoelaces. The cardboard fold around each pair said, "Shoelaces, the Glue for Your Shoes." "Sell these," the red-sweater man said, handing Marcus a black Sharpie. Marcus knew just what to do and wrote on the cardboard box, "Shoelaces, $.50," and added a redundant, "Cents." Slowly and surely as the sun faded, the mannequins worked an enchantment upon the boy sitting below their plastic feet and under the window frame. A line of Christmas shoppers formed to purchase shoelaces. All told, Marcus sold two hundred pairs in one night; his full lot of cash was, of course, "$100.00 Dollars," as he wrote in monetary redundancy in his diary at home before falling into a deep, well-earned sleep. He left the empty box outside on the porch, for he thought he'd recycle it the next day.

In the morning, when he left his city-owned, brick apartment in "The Projects," his cold toes kicked what he thought was his empty shoelace box. It didn't budge. Marcus found the box filled to the brim with shoelaces. After school, he sat beneath the mannequins, and once again a line formed and he sold out. He logged another "$100.00 Dollars." This continued the entire Christmas season until Marcus amassed "$3,000.00 Dollars," which happened to be just enough to fund a year's rent for an old coat closet with a half-door within the department store (the manager having noticed Marcus during Christmas and thus giving him a serious break). Marcus recalled his mother's oft-repeated refrain: "Success is always and only the exploitation of a seed of luck." With the relentless elbow grease of the literally and figuratively hungry, Marcus upgraded the closet to a room-sized space. He then expanded over the years to a storefront of his own, stocking it with shoelaces and simple sneakers on sparse racks, which later filled and bulged into three local stores. Upon misfortune later in his life, he dug deeper and multiplied his city-chain into a regional chain with nearly every conceivable shoe and shoelace known to man. Marcus never relented on his hard work and mastery of the sale, and he was forever thankful for the chance he was given when he was fourteen.

One May day, Marcus took his mother on a picnic and told her the story of his start, which he had never confessed before. While handing her a jumble of eight shoelaces, he searched her eyes to believe him. Her response was not of disbelief, but of prayerful thanks. She fingered the lacey mass as though the knots were the beads of a rosary and then threw it in a fast-moving babbling brook beyond their picnic blanket. "We give thanks to the angels for that, my son." She did not reveal how for three years she had secretly worked the nightshift at a shoelace factory in Nashua and had convinced a red-sweater-wearing co-worker to bring her son the day's rejects one winter day, long ago. She kept the magic box going for a month straight, until her son's wings unfolded and he flew himself, finding a way to fill his own inventory. Marcus, for his part, thought his mother worked her second job at a diner on lower Elm. Why he never went to visit her there is a mystery only he can answer. Perhaps believing a box of dreams can replenish itself is easier to swallow than the image of your mother slinging coffee or sorting laces at 3 a.m.

After reading this plaque, I determine to later ask Marty to write the following note to my father:

Dad, you may want to ask Nana about your shoelaces. Perhaps she will explain your lovely miracle after all. Please help Ivan understand the value of hard work. I want him to be just like you.

Love,

Viv

CHAPTER XII
Ivan

May 11, 2023, Ele and I got married even though we're still in college; we talked about the anniversary of my mother's death. Ele hugged me and fed me some wedding cake. I didn't tell her she had frosting on her nose. I licked it off. She promised to do whatever it took to get me through college and med school—but somewhere close to our home. And I promised to do whatever it took to get her a degree in history, also close to our home, which she wants because she imagines herself a history professor. I'm going to train to be a spinal doctor. But I'm not going to practice medicine. I'm going into research. But first, our two-week honeymoon in Maui.

June 2023, Ele has finally moved in with me. We live together in the same house. This is the happiest day of my life. She and I will live in the same house I've lived in all my life, my mother's house, my and Ele's home. My father and stepmother and stepsiblings moved two towns over to a log house we've spent the last two years building. My and Ele's children will grow up here. And not one of them will know the "secret" Ele and I keep to this day, the one that kept us together.

February 16, 2024, I read *Ivan* to Jacob, our first-born son, all night of his birth and into the dawn while sweet Ele slept (honeymoon—or maybe pre-honeymoon—baby ☺). Ele has chosen to go to night school, given our "surprise."

February 17, 2025, I read *Ivan* to Celia, our second-born child, all night of her birth and into the dawn while sweet, sweet Ele slept. Ele has decided to put off the rest of college for now, and when she told me, she giggled and kissed the puffed cheeks of our babies, blowing bubbles on Jacob's bullfrog tummy until he gave that wonderful baby laugh. I'm concerned she might regret this decision, but who am I to argue with Fortress Ele. Plus she seems so in love.

February 28, 2025, although many years have gone by, I walked to the place where Ele and I set out to solve our "problem." I then walked to the spot I went to four years later to finally dispatch with our "problem." I read my old notes in *Ivan*, tearful, but happy.

February 18, 2027, I read *Ivan* to Lucy and Alice, our newborn twins, all night of their birth and into the dawn while sweet, sweet, sweet, sweet Ele slept. Ele announced she doesn't want to teach history anymore. She says she has no regrets because, as she says, "Why be shackled to someone else's past when I'm creating history myself." And who can argue with Fortress Ele?

I read *Ivan* to all of our children during the one-week celebration of their combined February birthdays. I think I'll do this every year, so I'll add the years as they roll by: 2028, 2029, 2030, 2031, 2032, 2033, 2034, 2035, 2036, 2037, 2038, 2039, 2040, 2041, 2042, 2043, 2044, 2045, 2046, 2047, 2048, etc.

July 17, 2033, I got a business loan today. I'm going to find a way to cure spinal injuries. I will spend my life doing this, and I can only hope my mother would be proud. Although I am thirty years old and happily married ten years now, I have taken myself to sit alone in a botanical garden. My mother once admitted to me that she would do this when she needed to be alone or to be thankful for something. So here I am, missing her so, and I am reading *Ivan* once again. I have paused to write this note because a flock of yellow butterflies, which look like flying buttercups, have taken to rest upon my backpack. And a red cardinal dances on a fountain's edge at my side, winging water at me, and I swear he's winking my way.

CHAPTER XIII
The Science of Luck and Misfortune

From the point of our runaway attempt at thirteen to the age of fifteen, Noah and I were still best friends, but also, declared boyfriend and girlfriend. We ate lunch together. I went to all his soccer games. He read the stories I wrote and came to my plays to throw flowers—fistfuls of roadside black-eyed Susans or devil's paintbrush or whatever was free and in season. One night, after catching us making out on the school's play structure after a long soccer game, my father gave a disastrously embarrassing speech about where babies come from. My mother hobbled into the room and relieved him by sending him off to buy himself a six-pack. In her blunt, tough-love way, she cleared things up: "If you have sex, you will get pregnant."

From then on, she held a tight tether from her medical bed upstairs, keeping air-striker track of my and Noah's comings and goings. She had the pained hope of a teenager parent that I would not become a statistic. And she wasn't alone in her war effort.

As though they were commanding generals, I think she and Josie shared pinned wall maps of their enemies: Noah and me, puberty, hormones, and something far beyond puppy love they could not explain.

Despite all of these protections, no one on the living earth could pry Noah and I apart. By the time we were well into fifteen, we began to truly test the boundaries of our physical attraction.

If I find myself in a place of solitude and I focus, I can picture us up in our old fort. I feel his almost-a-man lips on my almost-a-woman neck, then those red, wet lips down to my uncovered breasts. A breeze blows the treetops above our patchy roof. While I lay beneath the rustling leaves, my eyelids skip and flicker an involuntary dance, and his lips linger at my breasts, around my, a rise of heat and there I flicker, again, a trailing line of kisses to my stomach. He, skip, urges those lips into my skin, to my, skip, back up to my, to my, to my heart that will burst. The leaves shake; he's up to my neck. His hands everywhere all over me.

He used to say he loved my back most.

At the end of August of our fifteenth year, it was hot. Everything was in respite, even my mother seemed fine, and although she would strain through wheezing steps, she'd amble outside to sit in her wildflower garden to study with Josie. They had taken up a home college course because my mother was determined to cure herself; and Josie was determined to cure her friend. They'd gossip and snigger, and my mother would cough as they worked through the syllabus, sitting in the garden, sipping lemonade like the fine southern ladies they really were.

In an effort to explain why she'd taken up her medical studies, my mother would lecture, "Only one person in this good life will look out for you and it's you, don't you forget, Viv. Can't rely on me, your father, your grandparents, some guy you might marry someday, no one. You got you. But I do love you too much, so I'll try the best I can, babe."

"Noah, Mama," I said.

"What?"

"I'm going to marry Noah. You said 'some guy,' but it will be Noah."

"I don't care if you marry the Pope! Just look out for yourself."

"Mom," I was giggling, "You can't marry the Pope."

Then she was giggling with me, snorting in her laughter, and spitting and stumbling over other possible suitors she had to make up because apparently no realistic humans might marry me, other than the Pope. "Marry Tucan-Sam, marry, marry, whatever, marry Harry Barry, marry the damn Mayor of Mazatlán, what do I care."

Thereafter, whenever she couldn't remember something, I'd tease her by telling her to call the Mayor of Mazatlán and ask him if he knew.

And she would giggle as though tickled every time.

She was gorgeous when she laughed, and she owned the world.

The very next week, Noah and I would start school. On Monday afternoon, I made my mother a grilled cheese sandwich and cut it into the shape of a heart because it felt so good to see her big eyes dance in a surprise. Everything seemed primary-color rich that August Monday: her reading amongst royal-blue delphinium and shocks of pink petunias, Josie sitting with her, not reading anything, painting her nails and cooing at another Vinet baby, and best of all, Noah to myself. All the boys in the neighborhood went to a football camp for their last week of summer vacation, except Noah, who favored soccer, which left him and me alone for one whole week, uninterrupted.

After lunch, we went to his basement to begin a game of Monopoly. We played eight straight hours. The next day we played Payday. Eight hours again. Next, Life, then a day of Battleship and Clue. We played in his basement or on a card table in the backyard under a navy-blue umbrella or at a picnic table in my mother's garden. We'd move base when we were forced to eat meals.

Odd, how we were so simultaneously engrossed for so many hours despite the height of a blazing summer. The brilliant sun was but a backdrop to us. Heat crickets and invisible beetles sizzled in their hot electricity, sending a radio wave of blisters through the air. If our game-playing was outside, we ran an extension cord to wherever we were and directed two fans on our faces. We collected rocks to secure the board and fake money and cards of whatever game we played.

By Friday, we were back to Monopoly. This was the last time I ever played Monopoly, because as with an Ouija board, that last game scared the hell out of me—like watching a prophecy be told and unfold all at once.

We were in Noah's backyard, sitting at the circular picnic table with the navy umbrella. Sharing one side of the circle, the Monopoly board was between us; two fans spun on high, one directed at him, one at me. The morning cicadas and chirping sparrows sent a serenade of bug declarations and bird questions. The sky was pool-blue cloudless, and the air smelled like cut grass. Game after game after game, we played.

Late into the afternoon of our Friday Monopoly Marathon, Noah rolled a seven. Then he rolled a seven on his next turn. Then a seven again. And again. Then he rolled some random other number. Then a seven. Then a random other number. Then a seven. And so on and so forth. Sometimes he seemed to fall off his pattern, but soon enough was back to a rash of sevens. Roll after roll after roll, the sevens coming in one of three ways: a four and a three, a six and a one, a two and a five. We became so boisterous over the strangeness, we attracted the attention of Josie and Noah's brothers, who formed a semi-circle around the table. By the time we filled the board with homes and hotels, Mr. Vinet was home and my parents were present. Now a full circle of family and even some nameless neighbors surrounded us. We piled red hotels and green houses on our respective properties, and Noah kept rolling those sevens on a fairly constant basis. I'd get some streaks of sevens, but only two in a row, and I'd return to a variety of rolls: a twelve, an eight, a three, so on.

The crowd around us murmured at first, but soon began hooting, repeating their collective awe: "I can't believe this"; "We should be taping this"; "Seriously, all game like this?" Someone made a cheesy bean dip, and our dads fired up the grill. Beers were uncapped. The pack of brothers fought for space on our respective sides, as though towel boys in the corners of a boxing ring. High fives flew, empty beer bottles piled up. Josie turned on the garage floodlights and lit citronella candles for her impromptu party.

When Noah put one hotel on Boardwalk and one on Park, I asked my mother for an icy Coke. She left and filled my order, handing me a frosted mug through the crowd as though dabbing sweat from my forehead. "Here you go, babydoll," she said, clasping my shoulder and squeezing.

Then, when Noah should have rolled a seven, he rolled snake eyes, those two beady dots equaling a two, and our neighborhood audience hushed. Someone said, "Ooohhhhhwwww," as though they'd watched him fall and scrape his knee. On snake eyes, you're allowed to roll twice in Monopoly, and when he did, Noah rolled a seven. Again. "AHHHHHHHHH!" his brothers yelled, and one jumped in the air, grabbed a tree branch meant for a swing, and hung like a monkey. Someone increased the volume on Magic 106.7 FM and our party was in full jam.

Then.

Noah rolled a ten, passed GO, collected $200, and landed on Chance. Chance said he had to pay street repairs of $40 for each house and $115 for each hotel on the board, which wiped him out, ending the game in my favor. The party was killed by one fatal card. All of Noah's luck and wise investments wiped out on the flip of One. Blue. Card. The sinister tip of the Monopoly Man's hat saying, *May be good, may be bad, you take your Chance.*

I think Noah used all the luck he had coming to him on that August Friday of Monopoly. All the sevens he might have rolled, sprinkled as they should have been, were clumped into one game. Had I known what was to come, I would have insisted we go to the beach instead.

Here's the thing about luck and misfortune. Neither one is smart enough to disperse across a lifetime. If they did, people would have a better way of staying consistently even. People would know they'd have luck one day and the next misfortune and next luck. So basically they could plan their emotions to be pretty much straight. Perhaps one day you are diagnosed with heart disease, but the next day the doctors find a cure, and the next day you find your best friend is moving, but the next day, as luck would change, they open up the school she needs one town over.

Looking back, Noah's streak of luck had started earlier in the year when he became the captain of the soccer team and won our town the state's junior division championship. He aced every test we had, becoming the academic star of our class. And he grew six inches, mostly legs, to become the most coveted commodity amongst the girls in our grade, the prom-eligible ones the year ahead, and all the pre-teens and grade-schoolers below, all the way down to some kindergarteners. One girl had an elaborate shrine devoted to Noah in her bedroom, which I learned when she had a birthday slumber party and forgot to cover her table of candles and newspaper clippings. His effigy landed on the carpet under the weight of her quick-thrown blanket. I stormed out, taking her present with me. Then I voo-drew her stick figure on a target for Armadillo to shoot, which, of course, she never did because she was gone.

My misfortune unfurled when Armadillo left and blossomed upon my mother's abrupt diagnosis and hospitalization. It flourished when the good heart doctors at Brigham & Women's deemed her health too precarious to do much of anything but lay in the new hospital bed my father rented for their room. This was when my father started diversifying products in his shoe stores so as to afford the part-time nurse and maid. My mother no longer baked all those curative chocolate chip cookies without the chocolate chips, or construct elaborate sheet-forts, or cannonball off the lake raft like a lunatic like she did, or braid my hair while doing calf raises, or take me shopping for too many shoes as though fashion were a diabolic plot against my father. She was no longer the state's waterski champion, a title she'd held until her heart failed, and no longer the physical force that would protect me from night robbers and demons. She was a shell of a once-mighty woman, a weakling, a gray ghost.

Some nights when my father worked the late shift at one of his three stores in Manchester, I'd lay in bed with her, and she'd cup my tummy with her hand while she told me secrets. Like how one time, when she was nineteen, she skipped class to go to a consignment shop in her hometown in Florida. There, she bought a wedding dress off the clearance rack for ten dollars, even though my father hadn't proposed yet. But, and here was her secret, she knew I was in her belly.

"How I loved you the instant I felt a molecule of you. I love you too much. Too much. I had to get that wedding dress," she said.

On the day Noah's streak of luck ended, the week after our Monopoly marathon, I tried on this very same cursed, premature wedding dress. It was the first day of sophomore year.

My mother slept in her bed and didn't notice—although I don't think she would have cared—me drowning in her clearance satin, just five feet from her. The white fabric pooled on the floor and melted off my shoulders. The day was as stark and quick as this: After school, while I played wedding, Noah went off to throw a Frisbee with those neighborhood boys.

Since nothing could harm Noah, he elected to save the day when the boys lost their Frisbee on the highest limb of a thirty-foot tree. If I were to overlay the events of his afternoon with mine, the outline would be as follows:

- [Noah and me] We get off the bus at the same time.
- [Noah] Peels off with pack of boys; [Me] Kick Keds off in "mud-room."
- [Noah] Arrives at park across the street from our homes; [Me] Arrive at mother's closet. With the windows open, I can hear them playing in the park.
- [Noah] Offers to get Frisbee in tree; [Me] Take wedding dress off hanger.
- [Noah] Climbing; [Me] Disrobing.
- [Noah] At ten feet, climbing; [Me] Pulling on dress, practicing vows.
- [Noah] At fifteen feet, reaching for Frisbee on limb; [Me] Pausing.
- [Noah] Slipping on tree knot; [Me] Twirling in front of mirror.
- [Noah] Falling; [Me] Watching a slight, slight wind move across my yard to his and rustling the leaves of my trees, then his.
- [Noah] Laying on his back on a rock below the tree; [Me] Racing down the stairs when I hear the screams.

The boys scattered around the tree when I tore up to the scene. Billy and Joel fled to call 911. My mother's wedding dress dragged in the dirt. And I'm not sure what happened after Noah said, "Help, Vivi, I can't move," and closed his eyes.

The next thing, some paramedic was prying my vice grip from Noah's hand and shining stick lights in my eyes, pleading with me to please blink. He spoke so softly, this man; he spoke as if his gentle words would wake me up. Mesmerized, I let go of Noah, at which point the man settled me on a log and handed my care off to his colleague. I watched the gentle paramedic blade his hands under Noah's side to roll him off the rock beneath his bent back. In slow motion, Noah's mouth opened wide and his jaw moved side to side. All I heard was a whooshing wind in my ears.

I didn't understand one bloody thing. I didn't understand what they were saying. I couldn't hear them. I couldn't listen. *What do you mean? What are you saying? What? No, no. You don't understand. He can walk. He can walk. He'll be able to walk. They can fix him. They'll be able to fix him. When is he coming home? No. You're wrong. He'll be home next week. He'll be fine. What did you say? I can't hear you.*

CHAPTER XIV
Marty

"Sunday night, doll. Sunday night. So good to see your eyes again, Precious. You been dippin' deeper into some place far from here. Where you go anyway when you leave us, eh? Anything you want to tell ol' Marty?"

"Hi," I manage, after Marty extracts a tube in my throat, this unnatural hard plastic that gags me. I cough. He adjusts my pillows a few inches higher, which does seem to help.

"Well, Precious. Wish you were awake last night. We had ourselves a rowdy party up in here, I tell you. Your boy slipped past us and somehow painted the wall." Marty directed me with his eyes to the wall behind the green guest chair, but continued talking just the same. "Smuggled in some real acrylics and painted you a big blue lake and a big round sun and he and you holdin' hands on a raft. Docs don't have the heart to repaint till you get yourself better and get up outa here."

Over on the wall, beyond the green chair and the now wilting bouquet of lilacs, is Ivan's get-well wall art. Above his painted raft and us holding hands is his child's handwriting: "I love you, Mama." The color of his words is a dripping green that has trickled into the lake and around our stick figure bodies. Where the green mixes with blue, pools of paint appear as sad as melted water. Several drops have made their way to the floor molding, apparently relieved at escaping the emotions in the brushstrokes above.

That damn monitor wails again, but this time Marty anticipates my reaction; he places a meaty hand over my heart, his face in my face. Stern, but kind, he says, "Oh hell no, darlin', you don't jump on me so quick. I have a story to tell y'all. Now you just breathe. Calm down. Count down with me. Together, let's go, ten, breathe." He breathes in deeply, an accentuated guzzle of air as though he were a yogite. "Nine, breathe, eight, breathe, breathe again, seven, breathe, six, breathe, five, breathe, four, breathe, my Precious, three, breathe, two, breathe a good one, and now, one."

This tactic works again because I am still with him. I don't dare look back at Ivan's wall of heartbreak art though. Instead, I steady my vision on Marty, allowing his demeanor to guide me in this real life. The only thing that might keep me from slipping is his voice, so I look in his eyes, hoping he'll read my mind and continue telling me his story.

"Precious. You won't believe my day yesterday. My lady, you know, my coma lady. Was here a year with her. Only once did anyone else, besides me, come to visit her. I've read you her journal a few times now, altho' I'm not sure my words are kickin' down the doors of your thick filters. Anyway, lady gave up her baby boy,

1973, to the nuns. Left the name of the baby's daddy, a fed'ral judge, I told you this much. The nuns, they went to that judge, and he took and adopted that baby. Raised him like his own. Ha. Cuz he was his own. Judge didn't tell his wife he was the baby's papa. Judge said after seeing so many sad cases in his courtroom, he wanted to do somethin' positive for this world. 'Let's adopt a baby,' he said to his wife. Can you believe it?

"But he loved my coma lady. Baby boy was conceived in love, I promise you, which don't make no sense. If he loved her, why'd he let her walk away? Poof, easy go. Demeanor like a steel trap. No contact. Left her a love letter though. I found it in my lady's journal. Real short, memorized the words already."

Marty tweezer-fingered within a pocket on his pink-mauve nurse's shirt, extracted a piece of paper, and unfolded it with his chin to his chest. He read the following upon a slow recitation and none of his regular accent:

> *How I will live this life without you, I don't know. But I must, my love. It has to be.*
>
> > *In sorrow,*
> > *~M*

Marty bounces his head as though trying to accept the words himself, as though the words and the sign-off are for him alone. "Mmm," he says to the letter.

"Tough pill to swallow, Precious," he says, although in the way he speaks, it's not clear if the pill is a pill for his lady or a pill Marty remembers he needs to take himself. Either way, I widen my eyes to tell Marty I agree with his reaction to the note.

"Ain't no crime greater than lovin' someone, telling them, then shutting them out of your life. But," Marty crunches his nose and slams his hands like banging cymbals, "leave that. Now Precious, let me get to what happened yesterday. Cuz' here now, here comes my confession. It's all tied up together."

He checks my vitals, jotting notes, and continues, "I don't work the mornin' shift on Saturdays or Sundays on account'a my addiction to estate and yard sales. So just so happens, I read this ad for an estate sale at my coma lady's house for yesterday morning, advertised right there in the Boston Globe. Sure, I knew her address and all from her chart. In actual fact, I'd been to her house before. Before she was ever even my patient for a whole year." Marty stalls, checking my response by adding, "Mmmhmm. You're wondering how I could have been to a patient's house before she became my patient, ain't ya? Well now, listen. Listen on.

"Since no one seemed to care for my coma lady, I'd go out and check her mail, make sure the gardener and all was comin.' You see, my lady had a daughter, she about thirty, and she hadn't talked to her mama in 'round nine years. She was no help while her mama was sick. Imagine. But those trips, those trips while my lady was still blessin' this rock with her tickin' heart, trapped in her coma, again now, those weren't my first trip to her house, no. Anyway, daughter hated her mama, some. Came up to me in the hospital a year ago and says, 'I'm going back to California. Here's my number when the old broad kicks.' I wanted to choke that bleach head out. Anyway, I was the one who goes and talks to my lady's lawyer to make sure all her bills gettin' paid. Got his name from her records. She had planned ahead." Marty bounces his index finger against his temple to accentuate the point.

I think, *Wow, he really got invested in this patient's life. Something's not adding up here.*

"Ain't none of these doctors know how far into my lady's life I was. So don't you go tellin' no one, Precious, okay? This here our secret."

I must indicate some assent because Marty continues.

"She got herself a grand ol' mansion up in Manchester-by-the-Sea. House overlookin' the ocean. Terrace with stone planters, trailing vines, and rosebushes like she holdin' some Victorian garden. Or like she stole a chunk of Lake Como, Italy. You know where I'm talkin', right, Precious? George Clooney, oh boy he a keeper, had a place there, accordin' to the gossip magazines. Well anyway, anyway, my lady married and divorced herself a plastic surgeon and she got their seaside mansion in the split. Set herself up real nice, my lady did. Husband got custody of their girl, my lady's second baby, and the daddy and daughter moved to California. My lady, she stayed in Manchester with the house, a'course. Now who knows what went on between mother and daughter. We can't judge my lady, okay, Precious. Yeah, she left her baby boy and then seems to have allowed a teenage daughter to go clear across the country. But let's not judge her just yet, darlin', alright?"

I can't speak an affirmation, a fractional head nod will have to suffice. It seems to be enough for Marty, for he stops fidgeting with my tubes and saline and heart monitor and pulls a rolling stool up to my bed. In sitting, he leans in to whisper more of his story, directly into my ear. A couple of times he looks nervously to the hall, just like he did the first time I met him.

"Precious, can you believe they already scheduled a sale at my lady's house? She died just over a week ago. Her body's still steamin' in the ground. Nasty daughter, well, soon as she heard 'bout her mama, she find the lawyer alright. She dug right in to her probate, flew out here, and had the auctioneer hired while they was taggin' my lady's toe in the morgue. I show up at the estate sale yestaday. First one there, Precious. I'd been waitin' at the gate by four in the a.m. Big ol' Dunkin D' thermos of coffee and a dozen doughnuts on the passenger seat.

"Here comes Miss-Lady in her tacky kitten heels and her tackier crop pants—made her stubby legs look even shorter. So Miss-Lady, she come clompering down the hilly drive. She opens the gate by curling her fluorescent pink, plastic nails around the middle rung. And like she some kind of grand host, she flings her flabby arms in the air, saying 'Come on in.' Girl ain't got no shame neither—out parading in the world with two inches of black roots, cutting a path through her frizzed blond helmet. You gettin' this picture, Precious?"

Yeah, I'm getting this picture. Lady probably cranks her air conditioning to subzero in her California house, not appreciating her climate, only bitching about humidity in a hermetically-sealed icebox and atop a velour couch. Probably snaps gum in public, chewing like a lazy, grazing cow. I say all of this to Marty by bouncing my eyelids as silent commentary. He open-mouth grins as though a boy served ice cream for dinner.

"'Welcome, come on in,' Miss Tackity-Tack says to me. So, I get outa my car and follow her up the driveway. Rhododendrons the size of wooly mammoths on both sides. She says, 'Please understand. My mother just died. So this is a little difficult.'"

Marty purses his lips tight as though trying to hold back his verbal reaction to this statement, and he rolls his eyes like they're ticking clocks. But his mouth pops open, unable to bear the work of holding his own tongue. "PalaEASE, Sister! I wanted to shout. For Real? You for Real? Here Miss-Lady actin' all sad for her mama, trying to drum up higher prices, and she ain't never once come to visit 'cept for one day, one year ago. She don't even recognize me as her mama's nurse! 'Course, I had a hat and sunglasses on and I do look different in my street clothes. Sure, I wasn't tryin' for her to rememba me. Oh, anyway.

"Now, Miss-Lady takes me to the garage first. Says, 'Pretty much everything is marked. If not, come find me. The house is open. I'll be on the terrace.'"

Marty pushes backwards on the wheeled stool to my wilted, purple lilacs by the green chair. Without asking my permission, he dumps the dying flowers into a foot-flip trashcan and holds the emptied vase under a stream of water in the steel sink. All the while, he remains on the round-seated stool. As if possessed by the ingrained actions of his nurse's routine, he bends to something beyond my view and withdraws a new bouquet, this time white lilies. Rolling once more, he arranges the flowers in the cleaned vase on the air vent under the window. He takes care to snap the stalks with his fat thumb and forefinger. Continuing his floral work in this manner, he resumes his story with his back to me, turning when he needs to emphasize a point.

"My lady's garage was fairly clean, had hanging yard tools and sealed bags of grass fertilizer. But I didn't want any of that. I moved into the lower floor of the house, same level as the garage. Must'a been guest quarters. Poked my way through empty bedrooms. Bedrooms, I presume, that had not been occupied for most of my lady's life. Miss Frizz-Roots musta plucked the best items out of each room because the carpet had furniture ghosts and the walls were blemished by picture hooks and plaster holes. I walked up a flighta' stairs to the second level, which was even with the terrace. In the upper hall, I see one thing on the wall: an unframed painting with the side staples visible on the canvas. The background has the brightest of yellow, which accents a turquoise glass, drying upside down. My lady's initials are signed in the corner. Now nothin' in my lady's journal said nothin' 'bout her paintin'. I unhooked the picture from the wall. It was an instant treasure to me. I would have paid thousands.

"'How much you want for this here paintin,' I asked Miss-Nasty on the terrace.

"Nasty say, 'That thing? Errr. Five bucks?'"

"And I think, you want just five bucks for some 'thing' your mama paint, you devil-woman? But I said, 'Sold.' Then I sneak behind her back 'cuz there I saw a stack'a more paintins', laying out in the sun, leanin' and fallin' off a lawn chair. Some on framed canvases, some on flat paper, must'a been about two hundred paintins'. I got real excited.

"'What's this here? More paintins'?' I say. She say, 'Oh, these ain't for sale, sorry.' 'Oh,' I say. But I kept looking over her shoulder anyway. She had her right arm across her belly, her left arm bent up to her face, and her hip jut sideways, like she smokin' a cigi on a street corner."

Marty recreates the woman's stance.

I really wish I had the ability to laugh in encouragement.

"Oh, damn, so here's where my story gets real, real fast. And I suppose this here's the climax of my secret, my grand confession. I hope you still like me, Precious." Marty moves fast to sit on a stool by my bed and wheels close to my face.

"You see, wasn't no simple visit to my lady's home for her estate sale, like I was just her nurse. I had a vested interest. I'm trying to get this confession out to you, Precious. Maybe I come at it sideways. Miss Tacky, she's noticing me spying those paintins' and there must'a been somethin' in the way I lost myself on the terrace because all of a sudden, she pokes her face up under the lid of my hat and peers into my sunglasses. Did she suspect me? Rememba me?

"'So,' she says, 'I'm real sorry. I can't part with those paintings. Truth is, I'm not sure what to do with them. I came over last night to get things ready, and I open up a closet in my mother's room, and out falls this giant stack of paintings. They're all hers. I didn't know she painted, and neither did my father. Some of them date all the way back to 1973. She has dozens from when she was married to my father, and, I tell you, he never knew. Why would she keep them a secret?' Miss-Lady asks me, her eyes almost crossed in confusion, her tone less toxic than before. I actually felt a moment with her, a thawing of her self and thus my conviction. I did try, Precious, I promise you I tried in damn vain to see her kitten heels as proper heels and those awful crop pants as a pencil skirt."

If Marty has concluded from my natural vertical challenge that I wouldn't be caught dead in shoes less than two-point-five inches, well he's right. Trying to view this woman in something other than what she was wearing means Marty wants to move beyond the shallow, but he has to joke his way there. He gets me. I get him. We're best friends in this moment, and I've only known him a grand total of twenty minutes in a semi-conscious state, which has been dulled further "on account'a'" Marty's merciful "vodka" cocktails. I believe deep connections are dredged fast.

"I asked Miss-Lady if I could see the oldest ones, the ones from 1973. 'Sure, I guess,' she says. Now recall, Precious, my lady gave her baby up in 1973. So what was she paintin' way back then? I wanted to know.

"I stepped over the granite pavers and weaved my way around Miss Thing, taking my sunglasses off only after hunching to hide my eyes. 'The oldest are at the bottom,' she said behind me. So I rifled through, one by one, and flipped past salt marshes and summer skies, New England homes, and white birds in the bay. As I reached the early eighties, a young boy started appearin' in nearly every paintin'. He'd be bendin' to work on a sandcastle or smilin' up into the clouds. I felt Miss-Lady hoverin' closer and over my shoulder. 'Not sure who the boy is, certainly isn't me' Miss-Lady says, and I swear I heard a rattle in her voice. 'Uhuh,' I said, hidin' the shakin' in my betrayin' hands.

"I got to the late seventies, when the boy she'd left would have been seven, six, five, and he was in every paintin', but instead of at the sea, she had him running through his yard in Mississippi, chestnut trees around him, an alligator in a pond. I let out a sharp exhale. Miss-Lady moved closer, tilting her head from the paintin' to me. I kept going. I got to the early seventies; the boy would've been four, three, two, one. He was an infant in these ones, off in the distance of a fadin' sunset, holdin' a woman in a white gown's hand. I gripped the one dated "March 1973" that showed two nuns clutching a note and bending over a basket. 'Mama,' I yelped, not intendin' to do so out loud. But my mouth ain't got the good mind to stop. 'Mama, I didn't mean to shock you. It's my fault. I'm so sorry, Mama.' I turned, and Miss Lady stiffened her arms straight at her sides like she about to pencil dive into a pool. Yes, I realized, she had heard. 'You?' she said, more as an accusation than a fact."

I lock eyes with Marty.

Marty moves his head slowly up and slowly down, confirming what I'm thinking.

A tear escapes him and plops on my sheet.

A confession. He was the boy in his lady's journal. But how was it he became her nurse, all the way up here in Massachusetts, when she'd left him in a basket in Mississippi to grow up by a pond with an alligator.

And why the apology? What shocked his mother?

How did Marty act his mother's nurse a whole year with no one knowing?

Will Ivan feel this way when I pass? Am I abandoning Ivan?

Machines around my bed beep and blare.

"Precious, I'm gonna give you some more of your vodka cocktail, so you rest now." Marty holds my wrist, which does calm me some, while he ups my medicines and continues to talk. "But know this. Fate—she's in a two-pronged war with time and circumstance. Sometimes circumstance wins battles by rippin' two people apart who should be together. And sometimes, time wins battles by slappin' everyone who should be clockwise, counter-clockwise. Fate, now, she waits, she maps the plan, and wham, she slams two people back together. The only problem is, circumstance and time play terrible tricks, and people may not recognize fate when she comes a'knockin—what with all the smoke screens. You see, when fate found me in Mississippi with a job offer in Massachusetts and fate gave me the nerve over a year ago to go on up and rang my long lost mama's door in Manchester-by-the-Sea, before she was my patient, and I told her I was her baby son, said I moved myself to Boston to be an ICU nurse, she screamed I was a thief come to mug her. She flopped on the floor, had a stroke in the foyer. Uh-huh. Well now, circumstance thinks she won this war." Marty cups his ear, his hand acting as a funnel for sound. "You hear her, Precious? She a clever foe, that circumstance, laughin' cruelly because she had my mama admitted to where I work. And wham, we back together, all alone, on this old round rock. Hilarious, ain't Miss Lady Circumstance? Anyway, Mama out cold, leavin' me abandoned once again."

Abandoned.

I black out.

CHAPTER XV
Barely Blowing Bubbles to Find the Surface

Two weeks and no letter. We were twenty-three. I ran to the wall mail slot hopeful once again. The block to my Back Bay, Boston apartment was in full spring: yellow forsythia bushes, lime leaves, and pink buds of double flowering plum trees. All of this concealed the rodent infestation of the townhomes lining my street, historical brick facades worthy of tourist drive-bys, but hiding health code violations within.

Clumps of fur, from my grad school study partner's cat, clung to my blue sweatshirt—well, Noah's faded Milberg High sweatshirt, the one I recovered from the trash when we were sixteen and Mr. Vinet cleaned Noah's closet. "Noah won't need these old clothes in Switzerland. The rehab has him in a uniform," Mr. Vinet had said, eyeing me with a mixture of apology and hope. In the year after his accident, fifteen to sixteen, Noah had been to nine different specialists. The one in Switzerland was yet another hope by way of experimental electrotherapy combined with a certain surgery not condoned in the United States. Mr. Vinet had leveraged all of his contacts at KPMG to start a rather well-funded charitable trust for Noah's welfare.

Seven years later, and I can tell you my and Noah's life in numbers:

- We were twenty-three;
- I lived at 429 Loudon Street in Boston, #33, four flights up, no elevator (Noah couldn't visit even if he would have);
- Noah lived at his eighth rehab facility, this time in Milan;
- He'd had ten different surgeries, thirty different doctors, nine false parts implanted;
- I had seen him in person one time since his accident, and that was directly after;
- Noah refused my pleas to visit him twenty-four thousand times;
- He wrote me constantly: 2,233 letters;
- I wrote him 2,333 letters.

Sometimes two or three letters were delivered to me in one day. All of Noah's letters ended with, "Love" or "I love you"; mine with "Please, I need to see you." He'd add constant P.S.'s with some form of the following: "Vivi, please, I can't let you see me like this. I want to come home to you, lift you up, and dance with you."

The longest, prior to the two-week dry spell when we were twenty-three, that he had gone without writing was a month when we were nineteen—the same month I went to the botanical garden with Lachlan. He had had a particularly rough surgery, which led to an infection, and then his therapist dropped him down two stairs. He was black and blue head to toe in the picture my mother slipped me—in secret. She had been to see him so as to accompany her best friend Josie. I, on the other hand, was begged by Noah not to come.

If not for his constant stream of lengthy letters, some with drawings, some with cutouts of articles, I would have likely abandoned my thoughts of Noah out of anger. Or, I might have stormed into his patient's rooms and knocked him upside the head. Instead, I chose to respect his wishes and live apart, loving him through letters and memories.

But two weeks of nothing and no excuse either. No surgeries, no injuries, no setbacks, no travel. He was just under care and in school in Milan.

I opened the mail slot, scared to confirm nothing was there, but praying he had written. A cable company card stabbed me corner-wise in the nose, having lost the door holding it in place. *Why do they advertise anyway? As if we have a choice.* A gas bill fell into my hands, a supermarket flyer too. *Great. Extortion charge in one and Pert coupons in the other. Just what I needed.* And shoved in the nether regions of the rectangular space was a postcard. *Oh please don't be from the dentist.*

The front had a picture of an elaborate church, gray stones and pyres of varying height, dripping into the sky, the way buttercream frosting drips on a cake that is too hot to ice. "Duomo, Milan, Italy," said the block font.

I sat on the first floor stairs by the apartment wall mailboxes. A second floor neighbor interrupted my fury to read my long-awaited card by edging past me with her bicycle. *Dammit, lock the damn thing outside. Don't you know I got a card from Noah? Noah!*

I flipped the card once she had bungled on by, her back wheel spinning in my face.

> *Vivi,*
>
> *This is the Duomo, a very large and old church in Milan. I hope you'll come and visit here some day. My mother brought me here to pray because the doctors have released me. For good. They say there is no more anyone can do. I wheeled up the aisle, wishing I was walking this march with your arm in the crook of my elbow. At the end you would become my wife. I am so sad this will never be. I hope to come see you when I'm back in the States next week. I won't be home long. I've decided to move to . . . I don't know where. I need to be on my own a bit. Away from doctors. Away.*
>
> *Much love, my love, I miss you a million years,*
>
> > *Noah*

I dropped the card from my limp hands between my sitting legs. *How can you say you want me as your wife and yet you're leaving again? How can you continue to abandon me? Abandon.* I whipped out my giant cell phone and dialed numbers by stabbing the buttons for concentration. The postcard was dated two weeks prior, which meant he had to be back home, our home, in Milberg, New Hampshire—only an hour-forty-five north on Highway 93. *How dare you come home and not call. And everyone else kept this secret?* If my phone were a neck, the person would have been strangled.

"Hello," came a woman's voice.

"Where is he?" I demanded.

"What? Who is this?"

"Mrs. Vinet, where is Noah? I know he's there."

"Viv, oh. Um, well . . ."

Josie put her hand on the receiver; muffled voices hushed beyond.

"Vivi, listen. Noah's sleeping."

"Yeah, I thought so. When exactly was he going to call me?"

"Honey, listen. This is so hard on him. I'll have him call as soon as he's up."

"Tell him not to bother. And not to send me anymore of his meaningless love letters if all he intends to do is give up and leave me waiting forever. What is this anyway? You told my mother not to tell me either? What?"

"Vivi, listen . . ."

But I hung up, crashing the flip on that giant phone.

I slammed up to my third-floor, rodent-infested hovel of an apartment, my one-bedroom war zone of dirty clothes to the left, my hallway kitchen to the right. The pervading scent was a constant propane. In the living room, which was really the other side of the hallway kitchen, was my one-person futon couch, on which I flopped, not knowing how to disentangle my tortured thoughts. People chatted in an inarticulate mumble at the bus stop below my window; a woman cackled, probably about ridiculous nonsense. The only relief I got was when the Number Nine groaned up, cracked open its rust-hinge door, and hauled the bus-waiters and cackler off. A mousetrap snapped under my futon.

My grad school apartment was like anyone's grad school apartment: a shithole.

I kicked the cushions, kicked and kicked, furious about everything.

My phone rang.

"Vivi, I'm coming to get you."

"Mama, you can't drive. Knock it off. I'm fine."

"I'm already leaving."

I see her still, sitting by my side at the diner's counter. She'd driven in her nightgown from Milberg to Back Bay. With a honk of her orange Volvo on the street, she'd summoned me from my rattrap apartment in an effort to lift my poisoned mood. Mama.

I was one of the lucky ones born to a selfless, wild-hearted woman.

The diner lights filled the interior gold, which, when juxtaposed against the black outside, suspended us in some surreal place—like an Ed Hopper painting.

And she in her nightgown, her blonde hair in a sloppy night twirl, her face a shade of gray—to me, she was color. And though she smelled of medicines, I'd catch a rose nostalgia whenever she brushed my cheek with her glossy lips.

I spun on the diner's stool, lifting my feet in the roundabout, hoping a revolution would switch my thoughts. My mother coaxed me along by teasing the waitress.

"Hey, Flo," she said.

"Name ain't Flo, lady. My name's Mirabelle," said the counter girl, smiling and bouncing her pigtails tied with blue ribbons.

"Mirabelle. Wow. Long way from Flo, I guess," my mother said.

"Long way, lady. Nice nightgown."

"Gee, thanks. Hey, Miraflo, you got any of those cow pitchers? You put milk in 'em. Pitcher cows. You know what I mean? I think my babydoll needs to use one—change her mood."

Mirabelle reached under the counter, pulled out a white cow pitcher, filled it with milk, and set it on my paper placemat. "Girl, I wish my mother was as lovin' nuts as yours. Nightgown out for dinner and all. My mother would never drop everything to come cheer me," she said, before sashaying off to fill a whistling customer's coffee cup.

As though in love with the cow pitcher and relieved by its long-awaited requited presence, my mother sank into an "ahhhhh."

"Babydoll, when I was little I used to drink my juice out of those cows. Your nana had to buy me a pack of cocktail straws so I could drink from them. Made me happy." She began to pet my head, smoothing my hair.

I swiveled to face her and pressed the deepened dimples of her cheeks with my fingers. I'd started this gesture as a toddler, thinking I might pop my mother's amusements to create a cloud of happy confetti. She'd always say, "Pop," and here again, she said:

"Pop," even though I was twenty-three years old.

"This cow makes me happy too, Mama."

The overhead speakers released the infamous night voice of David Allan Boucher and his pillow-talk selections of love songs and dedications. An acoustic version of "Maggie May" played, a song that always makes me wish to jump atop counters to sing along.

The door jangled in bells when a man entered, upon which a clap of thunder shook the room. An abrupt downpour bulleted the large glass windows of the diner, sounding as though water was fist-pounding to be let in to escape a chasing mob in the shadows. My mother's eyes shot a startled but then hypnotized stare outside, and a daring smile changed her sweetness to benevolent menace. And snap, as quick as unexpected thunder, she was suddenly well and suddenly young and suddenly full of mischief.

"Babydoll, look." She pointed to a field outside a side window.

"The field is a muddy slide—or can be. You ever body slide in mud?"

"Mama?"

"What, you never flung your body down a mudslide?"

"What on earth are you talking about?"

"Girl, I'll show you what I'm talking about."

Mama grabbed my hand, pulled me to a toppling stance, and weaved us around the tables of sitting patrons. Bumping a couple of plates along the way, she offered passing apologies.

Once outside, she lifted the skirt on her nightgown, kicked off her sneakers, and ran to the field. The rain had soaked us complete within ten seconds. I barely heard her taunting words over the pounding downpour, which tinged off the diner's metal awning and sizzled and frayed upon hitting the tar. She called through funneled hands, "Babydoll, come on. Come on."

Standing at the crest of a slight hill, she ground kicked her feet like a bull about to charge. A streetlamp flickered at the far end, revealing great puddles of mud. Mama pointed to the puddles as though a batter marking her aim—then she bolted, sprinting flat foot on the soft earth. About midway, she leaned into a slide, splashing and laughing like a lunatic when she landed in the mud beneath the flickering streetlamp.

"Mama!" I shouted, concerned for her heart, concerned she would raise her beat so dangerously high. But she sprang to and cantered back up the field, like a horse trotting a victory lap, horse head swaying high and proud.

The bizarre vision of her slapped me to silence: here she came, blonde beauty, sick beauty, mud splotched on her cheeks, globs splat in her untrussed hair, nightgown stained to ruin, feet soiled like Tom Sawyer's, and her right hand suspiciously closed at her side.

"Babydoll, you try."

"Your heart. Mama, you can't do this," I shouted through the loud rain.

"The hell I can't," she said with wild eyes, lifting her hand and throwing a fistful of mud in my face, laughing, laughing, laughing. And still the rain tinged and sizzled and frayed and boiled.

Whatever cure her glorious lilt, her leaf-shaking humor, whatever magic her happiness provided, I trusted her message—said and unsaid—and hurled myself down the mud field.

Do you see us on the ground in an eternity? There I glide, my body sopping up the mud; here she comes land-splashing by my side. Rain does little to wash us off—but at least our eyes are cleared. The streetlamp taps a luminescent tune, loud enough to rise above the pounding rain and our heavy breathing. I lay flat in the puddle, not caring about my hair in the dirt, and she does the same. Pins of water prick our faces. I shut my eyes.

"Babydoll?"

"Yeah, Mama?"

"You have to move on or you'll get stuck in a gray hell. You won't grow. Is this where you'll rest your love? Maybe someday he'll return. But Vivi, you have stalled. You'll have to let him go."

The sky exploded, and thunder drowned the sound of my heart shattering to bits.

"And, babydoll?"

"Yes, Mama?"

"Please help me up. I think we'll need to go to the hospital now."

As I raced her to the ER, as I dabbed the mud from her gray face with a wet towel, as I begged her to hang on—again—I heard her words, the words she spent a year of heartbeats to say, the words I'd have to follow: "You'll have to let him go." How impossible, those words.

They admitted her, once again, and by the time the late-late shift clocked in, they said I should drive home for rest. I was used to this actually. I'll skip all the details about her transplant years and the resulting rollercoaster of ever-changing immunotherapy treatments. Please just trust a simple premise: My mother's heart was borrowed and weak.

As I scraped my dragging legs through the hospital parking lot, leaving a trail of dried mud behind, a car slowed and stopped in my path. An electric passenger window, closest to me, buzzed down.

"Vivi," Noah said. And true enough, eight years after last seeing him, there was my love, driving a car equipped for cripples.

My knees buckled, I grabbed hold of the passenger door.

"Get in," he said.

I opened the door, aware of the mud wreck I was. Frantic he should see me so disheveled, I tried to smooth my unruly hair into some kind of reason, but stopped short when I focused on him. My hands remained on my head, stalled too long.

His legs are so thin. His legs are so thin. His face, his face is the same, the same. His legs are so thin, so thin, so thin.

He grimaced at my fixation upon his emaciated legs. On instinct, I knew what he thought: *This is why I had to refuse her for so long, her pity, her shock, it kills me.* He jammed some lever or pushed some buttons, I don't know, and we lurched forward and around the parking lot. Never once did he turn to meet my eyes as he spoke.

"Vivi, I'm sorry about your mother again."

"Noah, why? Why? How could you come home and not call?

"I'm leaving tomorrow. I'm going to Florida, to finish school."

"What? Why? I can't believe you're doing this. I miss you so much."

He jerked the steering wheel hard, and we shrieked around a corner. Repeating this action at each of the four corners, he'd twist his view further away from me. "Vivienne, you deserve a fuller life, and I can't give you what you deserve. I can't give you a child. Do you understand? Oh Vivi, it's so embarrassing to have to say the words. Do you understand what I'm saying? This is why I have avoided you for so long. You have to move on."

"We don't need children. We have each other. There's adoption. Noah, please look at me."

His legs are so thin. His legs are so thin. His legs are so thin. They're bones. They're bones. He can't have children. Why won't he look at me?

"You say that now. But I won't deprive you. Please move on. Please," he said with pitch rising and a crackling voice.

My heart expanded to fill my chest, heat rose into my throat, my cheeks, and burned my eyes. I began to sob fitful half-sentences, much like trying to scream for help in a dream.

His face is the same. His legs are bones.

"Vivi, please calm down. Vivi, Vivi. Where is your car?" he asked, avoiding me.

"Damn you, Noah. Look at my face!"

"No. I'll lose my resolve. Please, where is your car?"

Suddenly, without meaning to, my emotion sank to a cold indifference. Perhaps out of shock or anger or self-preservation. Perhaps because I was exhausted after all these years. But I still wanted him to hold me. *How dare he run away to Florida, this time for real, this time without me.*

I told him where my mother's Volvo was. I watched him drive away.

I do not know who should have fought harder. Goodbyes are like this: too quick and unreal, too divorced from the moment to allow timely reflection. Goodbyes are hellish tricks of space and time, leaving you incapable to say what should be said.

Do you see me sitting on the tar, leaning against Mama's car, stalled an eternity in the parking lot? I am thinking, *His legs are bones. Please come back.*

CHAPTER XVI
That Argentine Feeling

One month later, I was in Argentina. So I was in Argentina when I got the call. I packed a lavender suitcase with designer jeans, J.Crew t-shirts, and one obligatory black traveling dress and ran away for a six-week grad course. The school placed me with a woman who spoke no English. Instead of six weeks, I stayed three on account of the milk-poisoning incident, which was on account of that devil phone call.

My mother had recovered to a level that required nearly constant home bed rest, but she insisted the mud ride was worth the setback. Noah fled to Florida just as he warned, refusing to share with anyone any contact information. Churning my mother's impossible words with Noah's unacceptable resolution, I booked the Argentina trip as a necessary transition to accept the impossible.

My Argentine host, Mrs. Teglatere, lived in a building that had one of those one-man, iron grill elevators. The halls to her eighth floor apartment had hand-painted tiles from floor to shoulder in a rich blue and orange flower design. The feel was rather Italian. But the beauty of the tiles remained shadowed because the hall lights stayed a constant dim. Nonetheless, the building owners kept the common space as clean as an OR.

Mrs. Teglatere's apartment was likewise spotless. She laminated her couch in plastic, which didn't mute the orange velvet cushions or the matching trumpet vine flowers framing her balcony. Nor did the order of her apartment tame the red geraniums of incomprehensible volume filling her outside patio. When you entered Mrs. Teglatere's apartment, you were hit by a wall of orange and red, a wall of fire.

We ate in her kitchen on apple-green chairs with chrome frames. Each morning she made me French press coffee, which hinted of nut-chocolate, and a homemade toast she served with Nutella. My Spanish was fairly good, but not great, so we'd stumble through a conversation and somehow meet somewhere in the middle of some understanding.

I learned from Mrs. Teglatere's eyes that she was a widow, and the picture with candles how deeply she missed him. I learned from her Italian operas on the warbling record player that she suffered a foreign nostalgia. I learned from her soft hands and well-kept nails that she'd been cared for and cherished. And I learned from the lack of ringing and lack of toys in the guest room that she was childless. I diagnosed from the floral scent and dustless corners that she was healthy. And I learned from the cards in the bedroom on proud display that she combated her loneliness by housing exchange students in six-week allotments. But I also learned only those of a foreign tongue were allowed in that fire-clean apartment, for with the mismatched language, a safe distance would guard her from further loss.

I liked her willingness to let me get lost on my own. She didn't hover in my space with complex transportation directions or her suggestions on museums. She fostered a full-scale self-reliance, and her actions revealed her belief that the world should fend for itself, especially the female world, just as she was forced to do and did ever since her dear departed up and died. In this, I got a first-rate education on what it means to be deposited in a country where no one knows your name and no one cares.

More than once I nearly bit the dust when the Buenos Aires buses didn't stop on their four-lane roads to let me on; they only slowed, expecting me to jump on or off in transit. For three weeks, I thought only of the intricate strategy of foreign urban survival and expensed all energy in wrapping my mind around enough right words to find an American coffee and God willing, a bagel. I didn't try to grasp anything other than finding Argentine landmarks, watching their tangos, floating with awe through their above-ground cemetery, or losing my way in the four-block, gray-on-gray, stone University. Crumbling fortresses and ornate hotels hid a wealth that snubbed the cardboard villages I know I saw on the car ride from the airport.

Argentina's disdain for traffic laws or any traffic safety what-soever confounds me to this day, as does the country's farmhouse concept of food. I once ordered a "chicken sandwich" thinking I'd receive a civil-sized chicken breast between two pieces of bread. Instead, the waiter "Pffft" loudly to summon my fellow patrons to laugh when he plopped down a full-roasted chicken between a hard, crusty bun. The plate teetered as though a settling top.

"Americanos," he said with a mocking, not loving, snarl. I forced a chuckle—to blunt the awkward glances—and carved my own sandwich, biting into a grin and beckoning everyone to watch my gleeful chews. But they harrumphed into their meals as though I were a boring child at the Thanksgiving kids' table, unworthy of their adult and Spanish conversations. I was anonymous.

Wine was $2 a bottle, which I'd drain in uncrowded Italian restaurants over a mound of $2 spaghetti. And I liked when the natives considered me an alien and scowled at my US inferiority because I couldn't figure out how to read their menus or use their telephones. In this way, I became an observer, not a participant, a ghost around them watching their multi-casted, multi-plotted play.

Mrs. Teglatere insisted on cleaning my room and straightening my sheets. I often found her sitting on my single bed with legs crossed over the edge, reading her novellas. She kept books on several shelf units around the apartment, all of which came to mid-thigh. At first I wondered why she didn't consolidate her collection on one or two ceiling-high bookshelves in the guest room—so as to create a library—rather than filling her apartment with thigh-high bruise-makers. But then I remembered the one-person elevator and realized her vertical lift dictated her literary arrangement. Either that or she felt cushioned by the words lining her walls.

I suppose she'd recall a novel or novella whenever she dusted the shelving unit in my room, and thereupon lose herself on my bed. Actually, it was comforting to find her so absorbed. Unfortunately, me finding her embarrassed her and she'd shuttle off in her white slippers as though I'd caught her reading my diary, which I did not even have with me, nor could she read if I had. "*No problemo, no problemo, señora, no problemo,*" I'd call after her retreating back. "*Lo siento, señorita, lo siento,*" she'd say.

On the day of the infamous phone call, I awoke before Mrs. Teglatere. Just the day before, she had attempted to explain, as though an apology for her country, the cardboard communities littering the hillsides along the highway. "They are poor," she said in Spanish, not to state the obvious, but with her hands on her lap and her head bowed, her tone suggesting her true meaning: *We can do nothing to fix this for them, they are poor, the government* . . . But even her thoughts in her downcast demeanor were too cautious to remark further on her government. Her almost twitch of anger in a slight nose curl spoke of a suppressed shame, as if she were thinking, as she slit a quick look at me in asking about the poor in the boxes on the hill, *I am proud, American, shamed, because your poor live in high-rises, not boxes.*

But she didn't actually verbalize any of this. All she said was, "They are poor."

I think I understood her and I wanted to say, you're right, they don't live in boxes in America. They don't live in boxes in America. We are a superpower. We are strong. They don't live in boxes in America. They don't live in boxes in America. And if you say the phrase a hundred times it is true. Although in stark volume and in such unabashed hillside display, it is true by comparison, and you can say it just once.

I woke up early the day they called. Mrs. Teglatere was asleep. I tiptoed because if she heard me, she'd jump to action in her pale-pink, zip-up robe and create her daily squall in the kitchen with her French press coffee and her constant toast. She had catered me until then, three full weeks, so I wanted to slip out, do a run, and buy her some croissants before she woke.

I jogged along a safe, looping course, confined to the neighborhood Mrs. Teglatere said was "*bueno*" to be alone in while running. Slowing to a walk, I grabbed pesos from my pocket anticipating the bakery around the corner. At the doorway of a respectable office, about ten stories high, I paused to admire nine Romeo and Juliet balconies in a straight line up to the sky. About five colors of flowers dripped from the different ledges: fire orange of the neighborhood's ubiquitous trumpet vines, lemon yellow of four-petaled pansies, apple red of blood roses, peach of some fat flower I have never seen in America, and lime of potato vines, falling as full as Clydesdale tails. The colors were coming to life in the rising sun and seemed to stretch off the gray-black building.

Something scraped at my sneakers. I quickly kicked, thinking a rat had scurried over my toes. A boy pulled away from reaching for my feet and receded further onto the porch below; he huddled under a stained, brown blanket, alone. He was no more than six years old. A sign by his head said, "*Por favor, tengo hambre*," the same phrase I had used in my own desperate quest to find food: "Please, I am hungry."

A. Six. Year. Old. Boy. Alone. With a sign saying he was hungry. I felt winded. I spun around, thinking others must have noticed this atrocity and expecting a crowd to form. *Someone must have already gone for help*, I thought. But as I waited for the flurry, as I gasped at his cracked lips, shaking my head confused at how he seemed so helpless and dehydrated, no one came. No alarm stopped the world from spinning. No running mother tumbled upon us with a basket of food. Instead, birds started chirping, and the day began, just as it always did.

By then, I had lived in Boston and traveled to DC, Philadelphia, and New York, and never did I see a six-year-old sleeping alone in a doorway. Besides Argentina, at that point in my life, I hadn't ventured beyond America, so I'm sure I sound naïve to missionaries and world travelers. Yes, I'd read the statistics and was aware we have profoundly poor and homeless children. But never did I witness a child groping at a stranger's feet in any US city. Had I seen such a thing, never would I expect two women in matching, crest-patched capes to jaunt by, nor that they would practically skip, arm in arm, twirling tennis rackets, obviously on their way to a private club. Under no circumstance would I imagine they'd gossip through pointed fangs and continue on their way, as though a bewildered American with a homeless boy was a common scene.

I did not judge Argentina. I did not even judge those women. Instead, I fret in my inability to help the boy. My envied life, this boy, the comparison overwhelmed me. Was the walkathon last year enough? How about quarters in red buckets at Christmas? I figured I could not take him home. The seventy grand I'd borrowed for higher education, my access to more funds, these resources meant nothing, despite my probable ability to kick and scream and at least try to fight the hopelessness of the situation. Trancelike, I slipped into the bakery, used all my pesos to buy the boy three croissants, left them by his sleeping head, and returned to the apartment for the French press coffee and toast I figured would be waiting for me.

Emotionally misanalyzing the entire solo elevator ride, I tried to formulate questions for Mrs. Teglatere so we might generate a solution together. I sketched out the conversation in my mind as I fast-walked along the blue-orange wall, which cheered me none.

As I had expected, the aroma of coffee wafted in nearly visible plumes of caffeine clouds in her kitchen. Fresh toasted bread steamed on a dandelion-yellow plate. Yet, something was different. My Argentine host was not sitting in the apple-green chair as she normally did. Struggling to bring herself to say the words out loud, she nervously crinkled a note in her hands. Her English was bad, but she knew enough.

She sat me down with a solemn shoulder push, and I feared I had angered her in some way. I tried to speak when she poured my coffee, but she held out her hand to stop me, sat slow, placed one hand upon my shoulder and the other in her pocket. Her pupils glazed, announcing misfortune had returned in force. And since I had already primed tears from seeing the boy in the doorway, just her squished face of concern caused a waterfall to spill. "*Aye, popita, aye, aye, popita,*" she said, patting my back and handing me the note: "*Tu mamá* call. Noah die. *Lo siento, popita,*" she'd written. We were twenty-three.

I stopped thinking about the boy and went directly to my room, clasping the note limply in my hands. Absorbed in a fury similar to my Argentine host with her novellas, I read it one hundred times to make it true. When I began to wail hard, she shut the door with a soft click, leaving me to find my own way. For all she knew, Noah was an uncle or a brother or a lover or a friend. She never asked.

I lay on the bed with the sun bright and high, and since I thought the sun rude for intimating happiness upon his death, I shut the shades in a thick anger.

I didn't comprehend the words. I didn't listen to what they were saying. My mother, my father, they tried to explain. Aneurism. *What? And what, this happened when he was driving north from Florida, to find me, what? To apologize? Didn't anyone tell him I was away? He wouldn't listen? He crashed his van, he what? Didn't anyone tell him I was away? No one's fault. Would have happened anyway. At least no one else was hurt. No one? Really? What?*

There was no point in being on Earth if he was gone. Although I hadn't seen him much since his accident, I still looked to the moon or the sun for comfort, knowing he was under them too. I used to stand, in fact, anywhere outside, a lawn, a park, a botanical garden, a street, a forest, and sense a string from me to the sun or the moon and millions more strings from them to everyone else and one to him. I imagined we were all connected under the same sky pearl or blazing ball of fire, all of us dancing marionettes. In this, I sensed him with me, and I had hope that someday our night or day master might once again tangle our strings.

Around eleven in the morning, I stepped into the Argentine sunlight. Walking in a warped conscience, I had no intention of going to class that day. And whether the sun or the heat or my vast confusion caused my blindness, all I saw was white with yellow spears. This piercing spread to my brain in an apparent attempt to escape through my temples, which began to pulse. A migraine raged. I put on my shades, but they only clouded the edges. If I had had a walking stick, I would have dueled the mocking sun, stabbed the middle of its mocking blaze, and let her bleed liquid gold until reduced to a shriveled grape, a dry raisin in the sky. How dare it shine on this day. How dare it tease me by coming straight through my skull. How dare it hang there, holding just me on a tethered string while it cut him free. I slumped on the sidewalk, arms dragging, legs akimbo, a lonely marionette with a fire in her head.

As illogical as it may be, the only thought I had was to get some Frosted Flakes. For three weeks I'd eaten whole chickens between hard rolls, large plates of organic spaghetti, and French press coffee with a homemade toast. I wanted something processed. American. I needed comfort food. I stumbled along, literally edging my way by leaning against buildings, rubbing my skull in a stalled progress, and found a supermarket. This supermarket was like its American brothers by way of the aisles of food and cashiers. But it was unlike American brothers because while there were some boxes of prefabricated food with perfectly calibrated levels of salt, sugar, and fat for optimal addiction, most everything was perishable: vegetables, fruits, dairy, breads, and meats—literally hanging slabs of cow from hooks—in other words, the five food groups as God intended. I searched hard for something godless, worthy to withstand nuclear war.

Alone on a bottom shelf was a beaming box of hope: Tony the Tiger happily presenting his box of Frosted Flakes. I grabbed the coveted treasure with two hands and curled my body like Dracula to a chalice of blood. A girl with pink hair and several rings in her nose eyed me sidelong and shimmied away—maybe because I hissed at the non-existent competition.

I blew dust off the top of the box.

I'll need milk, I thought. But not thinking, I didn't consider the different pasteurization methods employed by the foreign organic bottler I selected.

You might say my grief over his death elicited strong contractions of muscle cramps, which led to a complete immobilization on Mrs. Teglatere's guest bed, and which increased to disabling bouts of sickness. For so long this cycle lasted, me fetal on the bed, you might have thought I suffered dysentery in the Congo. Mrs. Teglatere cooled my forehead, spooned me slices of ice, and insisted I go to Clínica La Sagrada Familia, which I refused. Instead, I endured a night of purging, called my mother, who rearranged my travel from her own bedside, and when I was well enough to hobble to the airport, I flew home, green or pale, depending on the light. You might say his death left me hollow or you might say milk uppercut my gut. Either way, I was too late for his funeral, for which I have never forgiven myself. I'd never forgive myself anyway because Noah died driving back to Boston to find me, not knowing I'd gone to Argentina. He suffered an aneurism as he drove; his special van curled around a despicable evergreen. Dead on impact. "He was spared a long drawn-out death," they said. But they were wrong: Noah started dying the second his foot slipped from the knot on that tree.

When the taxi swooshed the gravel in front of my childhood home, I barely had enough energy to open the passenger door. Thankfully, my mother was waiting on the front step, and the sight of her afforded the adrenaline I needed. Careless of her condition, she rose and ran to me and grabbed me as I buckled into her, falling on the lawn. She took the brunt of my heaving, absorbing the shock like only a mother can, allowing me to carry on for as long as the good Lord rolled the emotion through me. When I was empty, she carry-walked me inside and made a peanut butter pie, which we ate hot out of the oven with two tablespoons. She warmed hot chocolate too, and dashed it with cinnamon.

For two days, Mama held me, hugged me, listened, and collected every ache I let escape. Only once did she speak, at the end of day two. We were at the dining room table, her hand upon my hand. "I cannot imagine losing a true love in this life, Vivienne. Even though you lost him before in his accident, at least he was under the same stars, I get it, I do. But I'll tell you one thing you don't know yet. You will never love anything more than your own child, and your heart will be filled again when you have him or her. I feel no sorrow for Noah. My sorrow on his side rests solely with Josie. It is not a child who needs his parent to live; it is the parent who needs the child. And so I believe Josie thinks her life is over and there is no point to living. I know I'd be lost without you, Vivienne. We're going to have to get strong, if for no one else than her. Vivi, you simply have to let him go."

Having said her impossible words now twice, the second saying was a deeper tough love, her definite wake-up call. And her timing was sublime, for at that moment an animal moaned a death outside—a scraping with a pained pitch and wail. I hurried to the window for view of the side yard; my mother braced herself to stand. Slowly, as though hobbling with a cane she did not hold, she shuffled to the back door and waited.

At the window, I saw what she sensed: Josie crawling in the back lawns, a guttural groan spewing from her, although divorced from her vacant eyes. Imagine this pain. And then don't. Go blank. It is too much.

My mother met Josie, pulled her in through the mudroom, and held her head on her lap, as she lay flat on our kitchen floor. And I would not call this crying. I would call this boiling one's soul.

This unholy vision reminded me of the brilliance of the universe: taught me one tragedy will always trump the last; taught me my grief is nothing to another's; taught me past and future are mischievous liars—only fools fail to invest in real time. I would miss Noah, but in private. I would be strong, by moving on. Somehow.

The remainder of June, July, and August, I neglected my regular summer waitress job at the Lobster Hop and subleased my Boston hole to some poor traveler until fall. I opted to spend one hot season as a poor poet and live at home. I'd sit with Mama, leaning against her medical bed in my parents' room. While she raked my hair with her nails, I'd write tear-stained, three-line haikus and lonely poems that didn't rhyme:

That Argentine Feeling

This deep loneliness comes back
> *When here,*
> *When waiting for a train,*
> *Standing on a corner,*
> *Watching others together*
Me alone,
> *Without you*

Throughout my life, I continued writing—very distinct from my editing job: The former required pure creation (even if it was bad), the latter, mechanics and technique and rules. Free vs. form. I kept every half line, script, and trailing word of woe in a series of blue notebooks with a yellow butterfly printed on the cover, having purchased a box of them because I loved the image so much. It was the same butterfly I saw in Lachlan's botanical garden when I was nineteen.

Just last year, when I turned thirty-four, Amazon allowed for easy self-publishing, so I secretly published all of my poems under the pen name, Vivienne Solagracia, and under the title, *My Love*. Perhaps I sensed then my literary need coming to an end. If you were to review my poetry collection, surely you'd see the theme of a person as an island, the sole soul searching for answers, peace. The summer Noah died, a sense of the alone predominates, but also the ache of a foreign emptiness and guilt, as though I left something behind in the wake of my mourning. I believe I never shook the image of that Argentine boy, an image throttled from my immediate memory by the shock of Noah's death. *What might have come if I did something for the boy?* was a question I found myself asking from time to time throughout my life. What might have happened, how would life have shaped, for me, for others, had Noah not died?

I never forgot that boy.

"Noah, I'd like to see the homeless boy's Heaven."

Chapter XVII
The Reserve of a Nameless Boy

Imagine a poor, six-year-old, abandoned Argentine boy as he topples barefoot in his sleep along a crowded sidewalk in the gray brick and concrete busy Buenos Aires. He is tired. He is hungry. His vision is milky given his diet and the fact that he has never, not even on the day he was born, seen one single doctor. He is malnourished. He is sick in his belly, sore in his bruised feet, and vacant in his blue eyes, which hide in clouds of a severe vitamin deficiency.

A person within the sidewalk crowd is in a hurry.

This person does not see our little boy.

He is pushed.

Into traffic.

Much like myself, he is hit by a large vehicle.

A bus, in his case.

To add to the coincidence, the day he is so negligently kicked like a dented can, is the day I found him sleeping in a doorway.

And this accident happened in synch, I believe, with my discovery of another's death: Noah's.

"You and he died on the same day. In different countries. I didn't attend either of your funerals, and yet I find myself searching Heavens with you and visiting his," I say to Noah as we pass by the glorious bridge under the Van Gogh sky en route to the boy's Heaven.

Of course, I did not know the boy's heart stopped by way of a bus, or at all. I thought he kept living on and until we headed for his Heaven, I assumed he'd outlast me.

When we arrive at a thicket of dense bushes, Noah urges me through a double door made of woven bamboo. The entrance holds back an explosion of light and whirring rhythms of trilling laughter and trumpets. I pause before entering, noting the silence on our side of the doors and how the rays poke around the cracks but do not pour through. It could, the light. But even illumination doesn't want to leave the party beyond.

I push the swing doors, and the brightest sun erupts, tickling my cheeks, sourcing through my eyes. "Come in! Come in! Isn't this fantastic?" the rays seem to shout. The electricity and the light and the energy of a throng of people knot together in a dancing, dizzying circle. Hip-hop music thuds around us, making me want to thrust my shoulders to the beat.

The voice of my now favorite announcer in the universe returns over some invisible loudspeaker high in the Heavens: "A lovely Argentina boy, ah, his reserve, partly inspired when he once snuck into a circus tent, partly inspired when he once slept on carnival grounds. In both places, he fell in love. Come, come, look around."

A trampoline the size of a football field anchors a seemingly endless patchwork of fields and parks. Beyond the bouncing is a warehouse-sized safari tent, Indiana Jones style, which houses some large animals by the sounds of the deep neighing and horn blowing. A tall, narrow building stretches high into the sky to my right; the gray-brown bricks, the white mortar, the wall-sized windows, the ivory cornerstones, all match the office building I had seen the boy sleeping under in Argentina. Instead of Romeo and Juliet balconies, however, the windows open at each floor, each operating as a functioning kiosk. By stepping onto an outside elevator, similar to a window washer's perch, heavenly customers move vertical shop to vertical shop, pausing along the way to taste childhood delicacies. Hundreds of red cardinals twirl in a raucous aviary sky-dance, carrying paper messages between shop owners, or tying ribbons with their beaks in the hair of little girls decorating cookies or licking lollipops.

The snack choices rise into an endless sky. Noah and I step on the lift and ascend to the fifty-third floor, for no other reason than I pick a random number. On our way back down to the ground, we taste every possible concoction of empty calories, from berry-blue cotton candy to fried dough with an inch of powdered sugar. I rub my full belly when at last on the ground, and laugh at Noah because his blue lips are stuck together from too much sticky sugar.

To my left sprawls an ample, green, canopied park, with whistling leaves and a skinny stream trickling and bubbling and giggling and shimmering from one end to the other. One bench presides under a king-sized willow tree. The limbs are spring's bright lime green, and the branches spaced just so, angled perfectly to allow a gauze of sunlight to reach through and caress the face of the boy on the bench. His six-year-old skin glows in the sun's bathing warmth; straight on, he accepts it, for he lay on his back, his head on a woman's lap.

She is stroking his black hair.

No woman would gaze so, as she does, upon a child.

Except a mother.

A look of inconsolable love.

Tired eyes that acknowledge how irrelevant, yet how complete, she is in his presence.

And she rakes his hair to comfort him even further into a sedate happiness.

She is telling him a story, which makes abundant sense to me, for the one thing I know a child truly loves and would thus be in a child's Heaven, is a parent telling a story. How insatiable their thirst for stories—and here tales are endless, but also true.

I stand behind the willow out of sight so I can hear this raw mother-son encounter. In so doing, I realize my interest is rooted in my missing Ivan so terribly. I want to pretend the mother is me and the boy is Ivan; I want to experience his joy in hearing a story. Noah sits on the grass under the shade of the tree. He picks a fistful of white dandelions, blowing the weightless parachute balls as an invitation for me to hover in the magic of the woman's voice. Appreciating the patience he conveys, I calm in the slowness by which he follows the puffs of white and splits the flowerless stems into strips.

The woman sounds like soft authority, a slow and soothing rasp of comfort. In her telling, she controls the air around her and the boy, and in this way, she is a shield of perpetual safety. It doesn't really matter what she says or what words she uses, for her voice is what the child craves, along with her fiction, both of which form another Heaven altogether. I think of the billions of informational bits and bytes that tempted me to miss the true informational bits around me in life—nature's pixels and day-to-day miracles that came far closer to mimicking the perfect variety in which I am now steeped. Have you ever counted the colors on a late spring walk? Have you ever felt cushioned by the variegated greens of a mountain valley?

"There once was a girl named Ailene . . ." The mother begins her story in Spanish, which I somehow understand as if it's my own native language. All around the bench, the park seems to settle, even bees stop buzzing, lowering like hovercraft to land on blades of grass.

I'm not really following the story itself because I'm so mesmerized by the intensity of the boy's eyes at hearing his mother's voice, how the emotions on his face rise and fall with every climax of her tale. Just like Ivan. Like he's *living* the story. I turn to check Noah, who beckons me to continue with my observation by flicking his fingers for me to turn back and watch. Noah seems to have no interest in doing anything other than sitting in this lovely park among the settled bees, stripping stems, and counting the curves of the snaking stream. And supporting me. He must know this particular Heaven is both beautiful, but eternally painful for me. Watching the boy with his mother is like looking in a mirror.

A sweet squall erupts between the mother and the boy. He sits up from her lap, testing her about some details in her story. He apparently doesn't understand why the main character, Ailene, wears such colorful clothes. Ivan does this. He'll push me with a million questions about every last nuance of the characters I conjure up for him. Such as: "Mama, why would Carlos the Crab become friends with Cupid? Isn't one a crab and one a baby angel?" Point is, little boy questions litter any story I tell Ivan. With every question, I pretend to be annoyed, but I smile at him because my heart feels warm; and so, his interruptions only encourage me to tell more. And more.

The boy pesters his mother again, "What was Ailene wearing? Purple and also blue? But why?" he says.

The mother shakes her head in mock dismay. "It is sort of irrelevant what Ailene wore. Nevertheless, if you insist on knowing," and here she pauses to accentuate a loving sarcasm, "if you really insist. She wore bright blue overalls, the color of a raspberry freeze-pop, and from her front pocket poured a purple scarf. Around her neck, she wore a garland of poppy blossoms and also a garland of seashells. Her shoes. Well she had no shoes. Instead she painted her toes grape jelly to match the scarf that tumbled from her chest pocket."

The boy is apparently perplexed by this description and he sits straighter to punctuate his disbelief.

"Settle down, lay back down here," she says.

She waits until he is once again reclined and settled and smiling under her raking nails.

She breathes in the asparagus air under the willow, tracing the sun-dot freckles on her sweet son's face. She kisses each of his tiny fingers in a flurry of loving pecks, as though a hen to kernels in the grass, lifts his two square-inch palm to her cheek, and closes her eyes in a smiling satisfaction, a relief of love.

Opening her eyes, she raises her left eyebrow. Before the boy can rustle up frustration again, she continues, "Now listen, shhhh, hush, hush, let me finish." And off again she goes with her story.

Soon enough, the boy squishes his face and says something about how this Ailene character just simply could never exist because she's way too colorful. He doesn't seem to care about the actual plot; he's laser-focused on this apparently troubling detail of her colors. Again I think of Ivan. One time I had to stall in my reading of *Harry Potter* so we could have a half-hour conversation on the different candies the characters ate on the train to Hogwarts, which led to an explanation of the difference between magic and reality—and how sometimes the distinction is quite clear, but often, rather blurred.

The mother twitches her head as though lightly shaking a paint can. "Fine, Mr. Smarty-Pants. You want to meet Ailene?" she says.

The boy pops off the bench and bugs his eyes. I straighten within my hiding spot; a wispy branch from a willow tickles across my stiffened back. You mean meet Ailene? Meet a fictional character? Is this possible? I suppose, maybe. After all, I'm in a child's

Heaven. Ivan would be crazy with excitement if he could meet Ivan the gorilla. I'll have to follow them.

Once the boy and his mother pass by Noah and me at the tree and have trekked past the office building of desserts, I signal Noah with an elbow curl for us to follow them on feather feet. We catch up close enough to hear the continuation of the mother's story, and all I can think is how Ivan would bounce with uncontainable excitement to live in an unfolding plot.

"Sweetie, I haven't mentioned yet some critical facts about Ailene. Do you know the Faber-Castell crayon and colored pencils factory? That's where Ailene was born."

"In the factory?"

"On the very floor where they assemble wax crayons. So maybe she's so colorful because she's a product of her environment," the mother says.

I once again think of that college paper, the psychology or philosophy of aesthetics.

I pause in my listening, missing a paragraph or two of the mother's story. We are walking through a tunnel made of pink flowering bushes, and the ground is carpeted with petals. The sun shines in gold spears, through which birds weave in a synchronized flutter, their collective movement in keeping with a breeze. Noah walks a step behind, watching how I listen to this story. Trying to capture his thoughts, I believe we share an unsaid admission, one which makes my heart cave: Noah does not understand the emotion of loving a child to point of self-extinction. Jack, however, does share this emotion. Shrinking from Noah, I imagine how Ivan would race ahead, too anxious to meet Ailene, a fictional character.

Noah nudges his head, silently telling me to face front and listen. How connected I feel to him, so quickly redeemed. His act seems selfless: wanting me to enjoy memories of Ivan, as though the boy is Ivan, and wishing I not miss a word of the mother's story.

The boy floats in awe of his mother, his tiny hand tucked in hers. With eyes as wide as the moon, he watches her mouth move from the side. They do not acknowledge us behind them, although they must hear the crunch of the gravel and bending of petals beneath my and Noah's feet. Perhaps they are too absorbed in their own bubble to care, which is exactly how Ivan and I would be. The mother's voice returns. I listen once again.

"At the age of ten, after all these troubles growing up in a crayon factory, Ailene's father struck gold, literally. He found a baseball-sized nugget in a forest cave. Thereafter, Ailene and her father moved to the countryside and bought twelve groves of fruit farms," she says.

"Mama, so are you saying Ailene is so colorful because she grew up in a crayon factory and owns fruit farms?"

"Why don't you see for yourself."

I am so transfixed by the mother's voice, only now do I realize we have exited the flower tunnel and deposited ourselves in groves of fruit and citrus: purple-colored grapes, succulent-green pears, peaches you would die to try, pinkish plums as swelled as giants' fists, parrot-feather-lime limes, and indeed twelve hundred parrots too, and oranges of orange perfection. I feel like I'm swimming in a pool of Skittles.

A woman, who could only be Ailene, lengthens her wildly tall body to reach a peach from a high, arched branch; her thick, yellow hair is braided around a red streak. She's wearing blue overalls with a purple scarf that spills from her front pocket. Garlands of red poppies and seashells jangle about her neck and chest as she stretches. A royal blue parrot perches on her head, a rainbow parrot claws to her shoulder, and she hums a happy love song, as she fills her basket with more of the peaches.

"Ailene is a fruit farmer. I suspect she wears these colors to blend in and so her birds don't fly away from her. Go ask her."

The boy skips ahead, giggling along the way, and when he reaches Ailene, she bends, hands him a fat peach, and stoops to deliver a message in his ear. He bites the orange-pink fruit, which thereupon bursts into sprays of juice upon his face, forcing him to laugh without sound. He searches for his doting mother, who waits on the border of the fringe—literally a ghost. When the mother turns to me, either sorrow or peace fills her transparent eyes. Whatever the emotion, it's a competition at having been separated from him in life with seeing him happy in endless colors and food. Here, he'll remain young under her ache-loving care and the kindness of fictional characters, he'll play in bountiful groves of fruit, he'll rest on her lap in the park for incalculable hours of stories, and he'll bounce on his giant trampoline. For variation, he'll attend to his personal circus and pick through floors of desserts in a transformed office building, one that once both sheltered and plagued him.

I can't decide which piece of his Heaven I'll want to copy in mine, so I blink to force some focus. The colors fade. A peach fuzzes my vision to orange yellow, but clarify when I hear his lovely voice: Ivan's voice, here among the oranges. Squinting for better sight of my blond son running at the edge of the grove, I see him run away from me, scared in his heavy breathing, frantic in the way he tucks behind tree trunks and out of my view.

"Ivan! Ivan, stop," I yell.

And then flash, my peace is once again dampened by my sick reality. I am in my sterile hospital room and there is no Ivan, no Noah, no colors, no sugar scent, no fiction, no bliss. Nothing but white and a wilting bouquet of lilies.

CHAPTER XVIII
Ivan

I read *Ivan* to Ele in our lake-house cabin on the night our last-born child, the later of the twins, left for art school. We have an empty nest. Ele and I cry even at the funny parts. Ele wants me to note how I recite these words by heart, August 22, 2045.

I read *Ivan* to Jacob Jr., our first grandchild, in the afternoons after his birth when I visited him, September 2-23, 2050 (he may be a surprise, but he is my pride and joy).

I read *Ivan* to Wallace, my second grandchild, in the afternoons after his birth when I visited him, October 2-20, 2051 (he was not, I am told, a surprise, but he is also my pride and joy).

I read *Ivan* to my grown children on a camping trip to our summer house on Lake Suncook. Several families sleep in tents, but the ones who have blessed us with grandbabies get priority inside. *Ivan* brings us together each night by the campfire, July 4th week, 2052. One thing about this trip, and I don't know why this is so funny and profound to me, but Alice had everyone in stitches after the fireworks. She made up some cockamamie story about how our dolphin float and Ele's ropey sandal ran off to get hitched: We'd lost both at some point in the festivities. Ele was in an uproar for her sandal, and when I told her I'd buy her a new pair, she whacked me with a towel, but then bit my lip in a kiss and pinched my butt.

I read *Ivan* to Sara, my first-born granddaughter, in the afternoons after her birth when I visited her, November 4-14, 2053 (she is not going to fish with the boys, her mother tells me, but she is also my pride and joy).

December 24, 2053, after Ele and I finish being "Santa" and filling the entire living room and adjacent room with gifts for our children and grandchildren (I don't care that they are adults and the grandbabies are infants, Ele and I love nothing more than giving them gifts), we sit by the fire and down a good bottle of Chianti. For the first time in decades, Ele brings up our "secret" and "the problem" we solved so many moons ago. I thank the

Heavens and likely my mother that Ele and I were wise enough to solve our problem when we were so young. Oh Ele. Ele, Ele, Ele. What would I do without you? Merry Christmas, my love. And Merry Christmas, Mom, I miss you three million years and more. I snuck in a reading of *Ivan* by the fireplace, Ele snoring like an old diesel truck, her legs spread and falling off the couch, belly in the air, one arm overhead, the other hovering above the plate of cookies she dropped when she passed out from the wine. Cookie crumbs all over her face. I think she's beautiful like this.

I'm not sure when the children and grandchildren started to read *Ivan* along with me, not from strictly reading the words, but from our combined memorization. It may have been as early as 2065.

I read Ivan to Ele as she sleeps in the hospital waiting for the doctor's test results on her blessed heart. Why did she collapse in the garden today of all days? May 22, 2075.

Ele read *Ivan* to me on the night they discharged her from the hospital and I couldn't sleep, for the near miss of it all, May 23, 2075. Mom, whatever you did to intervene, thank you. I can't survive on this planet without my Ele, my rock.

CHAPTER XIX
Freshwater Memory Museum

After the reserve of the nameless Argentine boy, I have a quick blip of white hell in my hospital room, but am boomeranged back to the glorious bridge. The sky is still a rich blue, and the leaves of dense trees still chuckle. I have no mind to continue on to another Heaven at the moment, so I ask Noah to take me back to Lachlan's Freshwater Memory Museum.

When we enter, the inventory keeper nods me and Noah a hello as though we are regular employees, which, I admit on the spot, feels nice. We help ourselves to hot cider, doughnuts, and glasses of ice-cold water. A warm breeze washes in through the opened barn door, tickling a sea glass wind chime above the entrance; and a misty, heated fog begins to sizzle away, as the rising scent of a sugary nectar invades the space.

"Is the briefcase plaque done yet?" I ask the inventory keeper.

"Not yet. Got her up in the Quality Control department, working out the grammar. Should be done soon though," he says, checking items on his clipboard, going about his day.

Noah upturns his palms, appearing as though he's holding platters, and lifts his shoulders, saying I don't know in his gesture.

"Noah, why are they taking so long to finish with the briefcase?"

"No idea. Maybe they need time to set the words right is all."

Since he's already at my side, he drapes his arm over my shoulder and leans to kiss my jawline and neck. "Vivi, are you ready yet? Ready to choose your Heaven?"

I want to say yes, want him to continue with his lips on my neck—and beyond. But the question also seems sudden, as though I had been pushed from behind to stumble through a doorway I had intended to enter anyway. A pull makes me doubt answering Noah; another unanswered question drags me down. I distract the moment by walking to a corner shelf with a dog collar.

Jack, I think in reading about something stuck. *I haven't seen Jack's Heaven. Should I be in it anyway?*

Item #33015

One January morning, a cool wind whipped off Mount Washington, drew down the Kangamangus Highway like an icy, angry, howling ghost, and rolled with a cloud tsunami all the way south to Milberg, New Hampshire, to a pond or a lake or a river or a swamp, the nature of the water being up for debate.

A duck, who had forgotten to migrate to warmer soil or who had neglected to keep within his nest with his duck wife, waddled out for a morning quack along the banks of that questionable body of water. He didn't realize a wicked wind had dispersed the snow to dust evenly over the land; so he didn't know when he crossed the edge of the pond or the lake or the river or the swamp.

Now, this duck's webbed feet were warm because he had just untucked them from under his slumbering, feathered belly, which itself was extra warm given the nuzzling his duck wife gave him all night. And it did so happen that the clammy heat of his feet on the ice of the pond or the lake or the river or the swamp was much like the touch of a tongue on a cold steel flagpole. He became stuck. A truly stuck duck.

Along came a mutt or a hound or a beagle or a bulldog, the nature of the dog being up for debate. It is not quite clear how the dog knew, but the dog knew he had to, so he breathed his hot dog breath upon the duck's stuck feet, being smart enough not to allow his hot dog tongue to drag along the wind-swept ice. The dog accompanied his ferocious breath with violent headshakes so fierce, he loosened his already loose dog collar, which came to rest upon the frosty pond . . . or lake or river or swamp.

At once, the duck's frigid feet dislodged. And like a gallant knight, the dog bowed and lowered his head so the duck could waddle up his neck-come-ramp. In this way, the dog saved the duck and lost his collar, which stayed upon the ice all winter until the spring thaw, when it sank and floated to this place.

Ironically, the dog's collar announced the dog's name as though a prophecy, a fowl foretelling: "Duckie," was his name, his name having been chosen by the Heavens or his owners, Jack O'Neal and Ivan Marshall.

CHAPTER XX
The Lover Who Never Was

My hospital room is a lonely 2:33 a.m., according to the digital wall clock. No Marty. No Noah. No visitors. The lilies are brown on the edges and sad in their drooping. The light from the hall has a hint of black, leaving my room in half-shadow, the kind in which anything might hide. I shiver when I hear a book fall. Nothing I can see is there.

"Noah," I call out.

No response.

I inspect the window curtains for movement or bulges, anything at all obscuring my angel. Again, nothing.

On the rolling food tray next to my hip, a card stands open, revealing Jack's handwriting:

"'All our final decisions are made in a state of mind that does not last.' —Proust. I only hope you become well, so we might see your eyes dance again. With regret, Jack."

He can't let me be. Even here on my deathbed. And his wife? Does she know he's left this card? What does it mean anyway? To which decisions is he referring? He and I have made life-changing ones together, and a few on our own, which very seriously affected the other. What regret, Jack? Yours or mine? I picture how Jack knelt at my bedside only a couple of days before; I allow the familiar pull and doubt he has always evoked in me.

Another book falls.

I jump. Well, my inner self jumps. My plastered body merely seizes in confinement.

When I am scared, I try to think of something good, just like anyone would. And since Noah isn't around for me to announce a Heaven, I think of sex.

When I was twenty-five, my and Jack's employer, Harry Von Publishing, was acquired by a massive publishing corporation, whom I'm tempted to call MegaOverlordsWithBlackSoulsCorp., Inc., but was really called, Central Core Authors Corp. Inc, or CCA for short. Not sure why they needed the redundant Corp. and Inc, except it became clear they really wanted to be absolutely sure everyone in the world knew they were a corporation. It was the cat's meow for any author to be published by CCA and thus call themselves a *Core Author.* At book signings, I'd hear the wine-boozed followers of this crowd muffle into their cocktail napkins, "Now that he's Core, the sky's the bloody limit. And her, bahhh, look at her. She's not Core material! Pathetic. They should kick her out."

I knew Central Core wasn't right for me on the very first day they parachuted in a team from the Manhattan office (the "mother ship") to "help with the transition." I'm a little sensitive, if you hadn't guessed, about this whole mega-corporate-takeover-the-world stuff; so many times the big box chains have threatened to shut my dad and his small, yet growing, business down. I openly scowled when CCA execs marched into Boston.

Anyway, about an hour into our "transition meeting," my assigned "Corporate Liaison" admonished me for adding a period after Inc.

"Central Core Authors is spelled C-E-N-T-R-A-L space, C-O-R-E space, A-U-T-H-O-R-S comma, C-O-R-P period, Inc, *no period*. It is imperative [yes she actually did say imperative] that you do not put the period. You must absolutely skip the period because it is *corporate policy to never have your period*, I mean add the period, skip your period, er, skip the period. Whatever! Just don't put the period anymore after Inc."

I merged my lips to muzzle laughter exploding within and shot a look of stifled amusement over to Jack, who likewise swallowed his laughing shock. Together we raised eyebrows to our sell-out boss, H.V., who had abandoned his soul to these period-hating androids for the bargain-basement price of eight hundred thousand. H.V. guzzled the last of his full glass whisky, tipped his gentleman's straw hat, picked up a sticker-laden, vintage suitcase, and fled to his retirement hut in Bali. Son of a bitch, leaving his soldiers on the battlefield.

CCA executives soon planned an all-hands-on-deck meeting with a *very famous* (all of his books are blockbuster movies) author in Texas. They'd heard through the grapevine that he was scouting a competitor publishing house, a rather successful boutique, mind you, *boutique*. To woo the author back into the pack, they tapped Jack and me, precisely because they said we had a "boutique New England feel" they thought he wanted. CCA execs, however, deemed us too young to handle the kraken alone, so they paired us with his then editor, two senior staff members, and all of their administrative assistants. Personally, I thought the whole charade was a huge mistake, descending a squadron of mostly New Yorkers upon a Texan who apparently wanted the personal touch. Nevertheless, we set off for the Lone Star State, cell phones, laptops, protocols, memoed plans, written statements, roller ball pens, contracts, and promises packed. My first business trip.

At this point, Jack and I had worked together for one year. The last I explained him to you, I left off at him splitting a cinnamon apple doughnut in two, one half for him, one for me. A year later, we still shared the same closet in our brick townhome office in Boston. But something rather significant had changed our outward relationship. Very simply put, on the very day we sat eating that cinnamon doughnut, at the very minute I melted into my chair with his sweet pastry melting in my mouth, Jack placed his elbows on my desk.

"Vivienne, I have to tell you something, sweetheart."

Did he just call me sweetheart?

"Did you just call me sweetheart?"

He did one of those "hmph" laughs.

I was grinning wide and holding my breath. *He's finally going to make this real.*

"Listen, Vivi, I've let this fester too long. I can't believe I haven't told you before. I'm engaged. The wedding is under a year away. I proposed to her the day after we met. I've been hiding this from you all these weeks. Months, I suppose. Not sure why I didn't say anything. Actually, I'm pretty sure why."

Are you fucking kidding me?

"Uh, okay," was my response. I twirled my chair: I didn't want him to see me fighting with overpowering tears.

"Hey Jack," I said, while facing the wall. "Do you think you could maybe work out in the common room today?"

"Totally understand. And I'm sorry."

Sorry? You bastard.

And he left.

Jack's fiancé was a nice blonde from Michigan, the all-American farm girl, the Velvet Cake Princess in her town's Christmas Parade, the valedictorian at her Catholic school, the one who grew up in one of those Sunday-dinner-in-the-formal-dining-room kind of families. She had three brothers and four sisters, one of which was a younger replica, because the world just couldn't survive with only one perfect Stephany. To pile on her splendid attributes and thus to highlight my lack of feminine qualities, she was also the president of her Delta Gamma chapter, a longtime volunteer at the Greater Michigan Animal Shelter, and had won blue ribbons for cooking and sewing in 4-H. Hell, God might have formed her in His gold-standard mold for earth wives. In terms of a marital partner, I was no competition. My boxed brownies came out lumpy and burnt, no matter how I tried to follow the 1-2-3 "Easy Steps," and I considered paying the dry cleaner to hem my pants as sewing.

Still.

I loved Jack long before they married. But we met a day before he popped the question. They had been dating for ten years by then. Time and timing was not on my side.

Or maybe it was.

Jack never mentioned to me or to H.V. or to any of the rotating reader interns in the office a word about her, much less her name. As I think on it, I never mentioned Noah. Although later, long after the trip to Texas, I left a pretty darn big clue about him. Anyway, Jack didn't mention Stephany, I didn't mention Noah, and so, our pasts were not our presents, but in the closet in which we toiled, confined and mired in fiction, fantasy.

By the week of this business trip to Texas, Jack and Stephany had been engaged one-and-a-quarter years, which meant Jack and I had known and worked together one-and-a-quarter years plus one day. After Jack's cinnamon-apple confession, we brushed the topic under the braided rug and strangely acted as though he'd never said the words—there were, however, our somewhat mutual attempts to fend off a mutual beholding, which did continue to happen, albeit cut short by someone's forced jerk of the head: mine.

We'd have allegedly platonic lunches and shared safe laughs over work projects for many of the hours in the ensuing year, never once discussing his wedding plans or his bachelor party or his planned honeymoon or the absent band of gold on his long ring finger. Nor did we discuss her. Not once. I tried several times to bring her up in the context of happy things, as any good friend would. He'd shut me down every time.

Until that pivotal trip to Texas.

So there we were, having finished a heavy day of reviewing several of our famous author's manuscripts in a pressure-filled hotel conference room. Our merry corporate band had been silenced during the day by the author's insistence that he sit and watch our reactions while we read. Exhausted with balancing the need to appear boutique with corporate policy with appeasing—yet being honest with—one of our biggest clients, the team collectively needed a drink. So, as soon as he tire-burned out of the parking lot in his yellow Lamborghini, we huddled: "Ten minutes, hotel bar. Break!"

I slipped into jeans and a loose white shirt, but retained my peep-toe heels. Elizabeth Taylor once said, "Big girls need big diamonds," and I say, short girls need high heels. Whatever my appearance, I truly had no aspirations, good, bad, or indifferent. I simply wanted a Miller High Life, mozzarella sticks, and to unwind.

We congregated at the side of the bar, which was sectioned off with a low couch and square cushions for sitting. Several neon lamps bathed our skin in the shade of blue-lip corpses. I plopped on a cushion and threw my hair into a sloppy twist, securing the grease trap with a clip. It didn't dawn on me that I should care about the tufts of hair sticking out.

Jack entered the scene, having changed into jeans, but keeping his Brooks Brothers' dress shirt untucked, sans tie, unbuttoned, and sleeves rolled. I have a certain established weakness for the birthmarks on Jack's forearms and a tempting freckle that *come hithers* from beneath his left collarbone. Call them my Kryptonite. I bucktoothed my side-swept bottom lip. "Ah, shit," I said to myself.

There he came to be, standing in the crowd, and a calm I had never noticed in him trapped me in his bubble. He looked me dead on, ignoring everyone else. A complicit grin grew in an ever-so-slight upturn of his red-watery mouth.

I may have been his night's prey.

I played the willing victim.

I confess.

He sat next to me, and I don't think anyone noticed yet the tension between us. Although, the electrical wires were so unsheathed, I'm not sure how anyone could have missed the zapping.

And, truthfully, I wasn't trying to hide a thing.

His wedding was in three weeks, five days, and thirty minutes, which was the countdown to when I would again lose at love because of circumstances out of my control.

Inhibitions dissipated as the number of rounds became inappropriate. The unnatural blue lighting and the ever-present cocktail waitress are what I blame for the roughness in the atmo-sphere—the sandpaper air, coaxing us to go on and scratch those itches.

People started tripping off after round ten of some medieval shot only Texans would resurrect. I also tried to stumble away, but Jack pulled me, subtly, back down to my square cushion. "You're my prisoner," he said. *Well, indeed I am*, I thought upon lowering my eyes but raising my pupils. In front of the stragglers remaining, he took a sip of my beer. I took a sip of his. When he went to answer someone's question, we ended his response in an impromptu duet, quoting a Bob Dylan song: "The answer, my friend, is blowing in the wind, the answer is blowing in the wind."

"We're good together," he said, acknowledging how I'd anticipated his words.

"Uh-huh. I know."

The tips of his fingers stretched out from his bottle toward my fingers, and I did the same. Our fingers were so close but separate, it felt as though a magnet was pulling and pushing them together and apart, a force field of energy.

"Can I ask you a question?" he said, with a small slur.

"Anything," I answered, with a likewise small, but measured, slur.

"What do you think is going on between us?"

I bulged my eyes in the direction of the closest cocktail table.

"Do you even have an answer to that question?" he asked further.

"I have a very specific answer to that question."

"I see."

If I ever had a chance, it was now, I thought. I had to plunge ahead, no holds barred, take no prisoners.

"So?" he said, so close to my ear that I leaned toward his lips so they might touch me.

"Do you really think we should be talking here?" I said, pointing with my eyes to the three other co-workers pretending not to listen.

"No. Let's go."

Jack made a pathetic attempt to say we had to check some file in the rental car. I didn't have the wherewithal or the care to correct him or to come up with a better excuse. Several fiery arrows shot overhead, and a horse whinnied in dying pain as we walked out of the hotel lobby. We were in full-scale battle in this war.

Outside, the sky was black with tiny white stars, the moon a fingernail, and the hotel's exterior lights were dim. We leaned against our rented cranberry Mercury.

As though he hadn't been drinking heavy for the last two hours, Jack deepened his voice to draw me to some serious level. "Vivienne, can you answer my question. I really need to know."

I thought what he needed was a final gut check to his decision to get married. I was thus presented with an ethical choice: lie and say I had no feelings for him and suggest he better go to bed so as to not ruin his well-intentioned marriage; or, make things difficult and tell him the truth. Since I so deeply felt he was wrong for marrying her and I truly did love him, I chose the latter. I have no regrets for what I did. I own this choice.

"Jack, I am in love with you. You must know this by now." The granite beam resting on my spine rolled off my back and crashed to the ground, cracking to stone dust and setting me free to shake my shoulders once more. To me, the situation was complicated, but inside I felt everything was or would be right if I trusted this undying feeling, this love. Perhaps I was woefully naive.

Time can and does stand still, and people can and do freeze in place. Sometimes. Some very rare times that come but once or twice, maybe three times tops, in your life. Jack and I stayed glazed in a moment when the world stopped spinning in Texas one night. We may still be bolted on granite blocks, phantom statues in a hotel parking lot.

A cool breeze swung by down in Texas. It didn't matter if it was winter or spring or summer or fall. Might've been midnight or daybreak. The breeze came with no mind to the actual temperature of the air, as it brushed ever-so-smoothly across your body, dispensing the scent of cactus. And even if you've never smelled a cactus, you knew the fragrance when the breeze met your face. You wished to follow the hint of aloe, even if the promise was only a poisoned oasis and the temptation of inner water meant a heart full of sharp needles.

When I confessed out loud what Jack already knew, that cruel, cool wind pushed me closer to his skin, which smelled of cactus. He leaned in too, in a distress though, his forehead lined in deep conflict. But regardless of the conflict in his brow, his pupils dilated to dimes.

I did not relent.

"Jack, what do you see when you look at me like that?"

He pulled back some, leaned more against the trunk of the car, giving his answer an eyes-closed consideration. Finally, when the wicked cactus wind returned, he said, "Many things. It's more what I feel. I feel anxious, nervous, and I fidget around you. I'm afraid I will say something wrong. I feel safe, that I can trust you with anything. And, well, I feel mostly, happy. Ah shit, Vivienne. This is a mess. Stephany cheated on me. She told me last week."

Stephany cheated on him. Stephany cheated on him. What? This is the second time he's said her name to me.

I swallowed any hesitations that might have surfaced and I had ignored. His hand came to my ring hand and grazed my pinky.

"Jack . . ."

With the early forming of clouds in his eyes and a fraction of liquid collecting in one duct, he said, "Our wedding is supposed to be in a month."

I felt a cramp in my neck and a burning in my throat. I placed my palm on his heart. Someone from the hotel opened the staff door to throw out some trash. We didn't flinch at the company.

"I don't want you to get married."

There. Said. Done. Crime committed.

His shoulders sank.

"And yet, you could have said this many times before," he said, as though I was the one who had wasted our time to this point. "She tells me last week. Last week. One of our alleged friends. But I felt like this about you long before her confession."

I could not deliver a retort, for he grabbed my face with both of his hands and kissed me so deeply, the earth slipped out from under my spiked heels. The stone dust from the cracked granite puffed into a choking cloud and for this, I held my breath. His body collided with mine; leaning conjoined against the car, we shimmied, kissing, to the back passenger door. Groping, mad, insanely deprived of air, I unhinged his belt. He unbuttoned my jeans. A car alarm trumpeted on the street beyond the hotel.

"Jack, not here. Come on, we have to get back inside."

"Now," he said, pulling me with him back toward the hotel doors.

A whirl of activity collected me in a vicious spin, like I was cut grass in a tornado. We ziplined past registration, the lobby, and the bar, thinking we had gone unseen, and after fidgeting with my room key or his, it didn't matter at the time, we landed on one of our beds. His belt was undone, so I had just his damned button jeans to contend with. Mine were already lumped in a sloppy pyramid, my shoes flung to opposite corners.

Wild arms competed for space as though we were in a bar fight with the sheets. I scraped his smooth chest, licked the freckle under his collar, and thanked the medieval drink that gave me the courage to say everything I had ever wanted to say. And thanking Mercury for setting events in play, I arched to the heart of Texas, as the cactus breeze invaded the room through an open window and taunted me further along the path I had chosen—in good times and in bad.

I still feel aftershocks of the ache, the inconsolable urge I had setting my hips to his, lining our heat, me biting his shoulder. A pressure rose, a rising heat, a pulsing ache—a constant cresting, undying ache. The friction was the itch; the pulsing was the scratch. And when I thought the relentless need would never subside, a gush doused the flame, and I lay in an all-out pant, gasping for air, begging for water, and fell into an unfathomable, satisfied sleep.

In the wee hours of the rising sun, I awoke to the most gut-wrenching sound: a man weeping. I pried open my eyes to find Jack on his stomach with his head buried in his pillow. Unsticking my tongue from the roof of my dry mouth, I wished alcohol had never been invented.

"Jack? Are you alright?"

He stalled in his sorrow and lay quiet a minute.

"Jack?" I repeated, as gentle and as much without judgment as my waking voice would allow.

He faced me straight on unashamed, and for this moment, I might have been tricked into flattery, for one could interpret this to mean he trusted me in what must have been one of his darkest moments. But flattery is a transient pride, so I braced myself for the inevitable "regret for being drunk" conversation and "making a mistake" speech.

"Vivienne, listen. I'm a wreck. I'm so embarrassed to be . . . ah, forget it." He face-planted into the pillow, folding the ends around his ears.

"What are you talking about? Embarrassed? Don't be ridiculous."

My heart was beating so hard I feared the valves would burst. I sat to hold my bent knees. Jack flipped to perch on a folded elbow, wiping his face rough on the pillow in the movement.

"Vivienne, I just have to say it. I'll say it quick. I'm sorry, I can't make this easy for you. I did mean what I said last night. You do make me happy, I love to be around you, I'm sure I love you, which makes this so much harder for us, definitely for me. I love her. She's my best friend and has been for a long time. I can't leave her. I won't leave her. I have to marry her, because she is good for me. And I forgive her. I love you both. I am so torn."

I thought two things: First, *He loves me.* Second, *He didn't say her name. He never does.*

"But Vivienne, I won't say last night was a mistake. I can tell you, I've never cheated on her, on anyone. And I don't plan to ever cheat again."

Cheat? We were not cheating. I thought last night was a beginning. Cheat?

In hindsight, I allowed the delusion. I have no one to blame, but me. Back then, however, I was rather pissed, but also immediately struck guilty, and also sad for him, so pretty much a cauldron of emotions, which I could not contain nor filter into reason.

"You're not saying anything," he said, after I contemplated the wrinkled linens for an eternity.

"I don't know what to say, Jack."

"You don't have to say anything. I'm so sorry for making this hard. If I wasn't with her, there is no one else I would want to be with but you. You scare me, Vivienne."

What he said, how he loved me, how he looked at me, my own internal sense, all of it, everything made his resolution impossible to accept. I kicked the sheet off my naked legs, swung them over the edge, hopped off, stormed into the bathroom, kick-shut and locked the door, and sat on the frigid white floor. The hotel towel did not provide the comfort or warmth I needed. Jack pled with me through the hollow aluminum to speak. I asked him to leave, so he did. Click. Shut.

I didn't make it into the stifled conference room the next morning. I blamed my absence on the flu. With the strategy of a triage nurse, I avoided my own death by purging all thought to focus solely on changing my return flight to that afternoon, sneaking unseen out of the hotel, and calling on non-CCA professional contacts while in transit. The two things I thanked myself for were previously being good at networking and also building myself a solid—albeit young—reputation of quality work, which enabled me to quit CCA the next week after an old classmate-turned-entrepreneur asked me to join her freelance editors firm. Her job offer encouraged me to work at home—or anywhere in the galaxy with Internet—so long as deadlines were met. Sold. Once settled, the walls crumbled, and I wound up watching comedies and action films, anything without romance, long after Leno said goodnight. Pizza boxes, Chinese take-out containers, and balled tissues became the by-products of my emotional war.

Jack told his fiancée about the whole ordeal when we got back to Boston and before the wedding. To my great surprise, she took the news like the graceful, imperfect queen she was, having confessed her own mistake. And actually, their tandem confessions and mutual forgiveness caused a resurrection of initial love for the two. I'm told the ceremony was a deep-felt, tears-rolling, splendid affair. Of course, I wouldn't have a firsthand account: Jack personally disinvited me the night before, as if I would have sullied their sacramental day with my unholy presence anyway.

But think about this. Jack was at my apartment (the same Back Bay hell-hole since grad school) the morning before his Big Day. I wanted to slap him for thinking he had to actually ask me not to attend. I said as much, so he apologized. Awkwardly we sat on my one-person futon, my eyes red from not sleeping for the third night in a row. Despite Jack's apparent ongoing conflict, what with the way he looked at me, I suddenly had no strength to contemplate or fight or question him. Sleep is what I longed for, and also the bathroom: to throw up. Mistaking the nausea for heartbreak and the fatigue for guilt's insomnia, I fled, hand to mouth, nearly falling on the porcelain just in time. Once again, Jack begged for my forgiveness through the bathroom door, and I begged him to leave, so he did. Click. Shut.

Weeks later, I asked Jack to meet me at a four-table café on Boylston Street. Croissants and coffee rolls were packed in a refrigerated display case, and the aroma was thick with espresso beans. Jazz played as a mere hint, audible only to the solo patrons who had the heart to listen. Lighting came from the outside world. Further into the café, one might get lost in the negligible kitchen, or rather, in the shadows.

Jack approached the table, removed his light jacket, and sat.

"I'm pregnant," I said, without waiting for him to settle into the scene.

"I knew it."

"You did not."

"I absolutely did, Vivienne. And guess what, I'm not freaking out either."

"Well I am. You knew. You knew. What are you talking about? You did not know."

"I did."

"So what do we do now?"

"Well, that's up to you. If you keep . . . well . . . if you decide to . . . Whatever. If you decide to stay pregnant, I'm going to be in the baby's life."

"What about your wife?"

"She'll have to understand."

Turns out, I violated CCA corporate policy by having an affair with a co-worker, but I at least complied with the requirement to *skip my period.* As though we thought we were in Heaven, Jack and I used no protection, a fact I remembered two months later with the starkness of finding a scarecrow in my shower. When the pee stick said, "+," I called my mother and asked where babies come from, which was a question she first found amusing, until I didn't laugh along. She ended the call with acceptance, and said, "We got this, babydoll, we're a family. We fight and we love together, through everything, good and bad. At the end of the day, this is very good. You know I love you too much, and I sure am going to love that baby too much."

I was still living in my grad school, garbage apartment, the one that smelled of propane. You can go years with the same, monotonous routine. Day in, day out. Same place for coffee. Same hello to the same store cashier. Same gym. Same diner. Same grocery store. Years slipped by without much variation, which is time's trick, of course—a cruel sedation so you don't notice the passing years. And then, one night changed the world. Even finer, one second when his met mine and made a third. Science. Timing. Fate. Circumstance. Everything converged.

CHAPTER XXI
Ivan

I read *Ivan* to Jacob II, first-born great-grandchild, May 3, 2068 (huge surprise, but who are we to judge, we are all happy).

I read *Ivan* to Harkin (the derivation of this name eludes me, but he's my clone) and Lizener (perhaps the progression of years is creating these alien names), these grandbaby births bookending June of 2077.

I read *Ivan* to Sandaulan (again, derivation?) and Eleanor (THANK YOU!), twin great-grandbabies, September 5, 2078.

I read *Ivan* alone, sometime after my ninety-eighth birthday party. Ele was in the garden sitting with our daughters. It is May. The lilacs fill the air with their purple scent. I am ninety-eight, but I miss my mother on the ninetieth anniversary of her death, May 22, 2102. I think I stared at a yellow butterfly for an hour. He sat on the windowsill, keeping my company. The whole while, I thought of my mother's notebooks.

Adding this general commentary because this book has become my life's diary. No event of extreme tragedy or uncontained happiness ever forced a reading of *The One and Only Ivan*, beyond my regular readings in July and upon the birth of a baby, or the time Ele had the heart scare. Things have been pretty much even, and I am so blessed. There was, however, the one instance when I was forty-five and my spinal cord injury research company made an earth-shattering, life-changing breakthrough and the President of the United States called to thank me in my office. And so did the surgeons at Johns Hopkins. I couldn't read *Ivan* though. I couldn't read anything. So I wrote at dawn, while Ele made me celebratory M&M pancakes, naked. ☺

None of my four children or ten grandchildren or twenty-two great-grandchildren or two great-great grandchildren are named Vivienne. They have all been warned that no one can replace my mother.

July 4, 2102, at the lake for our annual week. I am ninety-nine years old. I reminded Ele we've kept our secret for over ninety years. "Shhh," she said, and I swear she looked nine years old. My lovely Ele.

CHAPTER XXII
Home

I'm back in my hospital room alone. The flowers are all dead, and the curtains unmoved. The clock ticks to 4:23 a.m., so I must have been daydreaming two hours, remembering my go with Jack. Noah is nowhere to be seen.

The card Jack had written with the Proust quote remains on my rolling tray, and as I read it again, I still cannot figure out whose decision he's referencing. Why is it always like jamming a corner puzzle piece into the center with Jack?

I suddenly miss a white house with green shutters and old, knotty oaks lining a long dirt drive. In the height of summer, this house is hidden from the road, what with the plump canopy on those wonderful, twisted trees. Noah and I used to pass the place on the school bus. He'd lean in and conceal an idea by speaking in my hair, "Viv, let's sneak in and investigate who lives there." "When?" I'd say, appearing to fellow bus-mates as if we were talking about trivial certainties. But for some reason, we never did the deed. Probably because we lived about two miles back in our own safe enclave, and to get to the white house, you had to cross the "Big Road." Nevertheless, we never went and for some odd reason, I never mentioned my draw to the property to my parents. Yet I always thought of this white house, through college, through grad school, at my job, when traveling—and I never understood why. I especially thought of it when I found myself pregnant and unmarried at the age of twenty-five.

And now, in my hospital bed, my mind once again wanders to this house.

One week after Jack and I left the clinic and I chose to keep the baby, I drove north to my hometown, Milberg, hoping to find a place to rent near my parents. I planned to work at home, but I thought it best to be around family with a new baby. Jack and Stephany lived outside of Boston, and he planned to have our child every other weekend. We had life all sketched out. Jack insisted on paying for his unborn child's medical bills, private school, and food. I tried to refuse—actually, I wanted to pay everything and also have Jack in the baby's life; truly, I wanted him around for the baby, not me. Jack, however, argued that this was his way of protecting his parental rights and also because he thought it was the right thing to do. Still, lawyers drew up an agreement just to be sure everyone's rights were protected.

The day I drove up to Milberg, ten weeks pregnant, I took the Big Road with that splendid, white house, about which I knew nothing. I slowed to a crawl as I came upon the driveway; a VW Bug hissy-fit-beeped and swerved around me. With my mouth open in shock, I stopped and draped my arms on the steering wheel, leaning to the windshield for better view of a sign: "Seizure Auction, October 20, 2002, 8 a.m." Below the sign was a bin full of flyers. U-turning and skidding in a wave of road dust to a stop, I practically collided with the bin of flyers. I flew open my door and toppled forward to read the details. The house had been seized in a drug raid and was up for auction the very next day. "No reserve," said the superscript. My father later explained that technically, the place might sell for $1. "But this never happens, doll. Don't get your hopes up," he said. "I'll come with you though." "Me too," called my mother, holding herself up in the kitchen doorway.

On the day of the auction, I was pacing on the porch of the big white house—which was a Victorian by the way—by 7 a.m.; no other soul in sight. My parents had gone up the street to get us coffee. The day was a cool, crisp fall, the leaves in an autumn rainbow. The sky was like the Caribbean Sea in its cloudless turquoise, and the waking sun sprayed an orange-yellow over the treeline.

Wind rustled through the low branches, causing a cone of fallen leaves to spin up into a mini tornado in the lawn. A bird who had forgotten to flee south for the season swooped to perform a wing-dance: I, his solo audience, his grateful admirer.

I didn't care that the shutters were falling off or the siding had holes and should have been replaced a decade before. I didn't care that three windows were boarded with plywood tagged in graffiti, or that the barn was stuffed with rusted farm equipment. I didn't care that in looking through a broken window, the kitchen appliances appeared burned and the wood floor warped by flood-water. I didn't see the house in that state: I saw her as a Painted Lady with life inside, the life growing in my body. I was in love with this house or the image I had, one I'd carried ever since Noah suggested we sneak in to find out who lived there.

A car door closing broke my solitude, and the bird flitted away. The sun sat high in the sky, baking off the comforting wind. A man with a cowboy hat emerged from a whale of a Buick and checked me openly, head to toe, his eyes up over his BluBlockers.

"You here for the auction?" he asked.

"I am."

"Me too." He extended his André-the-Giant hand. "Nate Mercio of Mercio Land Trust and Development."

"Ah," I said, picking up my purse to rifle for my keys and walking to my parked car. Everyone in Milberg knew about Nate Mercio. He had purchased the development my childhood home (still my parents' house) was in years ago and had stuffed more houses on the lower half and along the ridgeline, then he did the same with three other plots of land in adjoining towns. His company was well known for buying up local property, tearing down old houses, and cramming in cookie-cutter new ones.

"Whoa, hold up. Hold on, young lady. You leaving on my account? You didn't even say your name."

"Listen, Nate, is it? Nate, I had a crazy hope of buying this place. If you're the competition, I might as well leave. And I'm Vivi-enne, sorry, didn't mean to be rude."

He laughed a rolling gut laugh. "Hold up now, Vivienne. Your name is Vivienne? Wow. That was my grandmother's name. Loved my grandmother." He smiled to the sky. "She made the best fried dough and penuche fudge. Vivienne. Vivienne. People don't name their daughters Vivienne anymore. What a shame."

"Yeah, well." I took a step to leave.

"Hold on now. What made you think you could handle this place anyway?" he said, laying a hand lightly on my elbow, urging me gently to stop, and fanning out his other hand to the crumbling house behind.

"I didn't. I have just always loved this house since I was a little girl. My boyfriend, Noah Vinet, and I rode past on the bus and would daydream about sneaking inside and finding out who lived here." *Why am I telling him this? Why did I say Noah's full name? What on earth am I talking about? Shut up and leave.* But I kept talking, "And I had a stupid idea I could raise my baby here."

Nate darted his head sharp, as though I'd slapped him.

"You're pregnant?"

"Yes, I am."

"Where's your husband."

"Don't have one. And won't either."

He rubbed his chin, widened his nostrils, and tightened his jaw. It appeared as though he was pushing some deep emotion down. I squinted, confused at the reaction from this stranger.

"I remember Noah. I was one of the first responders—the first, in fact, paramedic on the scene." Nate quickly twitched as though pinched. "Oh hell, no, you're her. You're the girl who wouldn't stop holding his hand. Well shit, dip me in molten metal and bronze me on this spot."

A chill from the South Pole riddled up through the earth and crackled through my spine. I pivoted to the road in a slow, possessed turn, keeping a look of suspicion on Nate Mercio. What is happening? Nate moved closer, hoisting his sunglasses atop his rounded head; his eyes did not leave my eyes.

"Oh I sure remember Noah. And I sure remember you. That night, I hugged my baby boys until the sun came up I was so rattled. I've never witnessed anything as horrible as finding him at the bottom of that tree, or you catatonic at his side. I quit the paramedic's crew because of that day. Flat out quit. Couldn't take the grief. I went into land development, all because of Noah. Noah, Noah, Noah. What a prince. Would've been a great athlete. Would've conquered the world."

I crossed my arms and tilted my body, leaning on air. I thought I was listening to someone speak from outside of my body.

"I can't believe you just said his name," Nate said.

"I can't believe you did."

He spun on his chunky cowboy heels a full 360 degrees, stopped, pursed his lips, and spun again. Shaking his head, he clapped his hands, as though slaking off the oddness of our conversation. And sure enough, he forced a change of topic.

"Well now. Anyway. Vivienne, you thought you could handle an old Victorian on your own? What about the renovation, the construction, the painting, the upkeep, the drafty walls, the acres of mowing and raking, shall I continue?"

"Just a foolish dream."

"Uh-huh. Do you even know what happened here?"

"Not really. I just know the cops busted some lady who lived here for meth or something. The most my parents heard was something about a drug raid and that the house has been empty two years."

"Close. Been empty two years, yes. Two years ago, a fifty-year-old woman was found with one of the largest meth labs in the state in this here basement. Dealers from Boston and Providence and Hartford, even New York, used to drive on down this sweet dirt drive and buy her meth right on this very porch. Went on about a decade. Worst kept secret in this town. Her bust was all over the news. I'm surprised your parents didn't know the details. They live in Milberg, you say?"

"Yup. Our house is in Batchelder Acres."

"I bought and expanded Batchelder Acres not long after Noah's accident."

"Yeah, I know."

"Well I'll be damned."

"Be damned then," I said and caught his stare, not blinking back. I believe an unspoken message transpired between our minds, which had not caught up to our present thinking. Perhaps the message was an eternal warning to Nate, or perhaps it was the imposition of a reality beyond the one we were living.

"You're a real spitfire, ain't ya, Vivienne?"

I didn't respond.

Nate straightened his lips while bouncing his head, appearing as though he was fighting back that deep emotion again. "Batchelder Acres was my first purchase, alright. Part of me wanted to own the spot where Noah fell. The first tree I had cleared was the one he fell from. I wonder if it's my fault, Vivienne. I was the first one on the scene and I moved him. Maybe I made his injury worse." He ground his teeth. "Ah, shit. I never said that to anyone. What am I saying to you?"

The chill from the deep regions of an arctic tundra rose again, so I sat on the rotting wood porch to concentrate. A squirrel poked through a hole in a floorboard, and I swear that animal held its breath to hear this conversation.

Nate turned on his heels again, coughed, and forced a tortured smile.

"Cops put the circus all over the news to send a message to meth dealers to steer clear. Also all over the news again a week later when the lady up and died in her jail cell. Not one living soul claimed to know her. No one came forward to claim any inheritance on this property, which was seized anyway. Still, no one. But all over the news, I promise you, and I should know because I've been praying for this day ever since. I have specs drawn up for ten condos. Blueprints are on my backseat." Nate pointed to his candy-carmel Buick, reflecting in wax enlivened by a spotlight of sun.

"Ten condos? You'd cut down these trees? They're so beautiful. So old."

"Oh, you're one of those."

"No, I'm not one of those. I mean, I love trees and nature. Look, I just love this house and the property."

Now I wanted to stay.

"How much you willing to go on this place?" he asked.

"I don't think I should be telling you my limit."

"No, no, probably not. Alright. Let's see what happens. Please don't go. Maybe my price is so low you'll win."

"I highly doubt that." I dropped my purse on the porch, relenting to torture myself in watching him win.

The most I could bid was $50,000: $15,000 I had in savings, plus my parent's insistence on lending me a piece of their nest egg, if I promised to pay them back. My mother was excited to have me close; she even said, "Please Vivienne, do this for me. Take the money if you can get the house for a low price. Crazy not to." A cent over $50,000, however, would obliterate the piggy bank. Coming into this auction, my chances were slim. There was absolutely no time for any applications for mortgages, and besides, this no-reserve auction was "Cash Only." But everything seemed so right to me, and the timing was so strange, I figured I should attempt the long shot. I was banking on the hope that no one would want a fixer-upper in such a decrepit state, nor a house with a reputation for drugs.

Nate Mercio kicked his cowboy boots up over the gravel drive and wandered off toward the barn. My parents walked down the driveway—my mother with gingerly-taken steps and holding my father's arm—having left their car up on the Big Road. I apprised them of the competition.

"Nate Mercio," my father said. "Forget it. You're done for."

"You're not giving up, Vivienne," my mother said.

Before long, a few more people arrived: the auctioneer, his assistant, some accountant, the town's sheriff, and two town officials. Nate Mercio emerged from behind the house, his hands clasped behind his back and his gait a contemplative kick-shuffle.

Not one other person showed to bid, even though the auctioneer gave an extra half hour for stragglers.

The auctioneer used the porch as his podium, and the others mingled close on his stage. Us bidders, Nate and I, stood on the dirt drive, along with my parents. There would be no permitted inspection. "This no-reserve auction is inside unseen, as is," the auctioneer explained.

I clutched the paddle the sheriff handed me on my stiff-straight legs. Nate dangled his from his limp right hand; his left stroked his tight-trimmed chin beard.

"We have here a hundred-year-old Victorian, original wood floors, four bedrooms, one in each turret, two baths, a barn, and twenty-five acres. A rock quarry can be mined for granite. A stream runs on the east side and borders the property on the left, national forest preserve takes up the two hundred acres on the right. Real private, secluded gem here. Can we start with $200,000?"

Neither Nate nor I budged.

The auctioneer reminded us of the attributes and the market value, "$500,000 land value alone," he said.

"Rubbish," my mother said, not trying to be subtle.

"Can we start with $100,000," the auctioneer tried when his two bidders didn't flinch over the land's qualities.

Again, no one moved. No one bid.

The sun rose and expanded, illuminating our odd play as if we were the only event on the earth that day.

Some time passed.

My bird returned, fluttering by my right shoulder. The auctioneer again rattled off the litany of the property's acres and resources. We remained unmovable stones in the audience.

"Can we start with $50,000?" the auctioneer said in a quiver, taking a swallow. "Come on Nate, I've been through these auctions with you a hundred times. This is robbery if you let the bid go lower."

Nate crossed his arms tight, burying the paddle into his midsection.

"Fifty thousand dollars won't even get you an acre in this town. Come on now, someone has to start this auction. $50,000?"

I went to bid, but my father forced my elbow down. Nate didn't move, and he didn't glance my way either.

I think my pulse could have fired up Google's worldwide server farms.

The town officials began to pull at their collars. The larger one wiped a rivet of sweat from his neck. The smaller one clenched his teeth so tight, I counted his molars through his thin skin. The smaller one shouted at the larger one, "I told you this would happen. Son of a bitch! Who's the damn moron who said no reserve would bring us more bidders. Huh? Did you even advertise this thing? Why the hell damn, damn hell, shit is no one here?"

"Can we start with $20,000?" The auctioneer tried, looking askance at the town officials as though apologizing.

Again my father pinned my arm.

"Shut this shit down," shouted the small town official.

"The hell you will," Nate barked, his back suddenly straight and his muscles twitching under his black button shirt. "Tony, you tell 'em. Damn illegal to shut her down now." Nate gestured to the sheriff, presumably the Tony in his tirade.

"Can't shut her down," Sheriff Tony parroted, practically laughing at the officials whose obvious stupidity amused the seasoned cop.

"Ten thousand dollars, come on people. This is seriously robbery now. Can we start at $10,000?"

Without turning his head, Nate clicked his tongue, which I accepted as a conspiracy between us. I raised my bidder's paddle.

"Ten thousand dollars. We got $10,000. Nate, come on, I know you won't let this place go for $10,000, come on now, can I get $20,000? Nate, you can get three hundred fold on this land. Think of the houses you can develop. Twenty-five acres. Give me $20,000, let's get this auction rolling."

Nate laid his paddle on the porch at the town officials' feet, saluted the auctioneer, heel-toed to his car, and drove away.

His Buick whipped up a brown-dust fog.

The auction stalled until the dirt settled and our collective awe snapped out of slow motion.

The larger town official squat-jumped off the porch and kicked a stone, which hit the granite foundation of the house. After watching him pace a circle like a rabid panther, the auctioneer slowly raised his attention to me. "Well now, young lady, you have yourself a house for $10,000. Sold. And you can thank Nate Mercio and the crackhead who owned this place for that."

"And don't forget to thank the dipshit who put no reserve on the flyer!" The skinny town official spat at his colleague, who was halfway gone up *my* driveway.

I suffered mental whiplash the rest of the day and all night, confused by the sudden changes in my life: one-night affair with someone I was still in love with, pregnant, new job, and a strange house I had thought of my whole life—all within a three-month span. Reality scared me, not for the upcoming challenges, but because as I lay in my childhood bed, my present seemed as though it should be in the future. My nine, ten, eleven, twelve-year-old brain considered my instant adulthood too foreign to believe. I switched on my blue bubble lamp throughout the night to view my grown hands as a reminder of my adult age. Tossing under my mother's quilts, I'd jam my thumbs into my biceps to prove I was indeed real.

The next morning, I awoke to the sound of mumbled talking in the foyer and the creak of the stairs and a knock at my bedroom door.

"Vivi, you up? Can I come in?"

"Yeah, Mama."

My mother handed me an envelope.

"Who's it from?"

"Just open it."

She lay on my bed, curling around me like a cat, like she always did. I unsealed the envelope:

Dear Vivienne,

I believe, with all the faith I have been able to cobble together in my simple life, that Noah bought you your new home. Please enjoy and make her the castle you've always dreamed of. Now you know who lives there.

~ Nate Mercio

As I sat reading these words, I slumped in a sadness I had forgotten. My mother read over my shoulder and cooed an "ahhh."

"Oh Vivi, that's right, Nate was the first responder for Noah. Wow, how did I forget?"

I buried my head in the crook of her neck. "Mom, I can't believe I still miss him. Will it ever stop?"

"It never will. And that's okay."

The clock reads 5:05 a.m. It's stone-cold dark. Not one person comes to see me or even pass by my hospital room.

For the first time in however long I have been holed up in this sterile, white room, I long for my own bed. My own comforter. My brilliant boy tumbling into my room to wake me up. I miss my office in the turreted room upstairs and the walnut desk I'd bought at the Derry Flea Market. I miss the red runner on the grand, curling stairs to the first floor, my coffee maker, and the back deck, which affords a view of ten thousand oaks. Maples and birch too. All of them ours, mine and Ivan's. I miss our red barn and the tree-lined driveway, so long you can't see the Big Road. I miss our brightly-painted yellow Victorian with pink and blue and purple accents in the complicated outside molding. I miss our renovated three-season sunroom, the light-green shutters, and the green grass for miles, punctuated by those wonderful, knotty trees with their squirrel-infested trunks. In the fall, we hang aluminum buckets on the sugar maples we tap for syrup. Our home. Ivan's and mine.

Perhaps my painkillers are low, for my head begins to throb and my monitor begins to squeal. A nurse who is not Marty enters, adjusts the drip, and documents my pulse. She doesn't care to calm me with a Precious-infused countdown or humor me by adding more Vodka to my drug line, or entertain me with readings from another patient's journal. Her downward frown is permanently etched in place. *Marty, I wish you were here.*

A burning creeps through my arm where the IV begins, and once again I feel awash in a physical peace. But sleep eludes me.

I try to picture myself in a happy place, my and Ivan's blue and white kitchen. I imagine him toddling on the hallway runner, taking his first steps. I flip through the years of his waking intellect, his three's, his four's, his kindergarten five's. I see his perfect penmanship and the letter from the school asking to test him for advancement, to skip ahead, all of which I refused. "Why speed up his life. Let him take his time. Be a child," I had said. Still, I hired a tutor to challenge him, so he didn't lose his gift. He wrote a beautiful sonnet at the age of six, which hangs framed, the centerpiece of our living room. His other works of art clutter the other walls in the other rooms and the other hallways, everywhere, from finger-painted butterfly gardens, to a rainbow mermaid, to stick figures running and smiling under a yellow circle sun, to eight stanza, rhyming poems. All framed. All displayed. Ivan is the center of the universe.

I wade through our once formal parlor room that Ivan and I converted into a playroom. His indoor basketball hoop, his electric train set, his mounds of stuffed animals as a quarry of friends.

I jump to last summer, when on a regular day, after we shared a Milberg House of Pizza pizza on our two-person kitchen table, he suddenly aged into a forty-year-old gentleman. I didn't see it coming, expect it, or ever ask for such growth or grace. He picked up our sauce-stained plates and said, "Sit, Mama. I will clean up," and he kissed my cheek, only to add, "I love you, Mama." Turning to the sink to rinse the dishes, he hummed a song I'd hummed since his birth: Sesame Street's Ladybugs' Picnic. *One. Two. Three. Four. Five. Six. Seven. Eight. Nine. Ten. Eleven. Twelve. And they chatted away . . . at the ladybugs' picnic.*

He returned to the table with two chocolate chip cookies without the chocolate chips: one for him, one for me.

"Why are you crying, Mama?"

"Because I love you too much. Too much."

Laughter tumbles through my memories as I recall this past Christmas. Can you hear Ivan and Jack in the living room? Jack is tickling Ivan. Ivan is squealing for Jack to stop, but not meaning to allow his father to lose hold of him, even for a second. "I love you, Papa," I overhear from upstairs, as I lean over the upper banister. "I love you too, boy," Jack says in his baritone, scratchy voice. I draw myself a deep, hot bath, resolving to allow Jack the extra time he asked for with Ivan, as he always asks for nearly every single one of their visits. And I shiver as I shuffle off in my Christmas bathrobe, not out of sadness, but because I love Jack and Ivan to the point of bursting.

Yes I do still love Jack. I can't help but love him, because I respect him as a father and a faithful husband. He may steal a peep my way when he thinks I'm not aware, and once he left a message on my cell phone while suffering an alcohol-inspired nostalgia. But never has he acted—since conceiving Ivan—upon any temptation brewing in him, or in me. Jack is the only person in the world who shares the same level of love for Ivan as me, and I, therefore, remain his prisoner. I choose not to date, mostly because I'd rather not waste time away from Ivan. Also, there is no match to Jack's throaty laughter or princely face. And not a soul can trump Noah. So what's the point in kissing a consolation prize?

I think about last month when I found *The One and Only Ivan*, which I had begun reading to Ivan. I bought it in the lobby of my Brigham & Women's heart doctor's office. Dr. Plaqueinvalves—my secret name for him—had just cleared me for the nine millionth time and said I didn't need to keep checking my "strong ticking organ." "No, no, doc. If I have what my mother has, I'll begin whatever preventative medicines I can. I don't want to leave Ivan, ever," I had said. After buying *Ivan*, and in retrospect in acting out my own prophecy, I hailed a cab to my lawyer's office and added the following codicil to my will, which I insisted on writing in my words, without all the legalese:

"If I die, Ivan is the sole beneficiary of my estate, which is held in trust. It may not be sold until Ivan is twenty-one, except if *he* needs money for *his own* medical emergency [a separate trust document was drawn up with the lawyer's words]. His guardian will be his father, Jack O'Neal, but Ivan should be allowed to live in our home. He is so happy playing in the trees and the eaves and the millions of corners of our home. Please do not remove him from his place of peace, Jack. Move in with him—plenty of room for a larger family. Stephany, I can only plead with you, one mother to a soon-to-be mother, please allow Ivan to have his home. You have always been so good to him, loving and kind, and I cannot thank you enough for being so understanding, accepting, and a better person than me. I am sorry for everything."

Chapter **XXIII**
The Solitude of Jack

I don't know who you are sometimes. I forget. But I always
think of you regardless, whoever you may be. Please, take
the beach-glass bottle top in my desk's middle drawer.
I thought of you when I found it.

> *Until,*
>
> *~Viv*

(This is the note I'll later ask Marty to write to Jack after
I visit a portion of his, well, afterlife. His Solitude.)

My hospital room is a frigid hole. Marty isn't anywhere, the
lilacs on the beside table have begun to decompose, and the
lilies' bloated stalks yellow the vase water. The hall lights are not
even on, and the slats of the shade are shut. I gag at the smell of
the floor's cleaning solution, a gritty, sour lemon with a hint of
relentless urine.

I squint to adjust to the darkness and finally I see a shadow in a corner, peering through the outside window. Noah's back is to me.

"What about hell?" I ask him.

He plays with the blinds, flicking them to clang as though falling dominos.

"Well, now, there is the catch, Vivienne."

"Does it exist?"

"Hell?"

"Yes, Noah, is this what you've been warning me about?"

"From what I understand, hell is personal."

"Show me your face."

He turns around, his shoulders rounded. A gray has taken over the sallow skin below his sunken eyes.

In awe, I say not a word.

"Vivi, do you remember Bobby Doaner, up on Salitor Road? He was in our grade."

"The kid with the white trailer and the cat named Stanley with the one eye?"

"Yeah, him. Did you know he shot himself?"

"I had no idea."

"Years ago. When he was about twenty-eight, twenty-nine. PTSD over memories of his daddy's belt, and crumbled from the bankruptcy he was facing. Anyway, pulled the trigger on an old Colt. Do you know what happened to him?"

"Not a clue. Noah? Why are you so lifeless, so pale and transparent tonight? I can barely see you." My voice cracks as I speak.

"Please, let me finish. Bobby's in a perpetual spiral, Viv. His own personal capsule, and he can't escape. Some would say this is hell. I've heard that's what happens if you take Bobby's road to death. I've also heard you might spiral if you offer something, like your soul, and it is refused. Might be why heartbreak to the living is so painful—it's a taste of an eternal confinement."

"I don't follow. What are you saying? Please come here. Step closer. You're scaring me."

"Please, Vivi. I've already said too much. I must not dissuade your choice. What is your next Heaven? Can you think of any more?"

I am prepared to tell him, "Jack's," but now I don't want to say his name out loud, even though I am saturated in thoughts of him. Nevertheless, upon conjuring his name in my mind, I'm pulled to the bridge, the tree limbs, and the white stars. A flash of lighting rips the sky open. I blink, and there is nothing.

A blank vacuum.

I cannot keep track of the time as I remain suspended in this nothing. I know only a wailing in my heart. And beyond the wailing in my heart, I sense another space so unreachable from my depth, I find it easier to bury further. In this way, I spin into a cocoon within a cocoon. My silky shell becomes so thick, my encasement is as hardened and black as a fallen walnut upon the frozen land. There is no chance for this walnut to set in this unforgiving, unrelenting, endless winter. And so it, and I, roll around untamed, unfruitful, forgetting even the simplest of new things, for it and I grow not, we only fold in further within our rolling caskets, growing older and darker in the memory of what we might have been—had we been permitted to root in the earth. Or hold his hand in full view. Walk around with him for everyone to see.

Is this guilt? Should I feel guilt for my act with Jack? And when Noah drove up in his van, did I shun him? His condition? Did I not fight hard enough to rattle him out of his absence? For sure I was wrong. And so I roll in again. Again and again. Again forever, beyond the wailing in my heart, I sense another space so unreachable from my depth. . . . So goes the cyclical churning of these thoughts.

A pinprick of light beckons me further on, and as illumination grows, the ground returns. A blank ground, but a soft, earthy ground nonetheless. I continue along until my vision becomes my destination.

Out before me stretches Jack's Heaven—or part of it, I hope: a long, white-sand beach. Empty, but for the driftwood bench. To my right, sand spreads like a light brown tarp sewn into a low green patch of beach grass, which sprawls until slamming into a black and gray wall of wet rock. Atop the wall, I dare not take myself for viewing.

To my left, crackles and crashes the forever running record of an endless rocking sea, whose name I know not nor care to discover. It has salt, for one from the rolling waves, but also the taste of an invisible crust I lick from my lips. He has come here to be alone sometimes in life. This he told me once—although he never brought me.

It is thus in Jack's solitude I inspect another option. He has not seen me arrive, given the distance between us on this long beach and his focused attention on something in the hemline of beach grass and sand. Whatever it is, he finds and pockets it, smiling to himself and in profile to me. Seemingly consoled, he meditates on the diamonds dancing on the stillness of the ocean beyond the swells. He runs to these illusory water gems, dusting up the sand as he makes his way. So taken in delight, he jumps, stretches his wingspan like the largest angel, bends his knees, and arches into a reverse crescent—a dancer this man, caught in unmitigated solitude and peaceful silence. He has no idea I see him in this state. And I will never tell him. Until the very moment he reads these words. Does he know how much I love to find him so happy?

I wait the right amount of time, allowing him to linger longer at the foot of the crashing water. He watches his heels sink into the shoreline—the meeting of water and earth—and they sink further with each crash, which soothes him, amuses him, as a kitten would a child. How soft the mud must be along the top bones of his feet. How lucky the grains are to lace between his toes and hold him there. What magic they have, that magic I don't. But even the soft sand and tickling pebbles, with their ability to hold and amuse him, will be pulled away by the receding tide. Perhaps a speck will have the honor of attaching to his stride, take steps with him to the hemline, and climb the path up the rock wall, or wherever he goes when he is not in his blessed solitude.

I watch him muddle in the mud until it reaches his ankles and I can take no more.

"Jack," I say.

He turns, only slightly startled.

"So you've come here," he says, and exhales in a relief of breath.

He removes his feet from the suction of the mud holes, one by one with some effort, for even the earth has difficulty letting him go. Or is this my vision of things? Perhaps another person would see just a man stepping away from the ocean. And who can tell whose view is most accurate?

When he reaches me, he takes my hand, and we follow the tire marks from absentee four-wheelers and dune buggies. We walk the long way down the beach, not the short way—to the hemline and rock wall. He could have taken and introduced me to it all, but this unspoken agreement to walk the long way says volumes, I think.

And so, I go along. Occasionally he jostles with the something he found in the hemline and placed in his pocket. An embroidered gold seahorse rounds the edges of his shorts, helping him to conceal his secret object.

He lifts his chin, contemplating the spectacle of the red setting sun ahead.

He holds my hand, more as a comfort to me, I believe, as though he knows this must be a difficult trip.

"Vivienne," he says.

"Yes."

"What if I told you I still love you? Would that change anything?"

"Change what?"

"Change what you choose, I suppose. Change what you take from here, from me, as inspiration?"

This question stalls me. Not much stops me from creating any Heaven I want. If I love Jack, he will be in my Heaven. I'd add this beach. The grass. The thing he hides in his pocket. The fire horizon. The tall rock wall. I might change the world beyond, if I choose. But would these items be real or replicas? Do I want a mirage of Heaven? Will fabrications satisfy my eternity? If he said he loved me, would I stay in his Heaven? His Solitude? Was there even a place for me?

Of course, Jack's real question is the inverse of his question: "If I don't say I love you, will you create a Heaven with me in it?"

We inch closer to the blazing horizon, and I get lost in my thoughts on his question. Forcing me to stop, he squares his body to mine and covers my breathing with his lips—and oh, the devilish cactus-breeze of Texas kicks up a storm, whips up a frenzy in this now burning solitude. My skin tingles as he traces my jaw¬line; my feet sink into the soft ground. I relive in memory the moments we made love, made Ivan.

Would it change anything if he said he loves me?

But did he say as much?

Really, my choice has nothing to do with what he actually says or doesn't say.

As he presses in closer and slips his electric fingers beneath the sleeves on my shoulders, I open my eyes. What I do not see changes, or solidifies, my answer. I do not see Noah in the grass or along the rocks or anywhere in my view. He is not here as he has been in every other afterlife.

I step away from Jack, although I crave to keep going.

"Jack, you need not say anything. Although, I note you haven't. I know you still love me. I feel it. I trust my own senses. So, if you said the words, things would not change. I don't belong here."

He touches the side of his chin to his right shoulder, a physical wince to my answer.

"You are here, Vivienne. I hold you in this place. Whenever I come to my solitude, you are here. And I sit with you. I talk with you. I've cried on your shoulder a thousand times. But perhaps I knew all along, all I had was the idea of you, and not as you are here today."

He reaches within his pocket and pulls out a shard of white sea glass. The top of a weathered, antique bottle.

"You put this glass in my palm when I last saw you. I dropped it by mistake, which seems irrelevant now. As soon as I realized it was missing, I've been in a mad search. And as today is the first day you come on your own without my making it so, naturally, today is the day I find it."

"Beyond, over the rock wall, am I with you?"

"Would that change your decision? Would you stay?"

"But I am not, right?"

He squints at the wall.

I am not.

"You could be," he says.

Even in death, he is torn. Even in death, I am torn. There are certain things in life that you are convinced will stay with you forever. You are right to feel that way, for it is true.

"Tell me," I say, "Before today, you only came to me upon this lonely beach?"

"I suppose."

"Then isn't that the decision, Jack?"

"I do not know."

I crane my neck to peer beyond his shoulder and again feel an awful ache when I realize Noah is not here. He will not urge me to move on to other options. He will not provide the answer by consuming me in a look or hold me upright from the quaking ground, helping avoid the hospital room for as long as possible. The peace of a Heaven and the fullness of completion become foreign, intangible fragments, which I struggle to collect and piece back together. Alone with Jack, I am halved—as though my legs have crossed the lawn to bounce in another bed, and my lungs to breathe in another house.

The weight of the descending horizon returns me to the enclosure I had when I first arrived, the same sense I'd suffered anytime Jack left me in life, a sense of another space beyond which I could not reach. A coiling begins in my chest, pushing me to the waves. A

churning, an emptiness, a confusion so intangible I'm barely able to harness a single word.

"Vivienne . . ."

I choke the beach glass as a prop to keep me upright.

"Vivienne . . ."

As I fall to the sand, the water crashes over my hips and legs. In time with the pounding surf, I let out my answer upon the full exhale of both lungs: "No," I shout, the one word I know through all of the confusion is the true answer, the one I'd struggled with so many times. The elusive answer to the most difficult question I was ever faced with: when to keep trying and when to walk away. Here on the outskirts of his Heaven, having avoided finality for so long, I want to say it a hundred times to make it true.

"No," I repeat, letting Jack go, leaving him in the serenity of his own creation.

There is no arguing, so desperate fight or plea; he, like in life, simply acquiesces and disappears into the hemline and over the rock wall.

I forget to hand back the bottle top.

A souvenir?

I intend never to return to Jack's Solitude, for I have something better and more complete on the other side of death, a place where tree limbs twist into beautiful asymmetry and Van Gogh paints the sky every night. I have a fury to hold and hug Noah, and also to find Ivan. But as my fury grows, Noah does not appear. The entombment thickens, as does the air, which becomes one color: gray. Rolling into myself, a horror strikes me: This is Hell, and I am stuck. Noah has left me. I chose too late.

CHAPTER **XXIV**
Hell is Gray. Hell is Personal.

Hell is not black. There are no fires. There are no demons hissing in your ear. You are not chained. You are not hot. You are not burning nor writhing in pain. You are not noticed. You are not speaking. You are not moving. You see only gray.

Hell is far worse than Queens, New York. At least in Queens you can find momentary relief by popping into a bodega for a fresh bialy.

I joke. For what else can I do? Nothing.

I am entombed in gray. Having spun into this forever cocoon, the worst fear a being can imagine is true: complete, eternal solitude with a vision of nothing. No movement either, thus no solace might be afforded by stepping to the edge of gray to inspect beyond into more gray. If I could say I feel trapped in a colorless bubble, I would say so, but I feel nothing at all, except fear, and I see nothing at all, except gray. Not even distant mumbles taunt from afar. And I would welcome the torture of such sound, for then I could experience anger.

But nothing.

Nothing.

Fear and gray.

I'm not sure what I've lost, what eternal strand of my being remains elsewhere, if anywhere. Perhaps a part of me resides only in this hell. For my sins, for my choice, for my inability to separate life from death, I do not know. A punishment nonetheless.

So I struggle in an all-encompassing fear. If I thought my previous maternal insomnia was terrible, at least then I had chamomile tea, lilac pillows, scented candles, and cherry juice to afford me some natural sleep. What was I thinking pitying myself so, for what? Loving my son to the point of paranoia? That was normal, but this is horror.

If I gathered my innumerable nightly worries, expanded each to last in a constant, slow-mo replay, and added 3-D visual depictions along with sensory fabrications for each diabolical *What if* my sick thoughts conjure up, then this, this is the fear. *What if* I really did forget to pick up Ivan after school, or neglected to take him to his doctor fast enough with that fever that was really pneumonia? *What if* I didn't notice that bully on the play yard at his school and Ivan had been pushed harder, on the concrete, or over the edge? *What if* this work doesn't ever slow down and I don't pay enough attention to him growing up and I miss everything, I miss everything? Next? *What if* I never see Ivan again? I don't. I see gray.

Ivan. It all comes back to Ivan.

I fight to reign in my scattered thoughts.

No. No. This is wrong. I do not belong here. Ivan. Ivan. Ivan. Where is Ivan?

What if I never see Ivan again? I don't. I see gray.

No. No. This is wrong. I do not belong here. Ivan. Ivan. Ivan. Oh Ivan!

What if Noah never walks again? He falls out of that cursed tree, each inch of the descent taking days. His spine snaps, like a car rolling over a dry stick. I taste his salty spit as he begs me to help him. I'm useless.

What if Noah never returns to me? He doesn't. I remain in gray.

And my Ivan! What if he forgets me? He does. I am nothing. I do not exist anywhere, probably not even in this gray.

NO! IVAN! At some point my fear does indeed shout these words, which I believe jostles a merciful nugget, a kernel of memory so buried in my beleaguered mind it may have been lost there forever had I not summoned some fierce defiance to this hell. A spark, his voice, his lovely, lovely voice.

"I love you, Mama," whispers through the gray.

I fight harder. I push for the kernel to say it again.

"I love you, Mama."

My chest, a burning, but a burning is something.

"I love you, Mama."

I push so hard on what I hope are my legs, a tingling begins. Can I walk?

"Oh Ivan, I love you. I love you too much," I scream and sprint to a burn hole of light in my fabric of gray. Not knowing where the light will lead, I go along anyway. I choose to trust in my love, for it has never led me astray. Maybe sideways and on a circuitous and indirect route. But always the right destination. Love is the only guide, it has never led me wrong.

Ivan.

Love is not easy. Love is not timely. Love does not follow some man-made laws. Love is not black. Love is not white. Love is endless color, sometimes obscured by layers of gray. One need only fight. And trust.

Chapter XXV
Freshwater Memory Museum

Like pixels that become blocks that become objects that become colors that form a world tumbling out of an unveiling videogame, my world becomes the glorious park with the wood-plank path, and I find myself at the bridge with hand-carved rungs. The trees are silent. But while their leaves do not ruffle in laughter—in fact, they seem to be watching me, waiting for some gesture—at least I am here.

"Noah!" I shout.

Nothing.

The stream beneath the bridge bubbles.

"Noah!"

Nothing.

I consider running to the other end of the bridge, the place Noah has so far denied me. Or have I denied myself? But when I dare step, a wind rustles loud through the leaves, which I take as a warning.

I slide down the hill to the grass door hut, hoping for view of Ivan, hoping to return to him somehow. But the birch branch handle is shuttered by a boulder, which I cannot budge. Searching the trees for answers, I land my eyes beyond the bridge where the end of a stone dust path mixes with the grass of the valley. I know exactly where it leads: Lachlan's Reserve. If I follow the path, perhaps Lachlan can help me find my way once again. To Noah. To Ivan. To some semblance of peace.

The crushed gravel crunches beneath my quick footfall. How long the trek takes is a mystery, but out of the valley I run, past a park of grazing deer, and into a forest of oaks and banyans, birch, and sycamore. The now familiar tree forts come into view, along with the tinkling sounds of piano and violin concertos wafting from tree knots. Every shade of green and blue conspire to swirl the scene into a liquid country summer. I tumble into a busy workday at The Reserve. Inhabitants whistle while sorting their piles of canoes and rafts and kayaks and fishing poles. Several people, including my friend Diamond, wave a cheery hello.

"Lachlan's in the FMM," Diamond says.

I burst in the direction of the FMM, sliding around corners and flinging my body by holding thin trees I'm going so fast. When at last I reach the barn, I slide open those fine red doors, as though I belong and do not need to knock. Sissy hoots from behind, "Ooh, babydoll's back and she's bright, woo! Wahh, the glow! I'll open the shop today!" Unsure why she should be so thrilled, I simply scrunch my nose and hop in place to share my amusement.

The corners, the beams, the table in center, all empty of Noah. Lachlan and the inventory keeper, however, sip coffee by a corner shelf, admiring a plaque.

"Vivienne, just in time. The plaque about the briefcase is done," Lachlan says.

At last! They are done with the briefcase plaque. And oh, how worth the wait.

The plaque is in my hands. I am reading engraved words. The first line causes me to tremble and my knees to buckle. Even here in Heaven, I am overcome with emotion.

Ivan Marshall and Ele Sanderstorm have lost a lot of stuff in fresh water. Here we are, once again, chiseling their objects in eternal brass.

Long before they married, when Ivan and Ele were nine, they followed a cardinal to Ivan's red barn, which housed Ivan's mother's old Volvo. Ivan did not permit his father or stepmother or anyone else to enter the barn since his mother died; everyone had complied because the boy had been so grief-stricken. "Are you sure?" Ele asked as Ivan pushed the barn door, entranced in following the red bird. "Yes, but, but only you can come in." "I am the only one here, the only one with you, Ivan." "Okay, then yes." "Ivan, hold my hand. We'll go in together." Ivan held Ele's hand, and they entered the barn together. The cardinal they followed seemed to tease them: He pranced on the hood of the Volvo, strutting as though mocking a lowly pigeon; he flew figure eights about Ivan and Ele's craning heads; he swooped and lay a piece of straw in Ele's hair. "Ivan, I don't think cardinals normally do that. I think he's trying to tell us something," Ele said with confidence, for only children are wise enough to interpret animals. The bird lunged and again lay a piece of straw on Ele's head, as though awarding her with a well done. "Where is he getting the straw?" "Up there. The ledge by the wood ladder and where all my mom's tools are." "I'm going up." "Me too." So they slowly walked to the ladder, still holding hands, and as they did, the bird settled, appearing relieved to dispense with the theatrics. At the top of the ladder, Ivan and Ele pushed their child arms under an old hay bale. Meanwhile, the fire-feathered bird squatted on the rafter above. Ivan's and Ele's hands met the clasp of a black briefcase. They pulled; they popped the lock; they dropped their jaws. They sat in the corner of the ledge, keeping the case of money between their legs. And the whole while, the red bird held guard. "Ele, if we show my dad, won't he make me move away to a mansion? Isn't that what grown ups do?" "No, Ivan. No, Ivan. You can't move." "Well, we have to hide the money." "No, not hide. Let's lose it completely."

Perhaps most children would have fallen dazed in their fortune, tripping over themselves to land fistfuls of cash on the counters of toy stores. The difference here: Ivan and Ele already owned the most valuable asset, even if their minds didn't yet understand in full. They each owned, jointly and severally, the love of their lives. And so young, and thus so lucky. Monetary value simply did not register in their forming minds, for they were lifted by a higher power, which fed the blood that filled their veins and allowed their hearts to beat in synch.

They trekked off into the woods, following the stream that divided their lawns. "Ivan, where do you think this money is from?" "I have a pretty good idea," Ivan said, but he halted his answer, not explaining further, even though he shared everything else with Ele. Ivan had a different secret to protect, remembering a note his mother left him on the day she died. Ele didn't press, for only children are wise enough to respect eternal promises.

The pair threw the case in the stream at the fork where the current picked up to join a rumbling river. Four years later, the stubborn case met upon Ivan, and the case's fate was thereafter lost, only to float here, to this place.

These words are an infinite relief. *My Ivan is loved. He loves. He lives happily. And long. My Ivan. My Ivan. My Ivan is safe.* A powerful and satisfying release grounds me in my place. And in this place, I peacefully accept: My time is coming in the wink of an owl.

My only fear now is the fear that Noah is gone forever. But as soon as I can leave my physical body, I will scour eternity to find him. I will come back to this reserve, ask Sissy to pack me a traveling bag of chocolate and coffee, and I'll set off to fine-tooth comb the infinite Heavens and the infinite Hells until I find my love—I trust my love to guide this search—and I am free to do so, because *Ivan is safe. And Jack is not my choice.*

I shock myself to the concrete floor and spin back into the living. I am furious to end the end and begin the beginning.

I return to Marty in a frantic pace, my breathless directions so urgent, I whiplash him into silence. This happens. I'd read about it once before. The dying will sometimes wake in a fit of energy, as though shot with ten epinephrine needles, appearing fully well and fully capable. But the vigor is a mirage, a short blip to allow one thing and one thing only: final goodbyes. Seeing as all I have before me is dependable Marty, I hurry to command him to fetch a pen and several pieces of paper. With a crystal clarity, I organize my messages while Marty vanishes to collect our implements. I experience an undivided connection so inextricably linked to the words in my mind, I believe I can scrawl out an entire novel, if only I could move my arms.

I dictate my final words: all of the letters I've already explained and lastly, the most important, a private letter to Ivan.

"Marty, on the envelope to Ivan, please write, 'For Ivan Only. Keep Private, Respect This!' And Marty, I trust only you to hand out these notes. Please be sure to give Ivan his directly."

"Precious, I'm crying here. Ain't no one gonna give Ivan this note but me. My lips sealed. They sealed. You kept my secret. I keep ya'all's. I never in all my career hear such proof. You down-right plain pretty precious. An angel is what."

Ivan,

Everyone will tell you you'll be fine and that over time you will heal and feel much better. You will not believe them. You will want to hit them, run, yell, and scream. And you should. But Ivan, I promise you, because I really do know, and I promise, promise, promise you will heal. You will be better. You will live an amazing life—beyond anything anyone could ever hope for, because you, you Ivan, will risk everything for love. For this risk, you will win.

My love, I love you too much. You are so young, but not too young to hear the only advice I think necessary for this life: You must do whatever it takes to be with your love—follow love, sacrifice for love, lose whole buckets of money, literally lose whole stacks of money—for love. Nana once told me that love is the science that pumps the blood through your heart. Please, please, Ivan, if you do nothing else, love far too much, more than anyone thinks appropriate. No one can define what love is for you, only you can recognize love, and when you do, you will recognize it as easily as you recognize your own eyes. Trust this.

I will forever, yes forever, remember reading The One and Only Ivan *with you as the happiest time in my life. I*

*will see you again—do not despair—but only after you've
lived the longest possible life your full heart can bear.*

All of the love in eternity,
Mama

*P.S. Remember when I told you the lady who used to own
our house was a bad lady and had to go to jail? Well, I'm
pretty sure she hid her crime money somewhere. And
if you find it, I support whatever you decide is the right
thing to do. Trust in your love, Ivan. It will guide you.*

If you think I should have advised Ivan more generally, maybe
pushed him to not squander money, perhaps we disagree over the
value of objects. Perhaps from my point of view, money might
actually buy love and happiness, but the payment is not to spend,
but to allow the loss of earthly items that lead us astray. As for
my specificity in Ivan's and the others' notes, sure, I've heard of
other dying proclamations and their general applicability to those
who witness them. I simply choose to be esoteric in my deathbed
guidance. Please afford me this, for I am the one who died.

Chapter XXVI
Green and Gray

May 25, 2012, A Reading at Two Women's Wakes as Told from Jack's Perspective

Branzwal Funeral Home kept the doors open given the unseasonably hot May morning. The weathermen said a shock of Caribbean air burst onto the New England scene at the break of day and would hover a week. They said this meant the start of an early summer. And wasn't the rest of the world outside Branzwal's just thrilled.

Inside, people sat on aluminum chairs with padded seats, lined in rows of five on each side of a thin aisle. My lovely son, my Ivan, swallowed in a black suit, sat in the front row with his head between his dandling legs. A pool of tears puddled beneath him. I sat on his right side and rubbed his back, dueling emotions of grief for myself and grief for him.

Taped recordings of violins filled the subtlety of background noise, barely audible above the humming ceiling fan. A lilac perfume overtook the room from bouquets in round, glass vases. Two caskets dominated a raised platform and indeed, our view.

A rustling of programs by anxious attendees mixed with sniffles and a deep sob that mushroomed from one pocket of the audience, and then another. Not one person said one word to his fellow man. A heavy truck drove past, its breaks aching a quick strain, but rolling loudly along, as though taunting the mourners within.

The undertaker, standing behind the back row, slammed the front door shut, which seemed either a rebuttal to the passing truck, a reaction to the dual event in the room, or a cue to the first reader to begin. Or all.

Taking her cue, a petite woman in a black hat and black empire-waist dress stepped to a podium beside the two closed caskets. She pulled the microphone arm closer to her mouth, which made a metal creaking noise and caused the speakers to scratch the air with feedback. We mourners stiffened further, uncomfortable by the sound, uncomfortable under the glare of this first speaker, uncomfortable in the mothball stench of black suits we wished remained closeted in attics forever.

The petite woman coughed. Her hands shook in holding a red leather journal, which she opened to a page marked by a purple ribbon. As she did, she looked vacantly to us mourners, her lids low in grief.

I had never seen this woman before in my life.

At first, her voice was soft and monotone, and I therefore missed her introductory preamble and nervous coughs to clear her throat. But as she settled into her speaking, the audience froze, hypnotized at the pitch and content of her speech. Her tone bellowed as though she were a Baptist preacher, but she never blinked from the page to ensure her subjects followed along—she must have known her tale would hold us transfixed. In fact, she was so compelling to me, each of her words sunk like hot lead, embedding themselves in my memory so deep, I can recite them verbatim.

"I'd like to read one of my journal entries from April 18, 2003," she said and shifted her attention to the open page below her now settled hands. In a firmer, stronger voice, she repeated, "Again, from my journal entry of April 18, 2003, nine years ago." She coughed and continued reading: "I went to visit Noah's grave today. As his mother, I thought I might be the only one left to bake him a cake. He would have been twenty-six. My baby, twenty-six. He's been gone almost three years. And no, my heartbreak has not lessened any. There is no such thing as 'time will heal' with a lost child, so save your Hallmark card for someone else. Noah is buried on a green acre in a memorial park on the coast of Florida. My husband and I live about five miles away, having fled cold New England winters and arrested memories of my son growing up in our New Hampshire house. We buried him here, by my childhood home, because he died not far on the interstate. And deep down, I knew I'd always come home.

"I visit Noah once a week and when I do, I am reminded of the power of two colors, gray and green, for when you arrive, this is all you see. Green lawn, green trees, and gray gravestones. No bursts of reds or blues, no invading streak of purple. Just a vast horizon of green and gray, which colors hold a spell on me. So as not to disturb the eternal sleep of the inhabitants, I usually dress in jeans and my green zip sweatshirt that says Fort Myers on the breast pocket. When I'm angry about losing my son, I wear a bright red blouse with a red shawl around my head, as if to say, 'Oh yeah, take him, did you. I will hunt you. Kill you.' This is irrational, I know, for whom would I kill? Any leads? Anyone to accuse? Trust me, if there were someone, the deed would be done.

"I came up to the familiar cemetery gate. I had a basket with a sandwich, for me, a bottle of water, for me, a bag of barbeque chips, for me, and a slice of cake, for Noah, but ultimately, for me. This is what I do, my personal tradition, for Noah's birthday. I don't let anyone else come with me; they will come later and pay their own respects. My family and I have endured in this manner. Tonight, we'll host an annual memorial service at the house, and someone will play "Angel," by Sarah McLachlan, meaning well, of course, and upon hearing the first notes, I will inevitably collapse into a puddle. So be it. I don't need to be strong for anyone in this, so shame the uninformed who ask me to be.

"I pulled past the gate today, parked the car, grabbed my basket, and walked along the stone dust paths. As usual, within ten steps, I was fully ensconced in a world of stone and green. Stone and green on my left, stone and green on my right, stone, stone, stone, green, green, green, and green edged out only by a sliver of blue, when I tipped my head up high. Such is expected, so I continued on, green and gray merged together and into a warping melancholy. Sound bled from my world, as it always does in this place.

"But, as quick as an unexpected kiss on the cheek, something new appeared, right in the path of my direction. I quickened my pace. As if seaside, a scene emerged around Noah's grave: a giant umbrella in rainbow stripes, shading a woman with long, black hair, who sat underneath in a blue beach chair. Her red sundress alone was like a sonic explosion amongst the green and gray. And there was something else about her: She was a full nine months pregnant. Big beach ball of a belly on which danced a yellow butterfly, which she watched in a rapt awe so completely absorbed, her mouth was agape, her hand, holding an orange, was limp to her side, and her concentration fixed to the point she did not hear or see me.

"'Vivienne?' I said.

"She dropped the orange and the butterfly fluttered away. 'Mrs. Vinet!' she shouted. Only one time has this little girl, now full-grown woman, called me by my proper name, Josie.

"'Vivienne, what are you doing here?' I asked."

"'Mom and I took the train down—she's at the hotel, upset I would travel so late in pregnancy—she wants to surprise you— anyway, I just had to take the train to tell Noah I'm having a boy, and to say Happy Birthday. It's our birthdays now,'" and twirling her hands nervously, she added, 'You know.'

"She steadied herself on the chair's wooden arms, bracing herself to stand. But I know how it is to carry fat babies in your belly, so I dropped to my knees, awe-struck myself. I had not seen Vivienne in years. Her mother, my Jessica, had kept me up to date in our constant phone calls and her winter visits, of course, so I'd heard Vivienne was pregnant; but since I couldn't bear a trip back to New England, I simply hadn't enjoyed, or suffered, the sight of the girl my son loved.

"She collapsed on my shoulder, heaving giant sobs on my Fort Myer's sweatshirt, and it was not I who cried back, but I who, for once, gave comfort in this despicable grief.

"Then, once calmed and caught up, Vivienne shared half of the slice of cake with me, and since she had the culinary shame of a pregnant woman, she didn't refuse half my sandwich or half my bag of chips. It was the happiest birthday celebration for Noah, for me, since he left."

The woman stopped reading and flipped the pages of her journal. After confirming to herself she'd landed on the page she needed, she continued.

"June 18, 2003. Two months since I found Vivienne and her colors at Noah's grave. She didn't tell me that she dropped a packet of wildflower seeds in the crack where the earth meets Noah's gravestone. So it wasn't until after our vacation when I realized my son's world was full of red poppies, banana-yellow buttercups, sky-blue delphinium, and a pink petunia, which grow in fierce response to the sea of green and gray." The woman tilted her head; her view was fixed on the space above the front door, the one behind those of us in the unwilling audience that the undertaker had slammed to begin this wretched ceremony. No longer reading, the woman, in a somewhat possessed monotone, added, "To lose Vivienne is a deep wound. For the last several years, she has joined me in Noah's birthdays. Just me and her, once a year.

In this way, I had part of him back; her colors changed everything for me. My husband and I leave town more often. I tried two new hobbies, running and painting. I replay comedies and read books. The world has been different, and I thank Vivienne. But now with the loss of her and also the loss of, I can't even speak of her. The loss of Vivienne and her . . . and her . . . and my . . . I don't accept these two caskets." The woman's voice broke and she ground her teeth to fight back the weaker emotion. A man, I presume her husband, tried to collect her, but she pushed him away with the faintest growl. She clutched the sides of the podium as though hanging on to the edge of a cliff—in a defiance of death.

Not one person in the room held their tears except the fire-eyed woman at the podium. The definition of her flexed biceps stretched the sleeves of her black dress. About thirty seconds passed before she jerked her head to the air above our sitting heads, a look one might mistake for pride if one didn't realize the unfathomable grief. Her eyes burned in the crimson of demonic anger. Without focusing on a soul in the audience, she spit out her venom, "Now I once again fear the green and the gray, the stone and the concrete, the tight cut of the lawn. I am sorry I cannot write a more uplifting eulogy. I write the truth. And the hard truth is, Vivienne died too young and so did my son. And so did . . . Oh, and so did she, she, the only rock I had is gone too." She exhaled from what must have been a burning throat, "I am not angry. There is no word for the murder I feel." She fled the podium, leaving by way of the rear fire exit. Slam. The room shook in her agony.

I had never heard of Noah before.

Naturally, that evening, given the base despair of the ceremony, made infinitely more horrific by the woman's speech, I slept with poor Ivan once all the guests finished their funeral cake. My boy was out of tears by nightfall, so we chatted about the day in a disconnected, awe-struck way, and this is when Ivan shocked me senseless. I will never be the same again, as miracles are a real possibility for me now.

"Papa, Noah is Mama's friend who fell out of a tree when they were young. He couldn't walk. Then he died when Mama was twenty-three, and Mama said she was very sad. But he can walk now. Didn't you see him in the hospital with her? He was sitting in the green chair or hiding in the curtains the whole time."

If a grown man can get chills, I tell you, I had them.

CHAPTER **XXVII**
A Soul-Mate's Heaven

Lachlan escorts me back to the knot-tree valley, and I'm not sure if I'm fully dead. Legs crossed, I sit at the end of the gas-lit bridge; the leaves have returned to laughter, and the sky is a painted picture, but I cannot bring myself to cross. This is why I doubt death, yet I no longer question life.

Shall I go to Armadillo and ask her to paint her old brown ranch, in the past, so I might travel to the time Noah held me on the beanbag? Kissed me in her bed? Or the oak tree on the way to Manchester, when Noah first said he loved me? Or our fort in the woods where we made love? Should I traverse the places he went without me, the places that did not heal him? Or the parking lot in which he or I did not try hard enough? I'll scour them all and everywhere else, even be re-born if I must.

Using the hand-carved rungs as a brace, I rise, intending to begin.

Something, someone, is standing across the way, across the bridge. He is watching me. Silent. Is that? *This seems a repetition.*

"Stay. Stay. I'll come to you, not much longer now," he says.

I do not say hello. He does not say hello. Instead, it seems natural to ask a question as soon as he crosses the bridge and comes into my space. "I've been here with you before. Right? Weren't you waiting for me by the gaslight when . . ." Of course I am joking, for I have no intention of making the rounds again. I know exactly the course I want to take.

"What is your Heaven, Noah? Can we go there?" I say. The trees practically collapse in their earthquaking laughter.

Noah forces our world to pause by breathing deep and collecting my soul in his air.

A sweet silence tickles my skin.

He becomes serious, but with a confident squint.

"But don't you see? This is my Heaven, walking through all of this with you."

"Even before I came?"

"It was always like this and always will be, but improved now. You are my Heaven. You, Vivienne. I was so scared though. Had you not chosen us, I'd be unable to retain even a replica of you. The consequence in death is the same as in life: If you offer your soul and it is refused, you cycle in a certain hell. Only here, it is eternal. I've been there, you know. Your decision was as difficult for you as for me. We are more connected than you might think."

My eyelids involuntarily flicker; my hands shake. In an attempt to regain some control in my overriding excitement, I figure I'll flirt some—even though such an act is laughably unnecessary.

"And yet, did I speak my choice? How do you even know my decision?"

"Ah, Vivi, my beautiful girl. Whatever you wish. I'll ask properly."

I cringe when we return to the hospital. I for sure do not ever want to be here again. Noah kneels by my bed and places my hand on his cheek.

"Will you come with me tonight?" he asks.

His chin quivers in an effort to control the water forming in his blinking eyes. A tear escapes to roll along his nose. This is when I die.

"Yes," I say. "I will come with you," which is in effect the purest marriage vow. No witnesses necessary. No specific religion implied. No certificate to sign. No law sanctifying what is already true. If this was a traditional ceremony, I would have played Simon & Garfunkel's "Kathy's Song" in the procession, just to hear the one line that feels so right in this moment: *The only truth I know is you.*

And there will be a dress and there will be heels and there will be a tuxedo. This is my afterlife. What did you expect?

I lift off the bed, swinging my unbroken and unbandaged legs over the edge. I brush Noah's shoulder and ask to be excused. Hanging on the bathroom door is a blood-red Valentino gown, which so happens to be my size, and in a box on a stool are a pair of glittering stilettos, made of literal rubies. When I come out formally changed, a tuxedoed Noah greets me with a genuine bow. He straightens his black bow tie with a sinister bite of the lip and possessive scan of my red-cloaked body, as if suggesting he can barely wait to satisfy his craving.

"They're playing *La Bohéme* at La Scala in Milan tonight," he says.

"Exactly what I was thinking." And it is exactly what I am thinking.

"First, we must visit someone."

"Who?"

"Your mother."

In the very next room, in the very same ICU, with her head facing my now empty head, lay my mother. She is gray once again, quite nearly a corpse herself. She too is encased in white sheets, a white comforter, and white walls. Dead lilacs sully a vase on her night-stand.

I crawl up on her medical bed and lay behind her, curling around her like a mother cat. "Vivienne, is it time? I've been holding on, baby. They said they'd give me your heart when you'd gone. They've been prepping me, poking me, but I allowed this decline knowing you were leaving. I told them to donate your lovely heart to someone younger, better than me. Two transplants, please, I won't take it. I've been sending the spirits away until you came for me. I will not leave this earth before you."

"Come, Mama. Come with me now."

She tilts her sweet rose face to me, and after I peck her nose with a kiss, she comes to color. As if a gun shot to start a race, she bolts out of bed and stretches in her newfound strength.

"Babydoll, you go tonight. Have fun with Noah. I'm back in training. Got some waterskiing to catch up on—and damn baby, we'll have an eternity to chat away. Now go."

I kiss her cheek, which again smells of rose.

Mama.

Noah helps me off the bed and we walk away, passing my hospital room in our departure. I am thus afforded a glimpse of my broken body and have to accept what they see: my head bolted in a halo of metal. The visible parts of my face are bruised, puffy, and splashed with tinges of yellow. My rib cage is encased in an exoskeleton of Velcro straps and plastic bars. Both legs are in casts, ankle to sternum, same with my arms. I wish they could see what I see though: me in a red gown next to the love of my soul in a tuxedo.

Noah and I walk down the hall, tiptoeing by Marty who is napping. Our movement causes his fly-swept hair to lift in our slight, slight wind. The hospital hall becomes our heavenly bridge, and the walls became tree limbs. For the first time, I cross to the other side, Noah holding my hand the entire journey. Soon our heels click on cobblestones, and here in Milan, we enter the haze blue of dusk. A crowd of people, likewise in gowns and tuxedos, moves in our same direction, all of us en masse to La Scala. Everyone has tickets to *La Bohéme*. Do you hear these fellow patrons' chatter? Their collective excitement is a divine melody, an opera itself.

In the main aisle, on our way to orchestra center seats, Noah meets my lips in a long, slow, meaningful, deep kiss to my soul. This is the moment I die, and no doctor or miracle or magic dust can drag me back. Thank the Almighty Lord, thank this good God, I'm not going back.

For me, for Noah, for whoever is blessed to listen, the singers of La Scala soar beyond all their practices and performances, causing more tears to shed than in the history of *La Bohéme*. I contribute buckets to the downpour, bawling in my red gown. Noah's constant supply of white tissues are worthless.

Afterwards, we eat a dinner of fried zucchini flowers at a restaurant in a field outside Milan, and then we make sweet, heavenly love under a tree in that same field by the short end of a castle's mote. I cry some more, out of unbridled joy.

Tomorrow, in your world, you may hear about this, I don't know. Milan will wake to find mysterious puddles around La Scala. City engineers will be perplexed because there has been no rain in two weeks. And, outside a farmhouse restaurant that shares a parking lot with a tiny, old castle in Malpensa, a busboy will catch glimpse of what looks to be a long red dress hanging from a tree limb. *How odd*, he'll think, lifting his legs up over the high grass, like a tiger creeping closer. The nearer he gets, the redder the object will become. When he's ten feet off, the dress will break into twenty-five pieces and fly off in varied directions. A flock of red cardinals will take the shape of a gown.

Yes, I wish they knew what I know. Because while they are planning my funeral, a boy I've loved my whole life is unzipping my dress and kissing my exposed spine while caressing my breasts from behind. And I wish they felt what I feel, because while they grieve, this boy lifts me off the ground, lays me on his spread jacket, and quenches my ache with his own. I wish they knew how we move together in eternity, his body in mine, mine working with his, in slow, deep lunges of our conjoined hips. With our movement, whole fleets of new souls are born in the magic of our lovemaking.

Chapter XXVIII
Ivan

I am an old man. Ancient, some would say. And, yes, I knew better. Of course a rickety-kneed, ninety-nine-year-old with arthritis and cataracts shouldn't waterski. But seriously, what's the difference? I had already lived a full life and all that jazz. For the most part, my life was rosy, but for the blackest of times when I was eight—when I truly experienced a 'clump of misfortune' (as my mother used to say), a clump so dense (imagine losing both your mother and grandmother two days before your ninth birthday), I believe the good Lord allowed me bottomless pots of luck thereafter. Many times I felt the protection of angels, even when I was so very alone.

I created a company that researches ways to cure disorders and damage of the spinal column, a subtle idea planted by my mother. I believe we made great strides. Pun fully intended. Two of my four children operate the ever-expanding business. Of the other two, one is a famous chef and the other is a painter with her own little gallery in the New York City SoHo. None of them are slouches; none of them a problem. I am blessed.

As for grandchildren and great-grandchildren and great-great grandchildren and nieces and nephews, I've stopped counting. Suffice it to say, when there is a wedding, we fill the whole church and the annex. And if the church is not a grand cathedral, we spill out onto the front steps and sidewalk, the littlest ones on the shoulders of the ones crammed standing. My dear wife Eleanor, whom I call Ele, has been with me through nearly every high and low ever since I spied her across the stream when we were nine: me in my lawn, her in hers. I still see her as a giant ladybug. She's been my best friend, my lover, my confidant, and my earth angel for ninety years. Imagine that, ninety years. Everyone calls us The Turtledoves. "Oh, here come The Turtledoves." Or, "Make sure we put The Turtledoves at the head table." Sure, we fight, but I can't remember a time when Ele didn't tell me she loved me before closing her book and her eyes for the night.

One time when we were both seventy, they told Ele she had an infection of the heart. I think this must have been a blip when my band of guardian angels turned their heads, as my mother now blames. Of all the low-down, dirty things to say to me, *a disease of the heart*. My grandmother passed of such a thing on the day my mother died. The very worst day of my existence. So for the doctors to accuse my Ele of having *a disease of the heart* sixty-two years later, well I literally dropped to the floor and sobbed at the nurse's feet. Picture this, a seventy-year-old man, slobbering on the white leather shoes of a woman in her thirties. I tried to gain some semblance of sanity by reading the brand name: "Naturalizers," the tag said. My wife though, and here's the kick, she's no shrinking flower. She's no light feather just a'dusting her china set. "Now, Ivan Noah Marshall, you get off that floor right now. I'm not going anywhere. I've got two weddings to plan this summer and eight to attend, for crying out loud! Get up, you fool, get my jacket. I've got a turkey in the oven."

And that was that. Ele swallowed her medicine and changed her diet exactly as the doctors said she must. Although, I'd catch her some nights slathering butter on toast, her hunched, caught red-handed in the middle of our pantry, the lights out. Ele always said no one butters toast properly. One of her oft-repeated tirades went something like this, "I don't understand why no one gets this right. First of all, when you butter damn toast, you do it right away, right when the slices pop out of the mouth of the toaster. Otherwise, the bread gets cold and the butter won't spread. A chunk of butter can't spread itself. I love you, though. I do love you. But fool, you can't butter toast to save your life."

So here I find myself, ninety-nine years old, ninety years with the same woman, three daughters and one son, countless grandbabies, and a company with, I hope, what some will consider a useful medical solution. I'm a strong, successful, very happy, accomplished man, but I cried when I saw my mother at the end of that bridge on the night I died.

I remember everything about her and mostly how close we were. The therapists thought I'd forget details, as I was only eight when I lost her. But I didn't forget one single thing. Perhaps because I kept replaying our times and our games and our conversations, and I filled twenty notebooks with these words as though a transcript, and memories as though a novel, and poems so as to capture all the emotions. Also, the therapists discovered I had some grip on memory. The experts suggested I become an author or historian because I might lend some value to civilization with my ability to remember and record. But I was always drawn, distracted even, whenever I met a child in a wheelchair. *How wretched,* I thought, *to know your legs and lose them.* I did not pity them; rather, I had real anger for their situation. And even though their immobilization most certainly was not my business, I made it my business. *Was science doing enough?* I'd wonder.

By the age of fourteen, I'd drag my poor father to children's wings of major hospitals when I heard of a tragic sports, play, or car accident. I would sit with these boys and girls and talk with them about their view on the situation. This was my life mission. Love did guide me, whether with Ele or whether in my occupation, and I was rewarded to trust my love. I do not believe there is another way to find happiness on earth.

I never forgot my mother and throughout my life, I reread and memorized those twenty notebooks and penned two hundred more. The cover of every notebook had just one image, for upon my mother's death, my father asked, "What would ease your pain? I will do anything. I will go to the ends of the earth for you. Anything at all you need." As he stiffened his jaw to control the pain evident in his face, I answered, "Papa, please buy me a whole lot of blue spiral notebooks with a yellow butterfly on the cover, the kind Mama has on her desk." He took me literally, because "a lot" was delivered, three hundred notebooks in a crate.

No matter everything I learned in life, every goal I fulfilled, the words I wrote, the emotions I conjured up and battled, none of it mattered when I regressed to eight years old in the instant of seeing my mother again on the bridge. "Van Gogh's *The Starry Night*, Son," she said, pointing to the crazy blue sky.

A grown man who is just a child will cry when he is with his mother, after so many years without her. I even shouted, "Mama," and fell into her arms. The emotion was so overpowering, my heart literally gave out, for the next thing, I'm in a surgical pod, my mouth's ajar, and a robot arm was prepping to deploy an army of nanobots to perform advanced work on my broken body—but one thousand years of technology would not undo what had been done by my elderly water acrobatics. Was nice of them to try though. An overhead light blinded me, so I blinked and was back again with my mother, burying into her sweet-rose shoulder—same smell my nana used to have.

"Mama, I miss you so much."

"No need, love. We're together now."

We spent some time on the glorious bridge while she offered me a week, or so, to choose a Heaven. She told me how she had done this with her, I guess now "husband," Noah—whom I met, but inexplicably already knew. Although I was a young boy before her, I had my earthly old mind and my response to the offer to search for Heavens was abrupt: "No Mama, no need. I can't imagine being in any Heaven other than yours. Will Ele and the others be able to join us too?"

My mother said, "Boy, my Heaven is no Heaven without you, and if yours is the same, they will be, or are, already there."

"Then we need not waste time. Can I say goodbye to Ele?"

"I think you've earned as much. Now go."

White lights, whooshing blurred edges, and a whirring mass of people appeared under that massive overhead light. A black-suited doctor and a team of silver-suited interns crammed in my pod, shouting, "He's back!" I lay half-naked on a cold steel table. I felt like a hamburger under a heat lamp.

"Go get my wife. I won't be around much longer. Now, go get her," I directed.

Perhaps my centurion authority morphed the medical personnel into true tin soldiers, because everyone quit checking vitals and reporting numbers and levels, and the young buck doc darted from the pod and returned with Ele, lickety split.

A slight, slight wind puffed the blond nurse's hair when Ele entered. At ninety-nine, my wife is amazingly still agile and sharp. She may take her time in an elderly shuffle, but she gets there eventually. Her robin's egg eyes pierced from her wrinkled-yet-smooth face and glowed against the accent of her full white hair. The girls at the salon had curled and set and shellacked her coif the day before, so not even a strand betrayed the queen.

Ele was majestic, cloaked in the red, boiled-wool cape I bought her from a New Hampshire artisan. Even in summer, my beloved gets her chills. Her gold dot earrings caught the overhead light and refracted in faint yellow strings around her face. Her green tattooed wedding band warped within the wrinkles on her left ring finger. When I met this total vision, I was again struck at how beautiful my Ele was. Is. Still.

Ele reached for me and pet my chin with her familiar, soft hands, and in so doing, filled my space with the scent of her ylang-ylang lotion. I knew the outlook was bad because her already watery eyes watered more, and this is a lady who rarely sheds a tear. She did not hit me with her titanium love to pull my sobbing body off the floor, nor berate me with lessons on how to properly butter toast. She didn't remind me yet again how many grandchildren we have, nor proclaim the events of the day to prepare me for whatever itinerary she had designed. Instead, she took my hand while wiping tears from the sagging pockets beneath her eyes.

"Darling," she said.

"Love, my love, my sweet, beautiful Ele."

"Is it time, Ivan? I don't know if I can bear to let you go."

"I am with my mother. She is holding my other hand."

It was true. Ele was holding one hand, my mother the other. Now Ele is a realist and never once did she voice belief in ghosts or spectres, or anything fanciful for that matter. She'd go so far as to dress our girls as princesses in pink, but only after a lecture on the struggles of women before their time. And I as a poet with a wistful heart tried to find that same bone in her, but instead forever met up with her wall of reality, which was my backboard, my own spine. So I knew life was indeed over when Fortress Ele didn't shutter nor blink in disbelief when I said my dead mother was holding my hand. Instead, in an unwavering acceptance, she lifted her eyes to look across my body to where my invisible mother was standing. Into what must have appeared like air to her, my Ele said in a tone of pure elegance, "Thank you for sharing your wonderful son with me. He has made me the happiest woman alive. I will meet you properly soon, and when I do, I hope to hug you first and shake your hand second."

How could you not love such a beautiful woman with the grace of polished royalty, who does not bend in age or shudder in the face of stone-cold death? My only hope is that I gave her everything she ever needed or wanted.

"Ele, darling, I'm going now, but we'll be together soon. I'm with my mother, and I am so happy. I had the very best life with you. Better than this man deserves. Before I go though, I need to confess something."

Ele shivered, but only slightly, as she squeezed my fingers, perhaps as a punishment. What did she expect me to say, there at the end of our long lives together?

"Ladybug, no, no. Not a confession of that sort. My sweet, Ele. I never deceived you. Now listen, here is my confession. You know our secret?"

She checked the room, scrunching her already hunched shoulders, just like a nine-year-old, making sure no one was listening.

"Yes, our secret," she said, swaying in a coquettish way.

"Ladybug, remember when we found the briefcase? Stuffed in the rafters under a floorboard in our old barn. I remember you saying as we disappeared into the woods, 'Ivan, you'll be gone from me. We have to lose this money.' I think that was the one and only time in our entire life together you showed me a vulnerability, and even though I didn't know it would be the only time, I vowed to never let you feel scared again. I promised you we would never be apart."

"Oh, Ivan. You've always been such a softy, my romantic, my wonderful Ivan. The one and only Ivan. My wonderful, wonderful Ivan."

"But wait, darling. I haven't confessed yet. So we threw the briefcase in the river between our houses. Remember how we passed an apple back and forth, you bit, then I bit, and our legs dangled from a tree as we watched the money drift into the current, which we presumed swept our problem to the ocean."

"Presumed?"

"Yes, darling, presumed."

"But you said you checked. You said it was gone."

"And this is my confession."

Ele leaned in closer. "Ivan, what do you mean? All these years, you had the briefcase? All that money?"

"No darling. Not all. When you asked me to go check four years later, I walked the entire river length on our property and into Epping. I nearly dropped dead of shock. Over the border into Epping, lodged between two rocks and mostly out of the water, I saw our briefcase. Same old, waterproof Samsonite, and because most was resting on a rock, the money was just fine. So weird that fishermen had not stumbled upon it; I suppose it was camouflaged, blending with the black of wet rocks. Ele, I was still worried I'd be separated from you, for only the week before I'd heard my father and stepmother talking about how they wished they could afford a new home. I jumped into their private conversation—I couldn't hold back—and begged my father to never peel me away from my mother's house or from you. My father, always so torn. I know anyone else would have used that money—how irrational it was to lose it, Ele. But I wasn't taking any chances, and plus I had the rationality of a thirteen-year-old boy. I hope people would understand."

"Who cares what other people think. They carry their cross. You carry yours."

"My Ele. Such a tough nut. In any event, I popped the case open, stuffed a stack of bills in my backpack, locked her back up, grabbed the handle, and ran to the quarry. I strapped my belt around a basketball-sized rock and the handle and chucked the contraption over the edge as though hurdling a bomb about to blow."

"A quarter of the bills in your backpack?"

"Mmmmhmmmm."

"Well then."

"So, Ele, do you know what I did with this $50,000?"

"No, Ivan, I certainly do not."

"I hid it right back under the floorboard in the barn. And not one of our one million rugrats ever found the loot, and neither did you."

"Oh, Ivan. Why?"

"I was thirteen. As we got older, I kept the money hidden in case we ever had a financial emergency. But we never did. We were so blessed, darling. One day, oh, we were probably forty, I figured out what to do with the money.

"Anytime I caught you looking at me with your blue eyes and you seemed paused in me—you know those moments, honey. Maybe you didn't realize I caught you at something so personal. You're so very strong. But anytime this happened, I sprung to life, and I couldn't love you more than in those moments. For someone like you to see me meant I was real. You gave me eternity and this emboldened my decision. I thought, if I was lucky to grow old and exit this world before you, having never had to suffer the loss of you, well I certainly didn't want you to wear black and mourn me. You mourn me? Never.

"Don't throw a funeral. I can't bear the thought of the kids gawking at me in a casket. Makes me think of my mother's and grandmother's funeral, and I never want anyone to feel so low. Please tell me you won't hold a funeral. Leave my corpse to morticians and spend the briefcase money on a black-tie party, the way you like, baby. Blow the whole lot on just one night. The whole fifty grand. Like a wedding. Why can't people wear tuxes and dance in celebration of a life and hire a band and a caterer and flowers and a candy bar and a doughnut bar—like at weddings? How many weddings have we been to? How many funerals? The weddings are better with the laughter and the drinking and the sloppy good fun. Please tell me you'll do this—it's all in my will anyway, so I think by law, you have to."

Ele's eye filled with tears; I rubbed her soft hands.

"Ele, have a barn burner. Have a grand old time, my love. And dance until your heart gives out, because I'll catch you on the other side."

I breathed deeply through my old man nose.

Ele bent and kissed my forehead. With her eyes only a fraction away from mine, she said, "You sweet man. I will miss you more in one minute of living than all the years tolled in Heaven."

She breathed in my exhale as though to capture my spent air and smooched me like the twenty-seven-year-old she was inside.

And my heart stopped.

Literally, it stopped.

The slight, slight wind returned, which cooled my shoulders and ruffled Ele's white hair. Suddenly I found my right arm stretched upward and my hand tucked within my mother's hand. We stood before a pile of canoes and a man with a clipboard.

"Where are we, and why is it so green and blue?" I asked.

Chapter XXIX
My Heaven

"'It was always like this and always will be. You've always been here with me. You are my Heaven.' That's what Noah said to me, which is exactly what I say to you. You've always been here with me. I carry you everywhere. I talk to you everywhere. As I said when we were alive, I love you too much. You are my Heaven. You, Ivan. It doesn't matter what Heaven I've created, because I choose whatever you wish.

"Although, I know you, my son. I knew you'd appreciate this reservoir and especially the miscellaneous pile. You have always loved stories so. And this is what we will do, we'll sort through miscellaneous objects and investigate their backstories and prequels and sequels. We'll delve into all their stories, stories about love, childhood mysteries, funny crimes, animal stories too, and comedies. Then we'll etch the best of tales in brass

"I'll never forget this glorious day. I was on waterski duty, filling in for Sam, the priest. He hiked off to escort Himalayan mountaineers who had fallen to their icy deaths. I was simply sorting waterskis, the black ones, blue ones, the O'Brien's, the Connelly's, ones with ripped boots, even one with a secret love pleading carved on the fin. And here comes this cracked waterski, but the image in the sky of the attendant story was filled with crackling laughter. I look up and there you were, this ninety-nine-year-old man waterskiing on Lake Suncook. And then you fell. The laughter stopped. The ski hit a floating log, sunk, and guess what, came here. Now, only happy, lost items come to this place, the Reservoir. But you were fatally injured. Yet, how better, what better, than to die at ninety-nine while defying gravity. Old man, you attempted a Triple Axel in your upturn and descent. Bravo, my son, bravo!

"But I didn't know today would be The Day. I actually didn't watch your life unfold. Whenever I tried to check in on you, those mist guardians turned, and I refused to allow their eyes on me and not you for one bloody second. When I saw your waterski and your fateful flip, I was overcome with anticipation, and I dropped the ski to meet you at the bridge. And like Noah did, I stopped you. I wouldn't let you cross—how could I deny you the choices and the opportunity to tell your family, my family too, how fantastic things are on the other side.

"And yet you refused. You wanted only to say goodbye to your one true love. You said you were home. Oh Ivan, I love you too much. Do you know you saved me?"

I've been through afterlife registration, passed preliminary angel training, sought forgiveness for some sins I committed—completed the requisite penance and all—and here I am fully enshrined in death. I have resolved to never complete my Heaven. Instead, Noah and I continue to examine multitudes of reserves as part of our conjoined Heaven, and thus, we pluck ideas whenever we roam, which is roughly every day.

Yes, every day, for I have made amends with time. I choose to allow time to keep a pace. Time can be a beautiful rhythm: think of music, think of poems. Harmony fails without the metronome. In Heavens, time does not equal decay. Time is in symmetry with color and music. *The psychology or philosophy of aesthetics.*

Between sampling Heavens, I work the Freshwater Memory Museum, which I've chosen as my chief place of Heavenly employment. I don't get paid, that's now how it works. Instead, for each plaque I scribe, I receive "boundless satisfaction and infinite entertainment." It's personal. I'll try to explain.

Imagine your favorite hobby on Earth and the moment in which you're working your hobby and you are one with the hobby, absorbed, and fully content—this is the feeling you become addicted to, and which draws you, calls to you, when you are doing anything else at all.

Say your activity of choice is skiing. Imagine your skis are tuned, the hill is empty, the lift is yours; imagine the temperature is a wintry-balm. But the cool air keeps the freshly fallen snow, which is a powder, in tact. You're riding up the lift, considering how the snow sticks to birch trees and how beautiful nature really is.

You reach the top. The view is of the winter world: ink lakes for ice-skaters, white-capped mountains, reflective blue sky, and roofs layered in two feet of snow, making them appear like real-life gingerbread houses. A waffle house to your right pumps out a maple sugar smoke from a sugar-shack; syrup is being heated to drip on hot waffles, made solely for the lucky souls who reach the summit, such as you.

You begin your swishing descent. You own this hill. You cut long S's, long, long S's in your excellent parallel. Your heart grows warm, a thrill runs up your spine to your brain, and you can't imagine being anywhere else ever again. You are in love with your action. You are satisfied. You are entertained.

Imagine this high does not dissipate, only amplifies. Imagine your body rivets to near explosion you are so damn happy. This is the best way I can equate the payment of "boundless satisfaction and infinite entertainment."

So, part of my Heaven is working the FMM barn.

Sometimes Noah and I take a break from eternity and spend a century holding hands underground as the combined root system of the largest organism on earth, the Trembling Aspen. Noah prefers Utah and I Montana, so we trade off. Our separate trees sway side by side and our roots are so intertwined, we truly are just one.

Our main home is a treehouse in Lachlan's Reserve, which resembles in many respects the fort Noah and I played in in our youth; except here, it is gold and it is bolted within a three-hundred foot banyan. Our interior is no solid interior, as you'd think in the living when you enter a home; our walls are covered in gold-framed paintings, courtesy Armadillo. One is of a botanical garden in some South American climate, which never suffers frost. This is my Solitude, where I go from time to time, by myself, to respect my personal faith. Whenever I am there, I am followed by scores of yellow butterflies and surrounded by orange trumpet vines, red petunias, forsythias, purple pansies, and beds upon beds upon beds of tropical botany. My God exists unfiltered in this place. Do you hear the whispering peace?

Remember Lachlan's musical trees? They're still here, of course, but I've added to their repertoire with a different genre of music that comes with a merciful divinity. Friday nights upon dusk, Jakob Dylan climbs the tallest sycamore, balances in his lovely boots on a limb, and sings his poems in a gravely *sotto voce* while strumming his acoustic guitar. And we all listen, our hearts in our throats.

Since this is my Heaven, after a day of selecting miscellaneous items to scrawl on plaques, Ivan and I hike off to share a picnic prepared by Sissy. She packs us a basket of chocolate, hot bread, a thermos of coffee, and a bowl of plump peaches she picks in a rainbow grove I showed her, one tended by a fictional character named Ailene, of course. As for the members of my family, Ivan, my mother, my father, they each have their own adjoining Héavens to attend to as well. But they're all here at some point, or I am with them, somewhere. Our walls are fluid, our borders undefined.

After we create plaques, Ivan and I take to an amphitheater carved in a seaside cliff where we write poems. Sea mist rises around us as if we're sitting in clouds, and water crashes against the seawall below and on the magnificent sea-glass beach. Armadillo usually waves to us from the dunes, where she paints mind-blowing masterpieces and molds glass remnants with copper wires into creatures of the sea. When Ivan and I are done with our writings, we send verses off in floating lanterns to earth angels who take and extinguish them over the heads of artists in life. I actually can't think of an act more Heavenly than this. Except when Noah and I create souls from our lovemaking in a field on the outskirts of Milan.

Postscript

His black cassock swayed in time to his hurried footsteps, creating a slight, slight wind as he passed the patients in their hospital rooms. With one hand he pulled to loosen his clerical collar, which itched his neck, given the expansion of his tight throat. In his other hand, he clutched a note the ICU nurse had just delivered. His note, separate from the other notes doled out to the others, who mourned collectively around the bed of a now departed loved one. *This woman, she, her, this woman, she was so young when I knew her, so many years ago. To have me called to her deathbed? This note, this note* . . . He failed to grasp a thought or a meaning as he continued on, passing doctors, reading a hall map, and on into the hospital's chapel.

He'd been beckoned to hurry to provide last rites. The emergency call reached him as he finished a separate funeral. Thus, not having had time to change, his clothing fit the occasion. *But this*

*note, this note. How does she know? The green bench. My green
bench. I haven't told a soul. How does she know?*

The cozy chapel, with its four pews, danced in the fractured
light of two arched, stained glass windows; a yellow mist, a blue
swath of sparkles, a grove of bouncing red, the sun leaving for the
day, lending to their deeper hues. Another Father exited a vestibule
at the rear of the altar, having finished filling the baptismal bath. A
hint of sandalwood incense came off his egg-white cassock, which
was bordered with a wide crimson ribbon and stitched with a thick
gold thread. No other soul busied their solemn encounter.

Father to Father, eyes locked, our Father fell to his knees in
the posture of prayer. Sobbing in his submittal, he dropped his
mop-blond head, extended the note to his comrade, and whispered, "It's true. It's all true."

Marty awoke when a slight, slight wind swept through his hair. His
folded arms, which served as a useless pillow, had fallen asleep.
The chart with her name, Vivienne Marshall, lay by his prickling
fingertips on the nurses' work desk in the hospital hall. From her
room rang a heart monitor, announcing the presence of death.
Marty slouched in a practiced acceptance into her room to confirm
what he fully expected: a buzzing flatline on the screen and a
Groundhog Day again. Another lost patient.

He took stock of his feet on the ground and removed a folded
note from his chest pocket. Reading once more the words he'd
already memorized the moment they were dictated, he wished

that for just once he'd catch a glimpse of the angels who came to take his precious patients away.

"Marty, I'm going to be your guardian angel. Hang on, you're my only case, and I mean to make this a wild ride. You are not alone on this old round rock, for I am the slight, slight wind that rocks you to sleep and tickles you to wake. Now, go roll this note in a glass bottle, cork it, throw it in a lake, and we'll laugh about it later. Later, that is, in a place where vodka cocktails fill bottomless glasses, and soaked celery appears upon the snap of your heavenly fingers."

~AND THEY LIVED AND DIED HAPPILY ON EARTH AND IN HEAVEN~

THE END

Acknowledgements

The One and Only Ivan is a charming Newbery Medal winning book by Katherine Applegate, published January 1, 2012, HarperCollins. It is worth a lifetime of rereading.

Thanks to Kimberley Cameron, an agent of grace, who has never given up on me or *The Extraordinary Journey of Vivienne Marshall*. *The Extraordinary Journey of Vivienne Marshall* owes her this publishing chance, for without her willingness to take a risk, for me, there would be no *The Extraordinary Journey of Vivienne Marshall*. Thanks to Mary Moore, Lisa Abellera, Dorian Maffei, and David Ivester of the Reputation Books team. Special thanks to Dorian for her keen editorial eye and patience in guiding me through her critical edits. What a joy she and the entire team are to work with. I am blessed.

About The Author

Photograph by Lara Keefe

Shannon Kirk is an award-winning author, lawyer, and law professor residing in Massachusetts' Cape Ann. Her debut, a psychological thriller, *Method 15/33*, garnered critical acclaim, has been translated in over a dozen languages, and is optioned for a major motion film. Shannon has been honored three times as a finalist in the William Faulkner-William Wisdom Writing Competition.

Visit her at ShannonKirkBooks.com

Reputation Books